anna magdalena

A NOVEL

maureen mcneil

Anna Magdalena

Copyright © 2022 by Maureen McNeil

All rights reserved.

Published by Emperor Books

Bellerose Village, New York

ISBN

Print 978-1-63777-344-4 / 978-1-63777-379-6

Digital 978-1-63777-345-1

Cover photo: Sergio Purtell / cover design: Melanie Roberts

No part of this book may be reproduced in any form or by any electronic or mechanical means, including information storage and retrieval systems, without written permission from the author, except for the use of brief quotations in a book review.

This is a work of fiction. All of the characters, names, incidents, organizations, and dialogue in this novel are either the products of the author's imagination or are used fictitiously.

For Herman and Lila

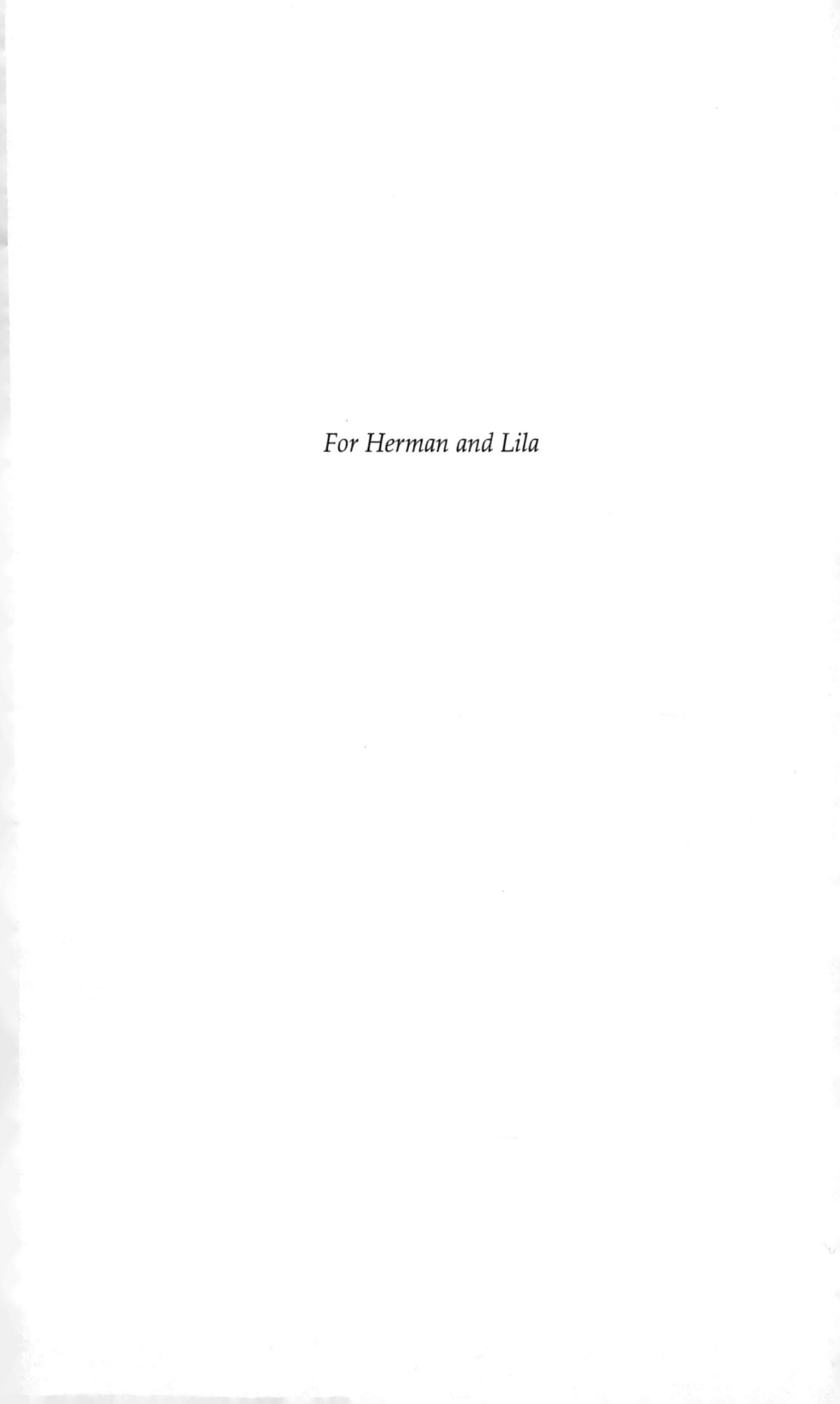

CONTENTS

One	1
Two	11
Three	23
Four	30
Five	40
Six	50
Seven	62
Eight	68
Nine	74
Ten	79
Eleven	85
Twelve	89
Thirteen	94
Fourteen	102
Fifteen	108
Sixteen	114
Seventeen	121
Eighteen	131
Nineteen	143
Twenty	154
Twenty-one	165
Twenty-two	171
Twenty-three	178
Twenty-four	185
Twenty-five	191
Twenty-six	196
Twenty-seven	201
Twenty-eight	210
Twenty-nine	218
Thirty	223
Thirty-one	230

Thirty-two	236
Thirty-three	243
Thirty-four	253
Thirty-five	260
Thirty-six	273
About the Author	285

ONE

AS THE PLANE banked over New York City, Reade opened the window shade and got his first glimpse of Manhattan. Skyscrapers saluted the dawn in pointed rows of gold. Even the Atlantic Ocean's undulating surface appeared gold-leafed as the plane circled back toward JFK Airport. Below, the Long Island beaches looked so much like Willapa. Reade remembered how, for a whole year, Anna Magdalena rolled out of his reach like a log in the surf every time he tried to kiss her.

The cab stopped in front of a gray, frost-bitten, four-story warehouse on a triangular piece of land, surrounded by a wire fence, woven with dead vines. He couldn't understand a word the driver said. Not wanting to get killed, fearful that he was in the wrong borough, he refused to get out. The driver pointed to his GPS and grabbed Reade by the armpits. Only then did

Reade notice a thin copper pipe draping a red cloth like a big red wound above the door, roughly painted with Anna Magdalena's initials. He apologized and pressed an extra twenty into the driver's palm.

The key was hidden in the drainpipe as promised, and opening the metal gray door, grit and cobwebs covered all but a narrow path through desks and cabinets shoved together in piles. A yellow envelope with his name leaned against the rubble. It contained a pictogram of male body parts cut from magazines taped in rows, titled: *What I Love about Reade*. Below this, in her familiar block print, she wrote, "Enter the door marked RESTROOM." And there she was in a sleeping bag, on a green couch, in a green-tiled bathroom, with three toilets, three mirrors, and three sinks. As Reade undressed, he noticed a drawing on the open concrete shower stall. The Empire State Building leaned toward The Statue of Liberty. In a cartoon bubble, it said: "Come on, light my fire." Liberty was drawn like an exhausted Virgin Mary in heavy drapery juggling a book and torch. She said, "I want updating, not a date."

This should have clued Reade to his next discovery. AM's jet-black bumble of hair was buzzed to the kind of cut his father gave him sitting on the kitchen table at age five. Nothing remained but a Tin Tin tuft of fluff over her forehead. As he maneuvered his cold feet into her sleeping bag, he worried. How would he save her if she tried to fly like Pegasus across the Atlantic? Only luck had kept them from drowning in the deadly Japanese current that swept down from the Aleutians along the Washington coast. His feet had landed on a sandbar, and knotting her thick unleashed hair in his fist, they had scrambled to shore. He should have been forewarned, that the black curls of her pubic were shaved, too, and the new sharp angle of her hip alarmed him. In her favor, she still had two small breasts, two dark, almond-shaped eyes, one sea lion nose, ten fingers, and ten toes. Sex was rehabilitating. Therapeutic. Restorative. When they rolled onto their backs, she offered him the secret fact regarding her disappearance.

"It was a certified letter from Honey Dearborn's attorneys. She left me a building in her will. I had to claim it in person. But before telling you, I needed to know if it was real. This is it, Reade. This warehouse is ours."

"Honey must have skyrocketed the value of your art," he said.

"Yeah, but remember," she said. "I was her last link to Frank, her only son. And she was dying of cancer. With Frank gone, she gave everything away."

Reade could hardly believe the strange scenario. It was so farfetched. Frank Dearborn was his eccentric neighbor in Willapa, and they only met his mother, Honey, after Frank died. Now Honey was dead and had left this building to AM. *More implausible,* Reade thought, *was that AM needed him.* There was work to do. A place to live. A building to renovate. A permanent performance space. AM's gallerist, Vivian Boo, already had a benefactor's ear about funding for the necessary renovations.

After a cold morning shower, Reade found her note taped to the door: Meet at sundown, 115 Central Park West and 72nd Street, apartment 6B. He found his way to the subway, got off at Union Square, and bought a cup of coffee. Sitting beneath a statue of Gandhi, he watched the great swirl of common: the patter of dogs looping around the dog run; NYC Parks Department workers bent in slow tai chi; the creaky tin-man walk of middle-age heroin addicts and their sorry sad eyes; preschoolers, hand-in-hand, dressed in oversized orange t-shirts; tall bronze models walking like jaguars —toe forward, shoulders back, rotating hips with each step—and their neatly unshaved equivalents dressed in business suits with suave, wet-looking hair swooped off their foreheads; shoppers at the green market carrying heavy recyclable bags; high school girls in a fistfight; the bell ringer's cry of *just one penny for the homeless*; lovers entwined like downed trees on the lawn; the steaming sculpture on the building to the south with electronic numbers counting every second; Lee Strasberg's blue banner, limp in the green leafy trees of 15th Street. Every so often, Reade looked for the sky between the buildings to guess how much longer before sunset.

Lulu Rose greeted Reade as he stepped off the elevator on the sixth floor. Her cropped white hair was cut severely, like Anna Magdalena's. Her eyes were painted black, and a flowing white dress emphasized her tan shoulders. Asymmetrical rings of silver clinked on her wrists. Reade selected a glass of sparkling water with lemon when a waiter approached with a tray of drinks. Resting his eyes on the row of Fifth Avenue buildings at the far side of Central Park, his ears tuned to two women sipping red wine on his left.

"Lulu's annual Thanksgiving Day Parade brunch was spectacular," said the tall one with a youthful-looking pixie haircut. The other woman wore bright green hair. Her eyes synchronized with her smile like a puppeteer pulling a string. The first woman continued, "The wind blew the giant Snoopy balloon into the window. We were lucky it didn't break!"

Feeling out of place in cowboy boots still dusty from his farm, a dull sport coat, hair bushy on top and long on his neck, Reade sauntered into the living room. He was taken by an oversized black and white photograph of a birch tree, its ancient curvaceous limbs carved with love notes and initials inside hearts pierced by arrows. Finally, escorted into the dining room, Reade saw Anna Magdalena seated next to Lulu at the head of the table. It was set with white roses, white china, white napkins, white candles, and an enormous amount of silverware, goblets, and wine glasses. He had never seen Anna Magdalena in a dress before and couldn't stop smiling in her direction. Like Lulu, her shoulders were bare. When she turned, he saw her back was also bare to her waist. He was wondering how he'd get through the evening sitting so far from her when the chatter stopped. The guests focused on Lulu, her hands circling over flames of candles. He remembered Anna Magdalena's stick drawings in the Willapa sand, her tales of Shakespeare's bad queens, disobedient wives, daughters in disguise, and stories of powerful women and their erotic likes and dislikes.

"Good evening. Kermit Fleur," said the elderly gentleman to Reade's left. He offered his soft, pale hand.

"Nice to meet you. I'm Reade Bordeaux." Reade lingered on Kermit's thick accent. He felt silly worrying about his own twisted tongue. Born with a speech impediment, Reade never learned to pronounce the letter R properly. His Ma told everyone he was born with a French accent, that is, until she heard the fourth-grade boys taunt him with *Weedy Bodo*.

"Have you seen Caravaggio's *The Denial of Saint Peter* at The Metropolitan Museum of Art? It is a very important picture," Kermit said between spoonfuls of chicken soup. "It was Caravaggio's last painting placed in a museum."

"No. I arrived in New York last night. This is my first visit."

"You must frequent the Metropolitan Museum," Kermit said. He pulled a small leather book from his breast pocket with writing paper and a pen and mapped a tour of his favorite rooms.

"Thank you," Reade said. "I am a friend of Anna Magdalena."

ONE 7

"Yes, I know," he said. "By the way, take a look at the Flemish Masters. Anna Magdalena's face is one they dearly loved. You will find her there. Every picture tells a story."

Waiters patiently bent over each guest with portions of what looked to Reade like his Ma's pot roast, slices of glistening chicken, greens, and noodles. He was beginning to enjoy himself when he noticed a man across the table spying on him through a vase of roses: his one dark pupil appeared between the white petals; his other was covered in a pirate patch. Reade fortified the wall between them with crystal water goblets and empty wine glasses and returned his attention to Kermit's art lecture.

"Neoclassicism was popular at the turn of the nineteenth century. With new engineering methods brought on by the industrial revolution, Greek revival, Gothic and Renaissance architecture appeared in the background of paintings. This was the beginning of modernity."

The one-eyed stranger across the table stood and tipped a bottle of wine toward Reade's glass.

Reade covered it with his hand. "No, thank you. I don't drink."

"Welcome to New York, Reade. And to my childhood home. My name is Saxton. You've met my mother, Lulu? And I see you've met my mother's partner, Kermit."

The two facts Reade recalled from Anna Magdalena's

description of her ex-lover practically crushed him on the spot: he wore a pistol in an ankle holster, and he preferred to sleep with strangers of either sex. Reade thought he might be challenged to a duel after dinner. Or worse.

"We worried when Maggie ghosted us," Saxton continued, "but here she is, back to haunt. And, I must add, it's good to have our whore at the table again."

"Whore," Reade said. His tongue was a bouquet of unpreparedness. He turned toward Anna Magdalena, but she wasn't in her seat. Scanning the room, he found her hugging a woman in a pink sari a few chairs away from Lulu. She noticed Reade's face-off with Saxton. The triangle—Anna Magdalena, her lover, and her ex-lover—caused a hushed ripple around the table.

"Call Anna Magdalena an esthetic terrorist, why don't you. Or an angel. Or an artist extraordinaire," Reade said.

"Whore is what I call myself," Saxton said. "Or anyone who makes sex the epicenter of their world. Perhaps virginity is still the aspired state in WILL-A-PA?"

Reade gave Saxton an abrupt nod. He sat down, refusing to engage further. Retrieving his napkin from the floor, he placed it over his lap and turned his attention back to Kermit.

"Mr. Bordeaux, we are breaking the fast. Today is Yom Kippur, the holiest day of the Jewish year. The day we ask both friends and enemies for forgiveness. You are not Jewish, are you?"

"No, I'm not religious."

"As an immigrant in New York, I survived on onion rolls placed on every table at Ratner's," Kermit continued. "Young Jewish immigrants who couldn't speak English like me were given the job of pouring water for customers. In return, we were allowed to eat all the onion rolls we wanted. I learned enough English to join the Army this way. U.S. intelligence needed German speakers. After the war, I started many businesses that failed. Eventually, I opened an exporting business to help Europe rebuild. I exported steel and began to buy impressionist prints and out-of-fashion nineteenth-century religious paintings. That is how I opened my gallery."

Kermit selected two pastel-colored cookies, pink and green, offered by a waiter. Reade selected a yellow cookie that melted into a sweet lemon paste in his mouth. He later learned they were called macarons, a favorite of Anna Magdalena.

"And what is your business?" Kermit asked.

"I'm a plumber by trade," Reade said.

"Oh," Kermit nodded. "That's a useful skill."

But the plain, dull word "plumber" tasted dry and brittle in his mouth so he elaborated. "Humans are driven by the need for fresh water. And like electricity, unless contained, water finds the path of least resistance. Water pipes are necessary yet it's common for them to break in a freeze or an earthquake. Water moves soil, so a broken water pipe can erode a hillside. Great amounts of soil run right over the biggest falls like Niagara and Victoria, sculpting graceful contours of deserts and mountains."

Kermit nodded. He gave Reade his card and untucked his napkin. As he stood, Reade noticed a slight hint of red in Kermit's silver waves of hair. A small plump pillow rested beneath each eye. "Please visit my gallery. I have some pictures I'd like to show you." He patted Reade's shoulder. "Good night, my friend."

Lulu linked Reade's arm and guided him past her friends, nodding and smiling. Anna Magdalena stood in a clutch of guests at the elevator: her stretchy black dress was calf-length; her shoulders now wrapped in petals of woven fabric like a peony. Walking toward her with Lulu, her eyes brightened.

"I hope you enjoyed yourself, Reade," Lulu said.

"I did. Thank you for inviting me. It was so nice to meet you and Kermit and," Reade hesitated, "Saxton."

Lulu paused their stroll. "I wasn't about to give up Maggie when she and Saxton broke up. She's mishpocha —that means family in Yiddish—and now you are mishpocha, too. You have nothing to worry about, Reade. Call me if you need anything."

TWO

IT WAS in the forgotten Victorian resort on the coast of Washington State where Reade met Anna Magdalena. He prepared a rich six-by-eight-foot bed in his garden and, deciding he wanted something more exotic, drove thirty miles up the peninsula to the Willapa Garlic Festival. Walking through the dozen or so vendors, a hand-painted sign caught his attention: *Trophies, Portraits of Wild and Domestic Creatures.* Locals hovered, reluctant to approach the papíer maché animal heads as the woman behind the counter was a stranger: blue-painted periwinkle covered her face. Her hair, tucked under a black knit cap, stood like a giant beehive on top of her head.

"I recognize my she-goat, Edna," Reade said. "That curl between her eyes and the dark streak of beard to the left of her chin."

"Ah! Yours must be the farm on the ocean, the one

with the little duck pond," she said. "I noticed your horse and goat have some sweet attachment. The goat butts the horse, he canters off, and she catches him and butts him again. Your horse doesn't seem to mind." The woman offered him her black-gloved hand. "Hi. I'm Anna Magdalena." Tilting her head, she pointed to the block-style letters, her signature, painted on her cheek. "Call me AM."

Her grip, strong and warm, surprised him. He was bewildered that this strange woman knew where he lived. "I'm Reade Bordeaux," he said. "He hates being alone. Buckeye, I mean. My horse."

AM spun the life-size goat head in one hand and offered it to him. Up close the head looked abstract; only from a distance of four or five feet was it strangely realistic. He turned the hollow head upside down and noticed strips of *The Willapa News* plastered inside.

"How much do you want for it?"

"Five braids of garlic," she said.

"What?"

"I don't take money for art."

"Why the hell not?"

"Because bartering brings out the quirks in people. You know, you get dialogue, facts, and fiction. I took a vow when I left New York: no sex, drugs, technology, or exchange of money for one year."

"That's bold," Reade said, looking around. "I see five braids of garlic goes for fifty bucks."

She leaned over the counter, her palm cupping his

shoulder. His eyes traced the edge of painted petals along her hairline. "If you hang around another hour," she said, "garlic braids go for half price. I'll hold your goat for you, Ree Dee. Or if you have some other trade in mind, shoot."

Handing the goat head back, he gazed upward at the wide, wet sky. The encounter was absurd, he thought; but after circling the festival tables, he purchased a bowl of ice cream and found himself wandering back to her booth. He set the bowl and spoon on her counter.

"It's garlic vanilla," he said and laughed, his mouth puckering.

As she lulled the first cold bite from side to side in her mouth, he decided she was beautiful: a cross between an owl and a sea otter. She was his height but slight, with eyes that were half-opened. And her nose was just a little bump with two, dark, tear-drop nostrils. If he didn't act now, he suspected that he would dwell on her periwinkle face all week long at the Seattle Pipefitting Company.

"I've got some organic garlic on my farm. I'll bring some by tomorrow."

"Okay," she said. "Take the trophy with you. My studio is the old gas station next to the Willapa store on the bay."

Her garage was heated with a wood stove. A makeshift worktable of plywood on sawhorses was covered with neatly arranged jars and tins full of pencils and brushes and large paper piled at one end. Behind the table was a closed door labeled "toilet." The other door, half-open, led to the itty-bitty office that served as her living quarters: a single bed, a hot plate poised on top of a half-refrigerator, and a space heater. Reade set his box of dried garlic on the studio floor, and she turned the electric dial on the hot plate to boil a pot of water. He watched as she placed fresh mint leaves in two cups. Her unpainted face was wide and smooth and her chin delicate as a quail egg. She poured the hot water into the cups, and they took their tea through a bit of woods to a damp, mossy log at the edge of Willapa Bay. Reade noticed an oysterman in yellow rain gear maneuvering a small barge with a pole off in the distance.

"This palette of horizontal grays has no distinction between water, earth, and sky," she said. "It's the embodiment of Einstein's thought: the past, present, and future as one."

Reade gazed at her profile. He wondered if her face was actually heart-shaped with that tiny point of a chin. He found himself shy and reverted to a childhood challenge of forming a sentence without R's to avoid his speech impediment, if only for a moment. "I hung the goat head on my mantle, and she glowed all night," he said. "She died a few months ago."

"What happened to the goat?" AM asked.

Reade smiled at her question. Was it a fluke that she also constructed her sentence without R's, or did she notice his game?

"Sheriff Fox blamed my neighbor, Frank Dearborn,

but it must have been my fault. I found tufts of her hair tangled in old wire fencing I left in her pasture. She probably died of dehydration. What did you paint her with?"

"I mix my own paints," AM said, "sometimes substituting ingredients such as horse piss and spider webs when I don't have them. Maybe phosphorus from Willapa Bay made it glow in the dark."

"Well, I've got a barn full of spider webs and a horse full of piss if you need any."

"Thank you, Ree-Dee."

"What are you doing in Willapa?" he asked.

"I'm planning my next season. I'm a performance artist. Technically, an esthetic terrorist."

"Terrorist?" He stared out at the sky. "Nobody dies, I hope."

"No, no, no. It's a movement," AM replied. "It refers to the process of making art—destroying outmoded ideas."

It was ebb tide. The waters of the Pacific poured into the bay through a deep channel, quickly covering the mudflats. "I've taken a vow, too," Reade said. "I'm married to Sergeant Becky Smith. It's sad to admit, but the marriage is failing."

"How's that?"

"She decided to make a career in the Army. I told her from the beginning I could never live that life. She's doing basic training in Fort Jackson, South Carolina as we speak."

Reade waited for her response, but none came. Anna Magdalena stared out at Einstein's picture. He could see it now—a picture of—not human time—but universal time. Or not even time, he decided, but movement or music. AM stood, stepped out of her sweatpants and sneakers, pulled her sweatshirt over her head, and sashayed into the water. As her bare ass set like gibbous moons into the bay, he tore off his clothes and splashed into the cold water after her, mud clouding his feet, grass slicing into his legs. She dove, porpoise-like, up and down in the shallow water. He walked behind her until, finally, she turned toward shore. Like his tongue never at home in his mouth, he never learned to swim.

The following Saturday, they rode Buckeye bareback to the Pacific. Slipping through the pasture gate into the dunes, a black bear ambled inland among the stubby dark pines. It was an unusual sighting. Weather was upon them. Buckeye dropped sharply down the last dune to the Pacific, and a sheet of hail bit their faces.

"Get under my jacket," Reade said.

But AM crawled under his shirt and pressed her cheek against his back, her teeth against his skin, her fingers clenching his ribs. Egging Buckeye on, Reade yodeled into the hail. AM yipped and squealed. By the time they arrived at the rocks below the North Head Lighthouse, she was moaning, her body limp as she slid off Buckeye. Reade tethered the horse at the edge of the woods, and they hunkered under a tarp tied between some stakes left by previous beachcombers.

"It doesn't take much to sexually excite me these days," she said.

"Really?" He laughed. "What about your vow? Doesn't that count as sex? What if you conceived? Who would be the father, me or Buckeye?"

She peeked through a hole in the plastic lean-to, her fists held like a telescope focusing on the foamy white ocean. "If I become pregnant, the babe will be lusty like me, with Buckeye's ears and hair, and your strong lean shoulders and butt."

AM's nails had broken his skin along his ribs, his shirt spotted with blood. She pulled out a pocket knife, poked her own finger, and dabbed her blood with his, like finger paints on the blue cotton.

"Brothers are gods, keepers of the status quo," she said.

"Oh, yeah?" Reade was unsure of what she meant. It didn't sound good. He was disappointed thinking that this was as close as they'd ever get. A gust of wind swept in off the ocean, rattling the plastic like a freight train. AM shivered. He mounted Buckeye and pulled her up behind.

She wrapped her arms around him again and said, "We'll call the babe Billie, and we'll roam the world of infinite possibilities, forever and ever."

The next adventure of Reade and AM took place when a second crop of Willapa blueberries ripened. Reade introduced AM to the field where he and his Ma picked seventy-five pounds most years of his childhood.

Eating while picking was part of the ritual, and when he stuck out his blue tongue, she jumped him and sucked on it. He held her shoulders close. She laughed and twisted her head free and he put his mouth on the curve of her neck. A rustling in the bushes brought them to attention, fearful of another bear.

"Knock it off," said an old man. He wore a baseball cap and a half-full tin of blueberries on a string around his neck. He shoved Reade, throwing him off balance.

"I'm Anna Magdalena," she said. "This is my friend Ree Dee. We were just laughing at our blue tongues." They stuck theirs out in unison and the old man followed, his tongue as blue as theirs. He gave them a silly smile and ambled off.

One rare, clear day Reade and AM rode Buckeye into the Coastal Range to view the trifecta of local Cascade peaks: Mount Hood, Mount Baker, and the famous one that blew its top, Mount Saint Helens. Up along Bear Creek, they ambled, twisting along a dirt road that narrowed to a path. Two eagles mid-air fought a buzzard with a small carcass in its claws; and when AM got off the horse to pee, a coyote stared Reade down without so much as an ear twitch. But it was a skinny, scraggly, bearded marijuana farmer aiming a rifle at them that turned them back. They skedaddled along deer trails, rooted through swamps and mudflats, past fallen houses and busted barns. Reaching the mouth of the Columbia River, they dismounted and warmed their fingers on a thermos of tea. They ate aged cheddar and new fall apples. Buckeye rebelled when they mounted him. He wanted a good brushing after the uphill sweat, a handful of grain, and a rest in the barn.

"I want to be you," AM said one Saturday.

They were canoeing to an island in the middle of Willapa Bay, famous for its 2,000-year-old cedar trees and home to the spotted owl. Steering in the rear, Reade meditated on the swirl of water that passed with her every stroke. They pulled the canoe through reeds and onto a beach strewn with agates. A path drew them inland, past remnants of fields and fences, evergreens overgrown with grapevines, old stone foundations, and a blackened fire pit to a great blue heron rookery. The majestic cedars were not grand like the California Redwoods as Reade expected, but wide with thick bark, stacked one inside the other like painted Russian nesting dolls. Awaiting tide change for the paddle back to the peninsula, they rested in tall grass. Thousands of migrating brants nested in the nearby spartina-choked mudflats. He pulled off her black knit cap and decorated her thick hair with tiny dried yellow flowers.

"I mean it. I want to be you," she said.

Reade laughed.

"I want you to teach me to shoot, Ree-Dee."

"Wouldn't a gun fall under the category of technology?"

"In my book, technology is mass communication and transportation."

"A farmer uses a firearm to put down sick animals. What do you want a gun for?"

"I want to know everything you know. I want to be you. It's possible."

"If brothers are gods, keepers of status quo," he said, "then sisters are revolutionaries."

She strolled along the edge of the bay. "I can walk like you. Talk like you. Actors do it all the time. When you look at me, you'll see yourself. Isn't that what happens? I can wear your clothes, cut my hair shoulder-length like yours, straighten it, and make it your shiny reddish-brown."

"If you become me, who am I?" he asked. "And where would you go? Would I be inside you?" He smiled. "I might like that."

She stood in front of him, her legs pressed together. "I'm going to click my ruby red slippers three times, Ree Dee."

"Wait!" He held her feet. "We might be airlifted like Dorothy to some strange Oz. Or sail over the edge of the globe. Or land on the moon. Or you might become the first female president of the United States."

At midnight, the last day of Anna Magdalena's year of celibacy, Reade woke to her slipping under his covers. He had quit his job at the Seattle Pipefitting Company by then and was working at the Ilwaco Marina to be closer to her. He loaned his house to Honey Dearborn's filmmakers, so he was staying on his boss's sailboat. They started gobbling where they left off in the blueberry field, the riggings of the sailboat chiming, the Styrofoam bumper squeaking against the dock until exhausted, dropping to whispers, she fell asleep. Reade held her close, naming all the lovely parts of her body he touched: soles to toes; calves, knees and thighs; abs and back; arms, hand, breast; cheek, and neck.

AM was gone when Reade woke the next morning. He looked for evidence, proof that she wasn't a dream. Days and weeks passed. He was miserable. She'd left a puzzle in the cab of his truck, a drawing of a female nude stretched inside the frothy curl of a wave, arms straight above her head, eyes closed, her mouth oval in an ecstatic scream. Under the drawing, she wrote, "v. excited." Instead of calling Sheriff Fox to send a search party, he rode Buckeye up and down the beach as they had for a year of Saturdays. Reade's boss at the Ilwaco Boatyard said he was sorry when he fired him for calling in sick three weeks straight. Reade didn't blame him. It was fishing season, and a shitload of broken propellers needed to be pulled from boats snagged in the shallows of the Columbia River or, worse, smashed onto the rocks on the Pacific coast.

Five hundred and fourteen hours after she disappeared, at 2:00 a.m. Pacific Standard Time, his cell rang.

"Ree Dee," she whispered into the phone. "I'm in New York. 1220 Front Street. A warehouse in Queens. Fly to JFK Airport and take a cab. Don't forget to say

Queens or the driver will take you to the wrong borough and dump you in the river."

His voice quaked. "I'll say take me to Queen Anna Banana Magdalena."

"Hurry up and don't be late!"

He threw back the covers and sat in the dark of his Willapa farmhouse, three thousand miles away. "Why'd you leave like that, AM? What took you so long to call? We were friends for a year, slept together once, and you poof into thin air?"

"I love you, Ree Dee."

She had never said anything close to that before. The pain of the last three weeks drained down through his legs and out his feet. "I love you, too, Anna Magdalena Pierce, but you can't disappear on me. My life has been a mess since you left. I'll book a flight, but if New York doesn't work out, sweet, this trip will be our grand finale."

"No poof. I promise."

THREE

FRANK DEARBORN WAS the most nervous guy Reade ever met. A skinny six-footer with a tight, thin face, reddish skin, and a slow, deliberate way of making him feel like shit. Reade remembered Frank saying, "How's your wife? Keeping her tied up in Seattle?" Then he'd finish his riff with, "I never did like you all that much, Reade."

What seemed to occupy Frank was nothing more than waxing and polishing the dozen or so spiffy vintage cars he kept in a garage in Chinook. One day, passing AM on her bike, Frank noticed her painted face —something she did when she went out in public—the way conventional women put on make-up when they go out. Frank rolled down his window and asked her to paint his face for an upcoming event, but Frank's unpredictable moods worried Reade. On the appointed day, he hid behind her studio. The paint session wasn't going well. Frank hadn't shaved, and she refused to paint his face. While Frank paced, AM rambled on about things she learned at the Ilwaco Museum, things he must have known concerning his great-great-grandfather, Oren Dearborn, and his friend, John Jacob Astor, IV. Astor named a small lumber mill on the Columbia River after himself and hired Washington Irving to write a novel billing Astoria as New York City west. The book was dull but Oren and John Jacob, the two friends, continued to scheme. They built a railway up the thirty-mile Willapa peninsula, a row of Victorian beach houses, and ran a steamboat from Portland to the fishing village of Ilwaco, turning Willapa of the 1890s into a vacation destination.

Frank finally settled into the old chair AM dragged in from the beach, and once his face was smooth, she dipped a little roller into blue paint, ran it over his whole face, a half-inch from his hairline, and signed her initials in yellow block letters on his cheekbone. A second dispute erupted when she refused his forty bucks. He threw the twenties at her, and she threw them back. She explained her vow not to exchange money for one year, but he refused to cooperate. The spat ended when Frank paused at the window and asked, "Will the paint wash off in the rain?"

"If it rains baby oil, baby, you are in trouble," AM said. "Otherwise, it stays on until you peel it off. Start at the chin and peel upward. You've got twelve hours before you turn into a pumpkin."

"Pumpkin!" he said with disgust.

Frank floored the gas pedal of his red and white '55 Chevy and drove off with a splash. Reade jumped into his old pick-up hidden behind a hill of oyster shells and followed as far as the turn-off to the Astoria Bridge. He was afraid Frank would see him in his rear-view mirror on the long three-mile crossing and do something dangerous on the bridge. AM later described Frank as having no skin, no outer organ to protect himself from the world. He was the kind of raw encounter she craved, edging close to the crevasses of human wilderness.

Sheriff Fox whipped his hand in the air like a lasso when he spotted Reade in the checkout line at Sid's grocery. He waited for Reade in the parking lot, his legs jittery even as his feet remained grounded. "Mr. Reade Bordeaux. It's my lucky day!" Sheriff Fox crowed. "Yes, sir! Frank Dearborn robbed a bank in Portland. Police cornered him in a gas station restroom. A crowd gathered when he wouldn't open up. Cops broke the door down and found Frank dead on the floor dressed as a clown. Authorities sent me a video that a local man took on his phone." He pointed a finger at Reade as he walked away. "Watch the news tonight. You'll see for yourself. Frank Dearborn is dead!"

Reade unexpectedly knocked at AM's studio door and found her reading on her bed. He had never shown up on a Friday night before. She tripped on a pile of books in the middle of her tiny floor and lurched forward, spilling her cup of tea. Reade waited for her to ask what was up before telling her about Frank's suicide.

"Let's ride over to the Depot Diner to watch the news. I'll buy you something to eat."

She grabbed her coat, slipped her stocking feet into her boots without lacing them, and they drove in the grumbling silence of his old truck through the clear, damp night. Weekenders had parked up and down the residential street, and they took the only two available seats in the far corner of the bar where people hang their coats. Reade ordered a pot of tea, a bowl of vegetarian chili, and a slice of blackberry pie. When an old photograph of Frank driving his red Cadillac in the annual car parade flashed on the screen, Reade asked the bartender to turn up the volume. The sound of gunshot silenced the diners as they watched the cop break down the men's room door at the Portland gas station. Frank's head was wedged against the toilet, his face painted purple. AM's initials were blocked in red. Only a trickle of blood issued from his mouth.

The next clip showed a reporter interviewing a teary woman from East Portland, the mother of three children, who claimed that Frank Dearborn dropped paper bags of cash on street corners in her neighborhood.

"Nobody believed it at first," she said. "I didn't believe it either, but I was on the lookout. When I found a brown paper bag, I shared the cash with everyone on my block."

AM turned to me, agitated, mystified. "Frank was an esthetic terrorist."

Reade protested. "But Frank wasn't an artist."

This newsclip was sent to Honey Dearborn by her detective and she had him track down AM. Unannounced, Honey showed up at AM's studio. A skinny, bird-like woman, Honey was a New York City art dealer who hadn't previously met AM, but it turned out they knew people in common.

"Did Frank make art?" AM asked Honey.

"As a child, I let him use the walls of his room to write and paint."

AM placed various life-size chalk drawings on the table in front of Honey, images she had drawn after each encounter with him: Frank as queen. Frank as a sea monster. Frank in the trunk of a tree.

"Did you sleep with him?"

"No. I've taken a vow of celibacy," AM said.

AM next placed a small holy-card-size image in Honey's hands that unfolded into a triptych. In the center was Frank as Christ on the cross with the crown of thorns.

Honey switched from her sunglasses to her reading glasses. "He makes a beautiful savior."

"This is you on the left in teal blue," AM said. "I found a photo of you in a stack of magazines at the recycling center."

"Yes, that's my dress! Who is this monk on the other side?"

"Me," AM said. "It's traditional that the patron and the artist include themselves in altarpieces, right?"

"Of course," Honey cooed. "Did Frank ever mention me?"

"He said you were alive."

"Mm," she said. "The last time I hugged my son, he was sixteen years old. I dropped him off at boarding school in Connecticut and by Thanksgiving, he had run away. I never lost track of him, though. My detectives sent me pictures. For a while, he lived a wild life in Miami with a group of artists I once represented. I don't know how he ended up here. Willapa must be one of the quietest places on earth."

"Why did he kill himself?" Reade asked. His voice startled Honey. He was warming his hands at the woodstove. "If you don't mind my asking."

She sighed. "The game was up. He would go to jail. But it wasn't *that* he feared. I think it was me. He would not be able to escape me."

Honey pointed to a sculpture on the pole in front of the studio where Pegasus once stood when the place was a gas station. Locals called AM's sculpture *The Bride* or *The Holy Ghost*. She called it *The Winged Woman*. It was constructed from four metal chairs pounded and tied into a female shape and stuffed with flotsam AM picked off the beach. Coated in plastic and in the constant Pacific Northwest rain, it glistened like ice.

"How much is the sculpture?"

"I don't take money for art," AM said. "You have to decide on its value and come up with an equivalent trade. I've taken a vow not to exchange money for a year."

"But darling, I've never met an artist who turned down my check. I can give you cash."

"I want a trade. I'm positive you have something that would please me."

Honey ruffled her short white hair like a bird fluffing its feathers. She pushed her arms into the sleeves of her black sleeping bag-like coat and shuffled out of AM's studio in big, soft boots to her waiting driver. He opened the backseat door for her and placed the cylinder of AM's drawings in the trunk.

"I'll speak with my attorneys," Honey said from the open car window. And she bowed her head.

FOUR

READE MET HIS WIFE, Becky Smith, in the dairy section of Sid's grocery in Willapa. She was clean-cut, cheery, and excellent at pulling off first impressions. Twelve years older than Becky and a whole head taller, Reade was dressed in his work clothes, coming straight from the Seattle Pipefitting Company. He was surprised when she struck up a conversation with him.

"What kind do you prefer?" she asked in a loud, articulate voice.

He gave a little chuckle. "The real thing, if I can find it. My kid goat needs a bottle. And you, if I may ask?"

"Skim. The responsible choice. I eat three bowls of cereal a day. Breakfast, lunch, and dinner."

"You don't cook?"

An old-timer with a boyish bearded face dropped his arm on her shoulder. Reade recognized his round belly, plaid Bermuda shorts, and thin legs. His first impression of Meyer had been that of a meth addict or a thief, with his hands cupped to the glass of his kitchen window, his eyeballs rolling side-to-side. Public paths to the Pacific Ocean existed on every block in Willapa, so it irritated Reade that Meyer trespassed twice a day, walking through the middle of his farm. Over time, Reade came to accept Meyer's presence as a creature with a right of way, like a woodchuck.

"I'd like to introduce you to my daughter, Becky," Meyer said. "She's in ROTC. Uncle Sam pays her college tuition at the University of Washington." He tapped her shoulder with his finger. "She's going to be a doctor. You're single, aren't you, Reade?" Without waiting for an answer, Meyer continued. "Hey, I like what you're doing with the old farm. It was the prime town property when I was a kid. You're making it look good again."

Becky and Meyer dined at Reade's place Saturday nights after that. Meyer liked Julia Child's white bean soup with eggplant and tomato and the buttery pie his mother taught him to bake. Becky didn't care much about eating but seemed to genuinely enjoy time with her dad. Meyer pitched in to help reroof the 1920s three-car garage when Reade hired Jeff, the sixteen-year-old next door, and they ended up building dormers and a sleeping loft and plumbing it for a kitchen and bathroom. When Becky began spending Saturday nights with Reade in the cottage, Meyer regarded Reade's farm as his and his daughter as Reade's.

"Dad thinks we should get married," Becky said two months after they met.

Reade laughed like heck. "Well, what do you think? I'm a lot older than you. You're twenty-three and want to go to medical school. Do you really want to get married? I mean, why would you want to marry me?"

She laughed. "You're tall, dark, and handsome. And doesn't Father know best?"

That Becky would break Reade's heart never crossed his mind. Maybe because he didn't ever feel the sensation of *falling in love.* Meyer orchestrated the marriage, enabling him to retire from his Boeing job and move full-time to Willapa. Becky got Reade's Ma's Eiffel Tower-shaped platinum diamond wedding ring, protection from the men at Fort Lewis during her ROTC weekends. And Reade, haunted by his Pa's last words, "Not enough love," married in case Pa was right. He didn't want to miss out if there really wasn't enough love to go around.

Between stories of women and fish, Reade's buddies at Seattle Pipefitting Company teased him about marrying a woman in the U.S. Army. Old-twisted-tongue married a straight shooter, they used to say. After his mother died he spent a couple of weekends with these guys drinking beer, smoking cigarettes, and fumbling through one-night stands with women he met in bars. It was buying the farm and planting an apple orchard that changed him. He cleaned the barn, built a new deck on the old ship watchtower, and with the help of a hypnotist, stopped drinking, smoking, and womanizing in one swoop. Soon after, he and Becky married, which was okay until Becky's spring graduation from college. She left for basic training and never returned Reade's texts or calls and they argued during their weekly Skype sessions.

"You don't get it, Reade," she whispered, leaning into her screen, her mouth opened so wide he could see down her throat. "Women have opportunities in the Army right now. Besides, I don't really have a choice. I'd have to pay back my scholarship and probably go into active service if I left the Army."

"Just tell me what do you like about the it, anyway?"

"It's exciting, she said. "Hey, you're the one who taught me to shoot a rifle."

"Yeah, exciting to everyone but the dead, the maimed, the orphaned, the widows, and the widowers. Why not go to Hollywood? War movies are a heck of a lot safer."

"Are you cooking dinner for Dad once a week like you promised?"

"He's here for Saturday dinner and Sunday breakfast, Beck. Like a stray, he shows up at my doorstep at all hours. Last Friday he was standing in my driveway when I pulled in from Seattle at 9:00 p.m. He said he found an article in a 1920 newspaper about the farm that he wanted to show me."

"That's not good."

"It's you he misses. He thought marrying me meant

you'd live a mile down the beach—at least on weekends."

After meeting AM, Reade worried less about his marriage. Becky was scheduled to be home December 20th but showed up the following Saturday, three days late. The four of them were sipping coffee in the driveway—AM, Meyer, Reade, and Bubba, owner of the Red Barn—when they heard the familiar downshift of her car. Her foxy red ponytail flew over the back seat of the convertible as she turned into the driveway. She jumped out dressed in fatigues and heavy black combat boots and gave her father a man-size slap on his back and a kiss on his bristly cheeks. She took three running steps and jumped into Reade's arms—a trick she perfected on their Hawaiian honeymoon—luckily, he caught her. Turning to Bubba, she socked him in the gut. Finally, stepping into a military pose, offered her hand to AM and introduced herself.

Reade's eyes popped seeing his two superheroes side by side: Becky was Artemis in military armor; and AM, Spider-Woman in her black ghetto clothes. Riffing on uniforms, guns, and the military—Becky's staccato and AM's drone—was amusing. They talked over each other like a dance until the conversation turned to Frank Dearborn, who had only recently died.

"I'd rather live across the street from an alien than Frank Dearborn," Becky said.

"Do you mean the little green Martians with antennas?" AM asked.

FOUR

"Whatever," Becky said. "Foreign is better than crazy."

"Pope Francis said if aliens land at the Vatican, he'll baptize them in case God allows extraterrestrials into heaven," AM said.

"Frank once did me a favor," Bubba interrupted, hesitantly.

Bubba was there to drop off an old pony that he claimed was born on Reade's farm. Reade knew the pony could no longer pay her way, but he let Bubba have his way. A few years back, Bubba's nose had been bitten off in a bar fight by his rival. Locals joked that the fierce little guy filed his teeth into daggers instead of brushing them. The doctor in Ilwaco was no surgeon: Bubba's nose had been sewn back, crooked and stuck out like a sore thumb.

"One dark night," Bubba continued, "I was headed toward Chinook and my truck broke down. I freaked when Frank pulled up behind me. But he handed me his keys to his '55 Chevy and told me to drop it off at his house when my truck's fixed. And he walked off into the night."

Reade laughed. "Sheriff Fox must have been looking for him."

Becky and Reade had sex three afternoons during Becky's December leave. She hated the old farmhouse and slept nights at her father's down the road. But in the evenings, Reade found Becky parked in his driveway when he came home from work and they headed to the cottage loft. After sex, she lit a joint, a new habit of hers, and turned talkative. Her stories eventually wound down to her Army career. Reade stated that he had no interest in living on an Army base or moving around with her. Every ragged conversation dragged him down. He was resigned to calling the marriage over. Still, he felt the sharp edge of guilt whenever he looked at her. Until the third afternoon.

"I forgot to remove my hat before entering the officer's club," Becky said. "I learned the protocol the hard way and had to buy a round of drinks for everyone at the bar, which cost a couple of hundred bucks and caused a lot of teasing. The incident singled me out. One of the Captains at the bar told me to follow her. She took me down the hall to an office, locked the door, ordered me to strip and lay on my back on the floor."

"Jesus, Peaches. Did you say fuck off or I'm reporting you?"

"I was paralyzed. I imagined a bullet from her Beretta M9 traveling up my spine and blasting out through a hole in my skull."

"What?" Becky didn't want his comfort. She wasn't emotional. She didn't seem to feel anything. Why did she even tell him? It reminded him of something her unlovely mother would say, just to unnerve him.

"Did you report it?" he repeated.

"I talked with a few of the girls. They weren't surprised. They'd heard of this kind of stuff and wrote it off as hazing. She was subsequently transferred, so no worry."

Becky flew off for officers training and Reade tried to erase the U.S. Army from his mind. Meyer continued to show up on his property, and he found it curious that he never questioned the Saturdays that AM spent at the farm. Meyer was a regular at AM's Sunday community art class and maybe, Reade thought, Meyer had fallen in love with AM, too. Each time Meyer asked where she lived, Reade came up with another answer: off the beaten path, the other side of Willapa, or I don't really know. He suggested to AM that she lock her door and hang a curtain over her one small window because Meyer Smith was, among other things, a Peeping Tom.

In the spring, Becky texted that she was undergoing tests at the hospital. Doctors thought she might have mono. Reade offered to visit. She said absolutely no. Lydia, her mother, had visited and that was enough company, which he understood. Lydia didn't care about much besides cigarettes, cards, and bourbon. Becky promised to send word when the doctors figured it out. But she didn't let on until maternity leave in August when she was eight months pregnant. And she ignored all of Reade's questions until he finally hit upon the one she wanted to answer.

"Am I the father?"

"You have to be the father," she said. "Fertilization only takes place when a sperm penetrates an egg and you're the only man I've slept with since December."

"But you were on birth control pills. At least, last we talked."

"I thought a baby might make a difference."

"Really? And?"

"Nothing has changed."

"Well, actually, a great deal has changed, Becky. We are going to be parents."

This news depressed him. He didn't want to think about it. And he didn't want AM to know. She had described Becky as dynamite when they met that morning at his farm, and Becky proved AM right.

Billie was born eight pounds, nine ounces after a long night of labor, and finally a C-section on September 17th. Reade peeked at him in the hospital and fell in love, but Becky didn't want him around until she was settled into her childhood bedroom at her mother's house. She refused to stay at their bungalow in West Seattle.

"William Meyer Smith Bordeaux," she said after she had filled out the birth certificate. Reade paused at "Meyer," but then, he reasoned, he got his Billie.

"Billie Bordeaux," Reade said. "Son of Becky and Reade Bordeaux."

She corrected him: "Son of Becky Smith and Reade Bordeaux."

It was a rough ride for Becky, camping out in her childhood bedroom with twin beds, matching yellow bedspreads, and ruffled curtains. Reade arrived each night after Lydia and her boyfriend left for the nearest card game. Becky showed him Billie's dried umbilical cord on the window sill; she gave instructions on how to support his neck while lifting him, how to change his diaper, and the correct ointment to use on his circumcision, how to bathe and swaddle him, and so on. Surprisingly, Billie was a balm for both of them. Reade prepared his bottles, fed, and burped him. He doted on Becky, too, running bubble baths, fetching bowls of her favorite cereal, making sure her phone was charged. She was plugged into headphones most of her waking hours, but Reade didn't mind. He was committed to Billie, even before the paternity test that his attorney, JT, an old high school friend, insisted he have done.

At sunrise he drove home to their empty bungalow in West Seattle to sleep, buoyed by this new little boy, and each day woke with the same nagging nightmare he had since buying Becky the convertible. It always started with her waving like a beauty queen from her car, but as she made the turn past the huge purple blooming rhododendrons and drove through the gate, she gunned the engine and drove straight out into the Pacific Ocean. Strangely, it was the look of happiness on her face as she drove past him that upset him so much, and her car sinking into the cold wet grave, the last strands of her long yellow hair being sucked under.

FIVE

IT WAS Reade's second cold shower in the Queens warehouse that sent him to the cellar. Ducking cobwebs in the light of one dim bulb, he was careful not to scrape his head on the low ceiling. Most of the cellar was taken up with a monstrous boiler. Reade poked buttons and pulled levers but the beast never ignited, it only blew cold stale air. With fall upon them, a lack of heat now loomed larger than a lack of hot water. An internet search brought up companies selling new gas or oil furnaces but no boiler repairmen. Reade pulled a 1991 Yellow Pages from one of the desks upstairs and called various non-working numbers until he reached Harry with a long Russian last name. Harry came right over. Short and muscular with small, clam-shaped ears, thick greasy hair, and a raspy voice, he spread a cloth on the dirt floor and named his tools in a song-like accent as he laid them out: pressure gauges, relief valves, standard jacket assemblies, brackets, panels. Not only did he breathe life into the metal monster, but by the end of the week, he had installed a hot water heater. Harry said he was on his way to Orlando to visit his daughter and left his tools with Reade in case he needed them. Ten days later, when Harry still hadn't answered his phone, Reade stopped by his small, two-family house. A neighbor with the same Russian accent told him that Harry had died of throat cancer.

AM's schedule was grueling: by day she performed and by night she was wined and dined by collectors who set up appointments through her publicist. When Reade heard that some art patron had died, he decided to take advantage of the somber occasion to spill his beans about Billie. He arrived twenty minutes early to the Park Avenue church with plenty of time to find AM and sit together, or so he thought. But all four hundred seats were taken and he was stuck standing in the lobby listening to the service through an intercom. AM was nowhere to be seen. He only got excited when he read in the program that refreshments were to be served on the third floor of the Metropolitan Museum of Art.

"Annie Appleseed, I've got news," Reade whispered in her ear. He stood behind her in a circle of women at the afterparty.

"Meet me on the roof at noon tomorrow, Ree Dee," she said without turning her attention away from the crowd.

"Okay, see you at home."

Reade slipped down the marble stairway as a quartet played. A guard pointed him in the direction of Caravaggio, but peeking into passing doorways, he wandered into rooms of Van Gogh and Monet, American native carvings and weavings, Greek sculptures, and painted pottery. Upon reaching *The Denial of St. Peter* from 1610, he found the subject dark, even spooky. St. Peter, a woman, and a soldier pointed their fingers at each other like the awkward triangular moment at the Yom Kippur dinner: Saxton was the soldier, the bully who tortured him in second grade; AM was the woman, the revolutionary; and Reade, the unfortunate St. Peter, the victim and three-time liar, keeper of the status quo.

In the Medieval section of the museum, he settled in front of a small 1492 Flemish *Madonna and Child* by Hans Memling. It was mounted in a round wooden frame made from a single piece of tree. The placard stated that small Madonnas of this sort were traditionally placed above a bed for private prayer. Memling's Mary had a tan oval face, a small chin, and bold eyes that held him tight. The Christ-child engaged him, too, with his Mama's thin arms and fingers. He imagined a portrait of AM in a round wooden frame on their wall and made up a little prayer. Why shouldn't he stare directly at her instead of a saint if it was she he wanted?

The next morning, he squeezed in a visit to Kermit's gallery at Park Avenue and 84th, even as he knew he'd probably be a little late for his roof date with AM. He wanted to prove Kermit right, that a plumber was a good study, worthy of Anna Magdalena. Kermit's assistant, Jules, greeted him and turned on a series of lamps as he led Reade through large, dark rooms. He described scenes from his childhood during the Holocaust, of his separation from his parents at their urging, of hiding for weeks alone in the woods, of holding his wits by writing poetry. They walked past gilt-framed paintings, heavy curtains, Persian rugs over glossy, carved wooden tables, and illuminated life-sized sculptures of lions and tigers. Pausing at Kermit's office door, he quickly gave Reade a happy ending to his grave story. "After the war, I married the eldest daughter of the family who hid me in Belgium. She was ten years my senior and considered by her parents to be an old maid. We have a son and three grandchildren."

Like an elderly Teddy Roosevelt, Kermit sat at a formidable desk in a dark three-piece suit and blue tie. His eyes closed, his hands folded together. Only the twiddling of his thumbs, like the workings of his brain going round and round a business deal, announced that he was awake. He stood as Jules and Reade entered, shook Reade's hand, and welcomed him with grace. Yet, a moment later, he barked instructions at Jules about preparations for shipment to the Getty Museum. Jules nodded as if this was business as usual. When Jules exited, Kermit continued in a gentle tone.

"Yesterday a buyer refused Granet's *The Choir of the Capuchin Church in Rome*, so I upped the price," he said.

"This is my strategy: when a painting doesn't sell, I raise the price. Let me show you this interesting painting."

The floorboards creaked beneath the thick carpet as Reade followed him down the hall, staring at the back of his impeccable suit. He walked as if weighted down by his full, long life. Jules placed the painting in its ornate gilt frame on upholstered steps built against the wall for display and adjusted the spotlight. Even so, like everything else in the room, the painting was dark, the exception being one brightly-lit square window on the back wall of the church. Beneath the window, dozens of monks knelt in prayer at the edges of the chapel, and in the center, two altar boys and a priest stood next to an oversized book of scripture open on a large stand.

"The Capuchin Church is in Rome," Kermit said. "The chapel is behind the church. The monks live in total seclusion and they are famous for mocking earthly life. Granet painted the picture looking through this tiny opening behind the altar. You will visit one day."

Kermit showed Reade a postcard of the crypt beneath the church with skulls arranged like flowers: their petals of pelvic bones, stems of femurs, and leaves of tiny bones of fingers and toes. "Granet painted seventeen pictures of this chapel, one for the king of Russia, one for the Queen of Naples, one for Pope Pius VII, and other royalty. The biggest, four times this size, is in the Metropolitan Museum. This is an excellent painting and an excellent investment. For you, the price is only twelve thousand."

Reade smiled with impossible delight. Still, he noticed that Kermit awaited an answer. He wondered if a businessman like Kermit saw everyone as a potential customer. "I don't know anything about art," Reade finally said.

"Like me, you will learn," he replied.

As Reade was leaving, Kermit gave him a bible-size book, Janson's *History of Art, the Western Tradition*, which he opened on the downtown 6 train. The cover was Jan van Eyck's *Portrait in a Red Turban*, a handsome and intelligent-looking man that made him wish he had a close-up of his Pa's face so he could read his eyes. Reade was only eleven when his Pa died and barely understood him beyond the stereotype of a lady's man, a Republican, and a Navy veteran, with WWII memories of the bombing of his battleship locked deep in his psyche.

Reade made it back to Queens by noon and got in line but was informed of a forty-five-minute wait to reach the roof. A volunteer greeted him at the bottom of the stairs, took his five-buck donation, and stamped "AM" on the back of his hand. He was told that she was expecting him but that he would need to step into the performance in order to speak with her.

Most visitors waiting with him on the stairs occupied themselves with texting and snapping selfies. Reade observed the moving gears of the city. He noticed the large green swath of cemetery beyond the Long Island Expressway and wondered if Harry might be buried there, or maybe even Frank and Honey Dearborn. Reade still wrestled with Frank as a possible Robin Hood. Even Bubba told a story of a generous Frank. But the only Frank Reade knew steered his car toward him on two-lane roads when Frank saw his truck coming, forcing him to swerve toward the ditch.

At the top of the stairs, another volunteer directed visitors wishing to participate in the performance to move left. A large sign became visible:

> *This exhibit is not meant to be a religious scene but a historical practice, part of a year-long discourse on how "humans treat humans," a collaboration by artist AM and Gallery A, funded in part by the National Endowment for the Arts. Please fill out a questionnaire on our website after witnessing the exhibit and post a comment on social media. Keep in mind not only historical injustice but social injustice today, here, and around the world. If you'd like to participate in the exhibition, let a volunteer know. Each participant is limited to ten minutes.*

AM was strapped to a metal cross against the Manhattan skyline clad in a tan bodysuit, a white loincloth, and a crown atop her head. A young bearded man hung on a cross to her left, a smirk on his face, his fingers on both hands forming a peace sign. On her right, a thin woman with braided hair looked anxious, her wrists and ankles bound to the metal cross, her eyes roaming from the edge of the roof to the traffic jam on the elevated Brooklyn-Queens Expressway to the cars inching toward the Queensboro Bridge. *She is an actress, appropriately anxious as if really facing death*, Reade thought.

Once she was helped down, the volunteer held a ladder for Reade and he was strapped to the cross at AM's right. As a kid, he never understood why the image of a man nailed to a cross hung in the church. He averted his eyes, never wanting to look at it, and eventually, he became numb to its meaning. Seeing AM on the rooftop brought back the nausea he felt at Sunday Mass. The catechism he hadn't considered in decades throbbed against his temples, this time like an elevator pitch: *Jesus Christ, conceived by the Holy Ghost, born of the Virgin Mary, suffered under Pontius Pilate, was crucified, died, and was buried. He descended into hell, on the third day ascended into heaven, and sits at the right hand of God.*

"Hey, beautiful, this is quite a scene but tell me: why does art have to be miserable?" Reade said.

Her eyes opened. She looked at him in character with full sorrowful attention. "Truth is painful, Ree Dee. Truth mixed with pain is memorable. Even outdated truths. But seeing this familiar scene, especially out of context or participating in it, we see the old story anew."

"I want to talk about love," he said.

A volunteer handed AM a cup of water with a straw and she pulled her whole body up on her toes, sipped, and relaxed again into the hanging pose. "Ree Dee," she whispered, "your love is so big; you expect too much. Oh, shit! I need to pee!" She waved her hand to get the volunteer's attention and winced. "Oops."

"You peed yourself!" Reade laughed. He noticed the dark stain down her leg and shifted the conversation. "Do you remember our first ride to the beach on Buckeye and you got so excited I teased you about who the father would be if you had an immaculate conception?"

"I said we'd call the babe Billie."

"That's my news," Reade said. "Billie was born a month ago. A son. Becky kept her pregnancy a secret."

"You have a son named Billie?" she cried. "A baby boy? Reade, you are a father?"

She took his hand, all she could reach from their perch, and kissed it. The audience whistled. Phones lifted into the air. The moment was posted in a nanosecond and tweeted as some pretend "forgive me for I have sinned" scenario.

"I'm doing a paternity test. I'm prepared to raise him."

"Reade," she said, totally out of character now. "I am a childless mother. Saxton and I lost a full-term baby two years ago: Georgie Saxton Pierce. He lived only three days. Doctors said his death was inexplicable. Bring Billie to New York, Reade. I will be Billie's second mother."

Her chin dropped onto her chest. The same male volunteer Reade met ten minutes earlier unwrapped his wrists and ankles, held out his hand, and guided him down. Up next was an Asian woman with short, fine, white hair, fit as a mountain climber and smelling of sunscreen. Reade floated down the stairs to AM's private quarters on the first floor and fell onto her green couch. His heart throbbed inside his head. He feared his unintended fatherhood would put AM off, that he would lose her, that one day Billie would accuse him of being a sad-ass old man. But AM kept her promise: No poof.

SIX

KERMIT FLEUR ASKED Reade to stop by his gallery and suggested he should wear a sports coat. He dropped what he was doing, brewed a pot of black tea, and sat at the wooden kitchen table determined to at least skim the entire seventh edition of Janson's *History of Art, The Western Tradition*. When Reade apologized for not having finished reading it, Kermit said to keep the book and gave Reade specific instructions regarding purchasing a painting by Jean-Louis Forain at Sotheby's auction house, with a ceiling of $25,000.

Reade found himself sitting on a stiff red upholstered chair, surrounded by serious businessmen and women, young and old. A few like him didn't fit in: a teenager wearing sunglasses with long greasy hair; and a woman wearing a big hat with paper pastel-colored flowers, her dress exposing ample cleavage. Reade's eyes roved between the bidders sitting around him to a small photograph of the Forain cupped secretly in his hand. He tried inconspicuously to memorize its details in small glimpses—a female nude perched on a disheveled bed—when he noticed a prim young woman seated at his left, eying him. She watched curiously without turning her head. He broke protocol, he was sure. Looking directly at her, he nodded. Paddles began to fly, and he found it challenging to track the bids. Each time the gavel came down, he got another chance to start over and try to follow what was happening. Never having heard of the artists' names before made it all the more difficult. A dozen small pictures by William Bouguereau, images of a single-seated woman or young child, sold for between six hundred thousand and a million. The catalog stated that Bouguereau's paintings had not been auctioned in decades. The women to his left bought the only still-life offered.

"Congratulations," Reade whispered. She brushed him off by looking away like a schoolgirl who didn't want to get in trouble. The unfinished quality of the Forain in the palm of his hand troubled him. Specifically, her ghostly hands and a foot in the foreground. Kermit mentioned that Forain had a fifty-year friendship with Degas and was interested in painting the poetic moment. Only the model's full milky breasts were solidly composed and brightly lit. The left nipple was prominent. *Perhaps she was a nursing mother*, Reade thought. Billie preferred the breast with the heartbeat, too.

He straightened in his chair when, in the second hour, the auctioneer called out Jean-Louis Forain. The picture, displayed in an ornately carved gold frame, glowed under the light which seemed to shrink the image. From where he sat, its dark background and the mattress she sat on was no more than a few quick wide strokes, and her thin strands of long topsy-turvy hair, even her facial features, seemed fuzzy. Her eyes, on the other hand, stared boldly at the viewer. Reade agreed with Kermit that the picture captured a rare eternal moment, and he raised his paddle with an opening bid of $12,000. Unable to look around, he listened as two bid against him. After a strange middle-earth moment of confusion, he lifted his paddle again at $18,000. No counter bid was offered and the gavel came down. "Sold," the auctioneer called out. Reade sighed visibly. The woman next to him turned to him now with a full-tilt of her head. When the auctioneer moved on, Reade got up and left.

Kermit was pleased with Reade's first purchase. His strategy to bring an outsider to bid for him was common practice. Kermit was well known at the auction houses, and he estimated that Reade saved him, in this case, at least ten grand. Kermit knew that the director of the Toledo Museum was looking to build his nineteenth-century collection, and when Kermit described the Forain, he flew to New York to take a look. Kermit was able to show him several other nineteenth-century paintings, and the director purchased a total of three.

Alberto was Reade's newest friend in New York. As a gentle six-foot-five multi-talented Black man, Alberto seemed to have acres between his shoulders. He didn't need to own a farm, as Reade did, to feel free. Reade guessed that if AM ever gave Alberto respite, he would do something radical, like end racism, poverty, and food insufficiency in New York City. In the meantime, in charge of the warehouse clean-up, Reade only had a month to prepare the first floor for AM's second performance of the season; and it was Alberto who hired three local young men to work alongside him. They filled dumpsters with broken metal desks, filing cabinets, and piles of dusty garbage from the first and second floors; moved their sleeping quarters one floor up, and steam cleaned the identical first and second-floor bathrooms. Reade hired a company to sand the floors, build walls, and paint everything white except the wooden struts of the ceiling. A king-size bed was delivered, the one prop AM needed for her performance. Vivian Boo and her Gallery A team were responsible for the lighting, videotaping, social media, and press. Alberto took care of the volunteers and everything else.

Alberto was originally hired by Gallery A to be AM's bodyguard during an ugly social media spat, but delighted in dressing AM and now also Reade, in evening attire. Alberto's long-term lover, a theater director, had given him borrowing privileges at his theater's warehouse. To attend *Tosca* with one of AM's collectors—which was to be Reade's first opera—Alberto dressed him in a tight gray designer suit with a ruffled silk shirt and cut and combed his hair into a man-bun. AM wore black velvet pantaloons, a see-through embroidered blouse, and swept her fist of hair down over her forehead into a single large curl. To this, AM added face paint: red roses and green leaves completely camouflaged her features. The audience quivered as they settled into their seats, and if getting to the opera wasn't enough drama, every emotion on the face of the soprano, Sonya Yoncheva, who played Tosca, was visible from their fourth-row seats. Tosca, like AM, dedicated her life to love and art. She had Reade bawling *before* she jumped off the roof.

AM's second performance piece of the season, Bed-In, opened to a crowd larger than the Crucifixion. The line snaked twice around the perimeter of the warehouse. The performance, inspired by John and Yoko's 1969 Love and Peace extravaganza, ran for five weeks, through the middle of December. Opening night, she wore a slinky Marilyn Monroe black slip beneath a sheet on the bed. Like the Crucifixion, the audience and participants had a list of rules to follow. Most participants were after a selfie under the covers with AM, but Alberto told Reade to expect some to fly the scene upside down. Sure enough, standing back against the wall, a guy wearing black horn-rimmed glasses, a 1960s haircut, and a black overcoat, carrying a suitcase, grabbed Reade's arm. Looking into the stranger's eyes, he recognized Saxton without an eyepatch. To Reade's surprise, neither eye seemed to have any problem. One of the videographers shined her spotlight on them in line.

"Reade, I beg you to stay and watch," Saxton said. "I'm up next."

A volunteer started the timer, and Saxton tore off his overcoat to reveal a smoking jacket. Opening the suitcase, he removed a bottle of champagne, popped it open and lit a cigar. AM feigned sleep, her head on the pillow, but she sat up to the snap of his fingers. He passed her a Chinese Kimono and a Cleopatra wig while he selected 1920s jazz on his phone. Presenting her with a long-stem rose, he then pulled an etched flute from each pocket, poured bubbly, and they toasted. Cell phones clicked as Saxton kissed her, breaking rule number one: no touching. AM slapped him. A buzzer rang. His cigar lit her paper wig on fire, orange flames blossomed over the bed, which Saxton doused with the champagne, making a swampy, smoky mess. Saxton winked at Reade and took a dramatic bow as volunteers ushered the audience out, closing the warehouse. Reade shook his head negatively and bit his tongue.

Deciding to stay away from the Bed-In after that depressing experience, he took the lump of keys AM inherited and strolled over to the old gas station leaning against the warehouse. A narrow path, littered with syringes and smelling of urine, led to a side door. He tried the various keys on the ring until one slipped in.

He jiggled it and slowly turned. Soft with rot, the wooden door bent under his weight. With a forceful shove of his foot, it opened to a small office. A counter was covered with a dusty cash register and typewriter, a 1972 calendar, coffee mug and spoon, tools, and stacks of papers piled with mouse turds. Opening the door into the double bay garage, streetlight glinted through a broken window revealing stacks of cardboard and old dusty cans of paint and oil. Flicking on his phone light, he recognized the dozen green trunks lining the far wall as Frank's, the ones he saw being loaded into the moving truck in Willapa after he died. Reade grabbed a hammer he had seen in the office and made a racket smashing the lock of the first trunk. Opening it, something furry and disgusting lay on top, which he flung to the floor: it was a long-haired, reddish, full-body monkey suit with a rubber face, hands, and feet. In fact, there were several of the monkey suits as well as a wooden cuckoo clock wrapped in cloth; a black cowboy hat in a box; a pair of pristine cowboy boots; and six little black leather books tied with string. At the bottom of the trunk were six gray cardboard boxes stamped in small black letters: Bank of New York. Reade opened the lid of the first box without removing it and counted twelve bundles of fifty one-hundred-dollar bills. $60,000! He smashed open the locks on the remaining trunks and unloaded the contents to get to the bottom. The same six Bank of New York boxes were stashed at the bottom of each trunk. *A lot of money, if real*, Reade said to himself. It wasn't until opening the first small black book that Reade got confirmation: Frank Dearborn's name was written on the inside cover.

Reade squatted on the cold concrete floor. What had his dear, strange, Willapa neighbor done? How was it that Reade was pawing through Frank's private stuff three thousand miles from Willapa? The very trunks that his other neighbor, Jeff, helped Frank carry up from his basement during a high tide. A car passed on the street, trailing an eerie sound of laughter. Reade promptly replaced everything except one monkey outfit, one box of cash, and the bundle of little black journals. He locked the rotten office door and hurried past the crowd outside the warehouse to the second-floor loft where he stashed everything under the bed. The trunks weren't safe in the old gas station garage. He had to get them into a storage unit pronto.

A few days later, Reade stood in the line that wrapped around the warehouse wearing the laundered monkey outfit. He had to endure the hour-long wait of strangers stroking his monkey fur and pulling his tail, which he ended up tying around his waist. Breathing through the old rubber face, now reeking of detergent, made him nauseous.

"Look into my eyes," Reade said when he finally curled up next to Anna Banana Magdalena. His head rested on the pillow facing her. Again, she pretended to sleep. Her hair had been whipped into a ruffled fluff with wispy curls. She looked like an exotic sea creature.

"Your eyes are the brownish-green of the Columbia River. It's dawn in the Ilwaco marina. Gulls cry for fishermen's scraps."

She opened her eyes. "Ree Dee, I dig your suit," she whispered. Now, propped up on one elbow, the strap of her slip fell off her shoulder, a nipple exposed.

"It's Frank's. I explored the gas station last night and discovered the twelve green trunks from his house in Willapa. I feel like King Kong right now, like I could climb the Empire State Building."

"That's the power of costume," she said. "It's the reason people dress up, endure make-up, spiked heels, and ratted hair."

"What do you get when you take the 'k' out of monkey?" he said. "Don't say it out loud. Whisper the answer in my ear."

"Where is your ear?"

"Oh, I only have fake ears. Whisper into my eye. I'll hear you."

"M-O-N-E-Y."

Reade held out his paw: "Put your chin in here," he said. Holding his open palm, he mouthed into her ear: "Funny Honey gave you monkey money. A lot, if it's real."

AM threw off the covers, pulling Reade up, and they jumped on top of the bed. The audience broke the line and clambered up to jump with them. The buzzer sounded. Reade pulled his tail out from under their feet and pushed through the front door, dragging his monkey-self down the sidewalk to the warehouse side door. A stranger ran after him and grabbed the rubber monkey's face and kissed it. He couldn't see through the eye holes but guessed it was Saxton.

Frank's journals made AM wheeze. Within minutes, she was headed for a full-blown asthma attack. She took a puff of her inhaler and stepped in the shower while Reade wrapped the journals in plastic, stashed all the treasure back under the bed, and made her a cup of mint tea.

Strangely, that same night, someone threw black oil-based paint over the front door of the warehouse. It had a gooey pitch-like consistency and covered the metal door, hinges, knob, keyhole, and the flagstone stoop. Reade had no idea how to clean it up, and the front door couldn't be used. Now the Bed-In audience had to enter through the side door and wind their way through the dusty garbage to get in and out. Reade had a gate installed so the general public could not go upstairs and informed Alberto that they needed an extra volunteer to stand guard.

"I want to find the culprit who tossed paint on the door," Reade said. He irrationally blamed Saxton for the kiss. The extravagant champagne fire. For ruining the mattress and closing down the show. And the blackened door.

"Leave it," AM said. "It's typical backlash. My performances provoke action by design."

Alberto agreed. "You want to fly, you got to give up

the shit that weighs you down, Reade. That's a Toni Morrison quote."

"What?" he asked. And suddenly, Reade shut up. He reminded himself of Sheriff Fox!

AM was dubbed by the press "Lady Magdalene." She was invited to countless interviews, which Viv accepted. Viv excelled at explaining AM's need for privacy, her embodiment of time and place, and her piggybacking on cultural myths to create a power shift. One host, in particular, dug into her background as an esthetic terrorist, dating back to Bach's second wife, Anna Magdalena, her namesake, an artist uncompromisingly devoted to art. In the same breath, he belittled her as a self-promoter.

"AM makes people angry," the radio host rebutted.

"Are you mad?" Viv asked.

"Not me," he said. "But she's dragging Honey Dearborn's legacy through the mud."

"Then you did not know Honey Dearborn. She considered artists revolutionaries, which is what you have to be to make art. You have to tear down the status quo, change the narrative, and get rid of outdated ideas. Honey was AM's supporter, her collector. AM was also Matt's last friend."

"You mean the bank robber who dressed as a clown...," the host laughed, unable to get hold of himself to finish his sentence.

Viv waited silently.

"Who killed himself in a gas station bathroom," he said, catching his breath.

"Make a point to see the new Garden Gates film premiering at the Independent Film Center in Greenwich Village this summer. It's called *Mother and Son: The Deaths of Honey and Frank Dearborn*. AM is interviewed in it, and she explains her position quite well. She talks about dropping a balm. That is spelled b-a-l-m."

Things at the Bed-In only escalated from there. Spectators were eager to not only get under the covers with AM but to provoke a reaction. Reade was upstairs when he heard AM yell GET THE FUCK OUT! He reached the first floor in time to see a naked man with a shock of gray hair somersault across the floor and crash into a videographer's tripod. Alberto was nowhere to be seen, and Reade ended up punching the guy.

"It was a performance, Reade," Alberto explained after the man pulled on a pair of sweatpants and left. "He's not a bad man. Yes, he broke the rules, but that is allowed. AM challenged him. We want the audience to practice using their imagination and know what it feels like to take action so when an opportunity for real change arises, they'll go vote, or protest, or donate their time or money."

SEVEN

READE'S second visit to the Metropolitan was again to Hans Memling's *Madonna and Child*. He was struck this time by her simple peasant dress. Mary looked like a teenage AM with brown eyes staring calmly at the viewer. He appreciated the quiet of the empty medieval gallery and the perspective that fourteenth-century art gave to his small life.

The guard, making his turns between rooms, broke his reverie and he headed to the eighteenth-century French paintings to study *The Choir of the Capuchin Church in Rome*, which Kermit insisted he see: the first and largest of the seventeen that Granet painted. It looked identical to Kermit's picture, except four times the size. The square window of yellow light illuminating the dark monks could be interpreted as revolutionary. Painters used the window as an invitation to step outside the church and into nature. To paint a landscape. He remembered AM telling him in Willapa that nature and imagination are equal and infinite.

Turning right and then left, feeling his way toward the museum exit, he stopped off at the small stone chapel that was set up with chairs for prayer, an artifact from some Italian villa. Not one for prayer, sitting in silence, he decided to phone Kermit again and made his call on the steps outside of the Metropolitan. Jules, Kermit's assistant, answered. Feeling for the bundles of cash through the outside of his bag, he told Jules that he wanted to buy the Granet. Jules said he would wrap the painting and have it ready for pick-up by noon. Reade had been carrying the cash for two days, and it felt right when he followed Jules into Kermit's office and handed him the money. Jules locked it in a safe without counting it, then picked up the phone and ordered chicken soup and sandwiches.

"What do you think is the most important thing to carry in your pocket at all times?" Jules asked.

"A phone?"

Jules pulled out a crust of bread wrapped in brown paper. "My wife gives me this every morning. This is the difference between life and death if you contract typhoid. You'd be surprised how long a crust of bread can last if it stays dry."

"Is this how you survived alone in the woods during the war?"

"No, I survived by luck," he said. "I had no choice. God abandoned me."

Reade stepped back onto the street with the heavy gilt-framed painting wrapped up in his arms. Once again, Jules' happy ending didn't shake off the deep sadness of his story. Reade missed Billie. The paternity test came back positive, and he was eager to settle the custody dispute. He propped the painting on his foot to hail a cab and made sure it was snug in the trunk before getting in. The cabbie and Reade rode in silence through slow Manhattan traffic toward the Queensboro Bridge. Living in New York seemed at times like he had entered a fairytale—as AM's lover and father of Billie, and working with an old master art dealer. Three months ago he would have been happy if he and AM sat at the ebb tide on Willapa Bay forever. But AM clicked her heels.

AM and her new assistant, Daisy, were celebrating a traditional Ghana holiday with a group of immigrant women and children making chocolate candies. He could hear their singing as he walked up to their private quarters on the second floor. He pounded two strong nails into the wall above the table and hung the Granet. Fingers of yellow light seemed to stretch across the loft from the center of the dark painting. Not God's fingers but something abstract: peace or acceptance. Were they the same thing, maybe? He flopped down on the bed. Googling the YMCA on 14th Street, he signed Billie up for the spring Water Baby class. In two weeks he and Billie and AM would live together as a family.

Kermit asked Reade to attend an auction of prints and ephemera, this time held at Christie's. Alberto took him shopping so Reade could look the part. He bought a dark gray Armani suit, a small-patterned tie, and a white shirt. He parted Reade's hair on the side and slicked it back, exposing his widow's peak. Thus dressed, Reade introduced himself to Kermit's friend Mr. Schue, head of the print department at a university in London. Kermit knew where he would be seated and described his curly gray halo of hair.

"Reade Bordeaux," he said, offering Mr. Schue his hand. Looking up from the catalog, Reade noted his quick, friendly eyes. "Greetings from Kermit Fleur."

Mr. Schue nodded. Reade continued to his seat, passing the same stiff young woman he noted at the Sotheby's auction. Kermit explained that she was probably from the Getty Museum, one of a handful of Getty staff bidding at every auction. It was a well-endowed museum, hungry for treasure.

First off the block was a typed letter signed 'A. Einstein' from 1948 which sold for over $10,000. Photographic prints followed. Kermit had given Reade a glossary of terms for the last visit. It explained the types of items collectors desired by size and category, but none of it had sunk in. He focused on his assignment to purchase a first edition of *The Caprichos* by Francisco Goya. Inspired by the French Revolutionary philosophers, it contained eighty images of humans depicted as hobgoblins, monsters, devils, broomsticks, monkeys, mice, and asses. AM would appreciate his depiction of social ills, but she would argue against depicting fallen humans as animals. She had no respect for hierarchy. To Reade, the real tragedy seemed to be the slow pace of human progress. Goya's *Caprichos* were from the 1790s. Curious, too, was the estimated price listed in the catalog of $30,000 when Kermit had given him a ceiling of $50,000. Reade learned in his crash course on printing that the most coveted was the first edition because of its dark brown sepia tint and deeply impressed plate marks. Later copies, made with worn plates, were cut up and sold as single prints or sold as a collection for as little as three hundred dollars.

The auctioneer finally moved on to Francisco Goya, warming up with a set of four lithographs titled *Bulls of Bordeaux*, followed by four more lithographs. When the first edition went up for auction, only one bidder raised the paddle against Reade and he quit at $40,000. Making the purchase, Reade signed his name as instructed. He hoped to get AM over to Kermit's gallery so they could look at the prints together.

A magazine cover in a coffee shop window on Lexington Avenue caught Reade's attention on his way home: *The Man with the Golden Helmet*. The article mentioned that Kermit Fleur bought the painting in the 1960s and within a year sold it to the Chicago Art Institute, quadrupling his investment. The painting was a sensation, millions of prints of the image hung in middle-class American homes. But in the 1980s, scholars determined that the picture was not painted in Rembrandt's characteristic brush strokes. This was a blow to the art world, the article stated. Kermit had cautioned Reade about this, that perceptions and circumstances change over time. Mistakes don't necessarily mean disaster or that a painting is a hoax. A provenance can change like a family story. Like Kermit's story. He was able to escape Germany before being hunted and killed by Nazis. In America, he found Lulu and became a multi-millionaire and an art dealer, caretaker of some of the most important pictures ever painted.

EIGHT

READE'S FATHER instructed him to keep a Bully List after a fistfight in third grade. He wanted Reade to note not only the name of the bully but his address so he could avoid walking down the wrong street. Every few weeks his father asked him to read the list aloud and explain any new incidents. This was only one of his Pa's lessons. Paralyzed by a spinal fracture, he was kept alive by the round-the-clock nurses, each prettier than the next as per his request. On the nurse's break after school, Reade visited his father. He lit his Pa a Marlboro, held the cigarette to his lips, and between puffs, held a glass of Jim Beam for him, patiently waiting as he sipped it through a straw. He also insisted that Reade practice the six basic boxing punches on his shoulder. Fearing he'd hurt him, Reade just touched his father's arm with his gloves, and he didn't seem to notice.

It was the naked man Reade boxed in the nose who was at the top of his current Bully List. Second from the top was Saxton; third, Frank Dearborn, who haunted Reade from the grave. Sheriff Fox of Willapa, the one who scapegoated Frank, was on the list, too, as was Reade's soon-to-be ex-mother-in-law, Lydia, and the anonymous person who threw black paint on the warehouse door. Since arriving in New York, the Bully List seemed juvenile and embarrassing to Reade. He imagined AM closing her eyes in a slow deliberate manner if she found out about it. This prompted Reade to ask her about the naked guy at the Bed-In. Reade wanted to scratch him off the list as soon as possible.

"Charlie Kim is one of the internet stalkers who claims he is my father," she said.

"So, he got ME involved in his performance?" Reade asked.

She stared at him.. "You have to learn to let the little irritating flies fly bye-bye. People are basically decent, Reade. At least fifty-one percent. We've all got to live together even if humans lie and cheat."

Charlie Kim resided in Manhattan, on East 72nd Street, in a black, five-story brick building with red doors, famous as the home of *The Paris Review*. Reade bought a box of macarons and took the number 6 train to 68th Street, and crossed York Avenue. A young mother pushed her son's two-wheeler bike around in a small park at the end of 72nd.

"Reade Bordeaux, welcome," Charlie said.

Surprised to be buzzed in and greeted in such a friendly manner, Reade gave him his hand and they shook. Charlie's bruised cheekbone was visible, and his left wrist was wrapped in white gauze. Ushered into the mid-century modern living room with a view of Roosevelt Island and the East River, Reade sat on a simple low, gray couch.

"I've come to apologize," Reade began. "I haven't hit anyone since fourth grade when my mother pulled me out of Catholic school."

"Well, it's lucky I'm here to nurse him," said a barefoot, gazelle-like creature wearing a tank top and loose flowing pants named Robert. He carried a tray of teacups, an antique metal teapot, and Reade's peace offering of cookies.

Mesmerized by the glittering sun on the East River, Reade's eye caught something else: the slowly-turning sculpture in the corner of the room. It was AM's Winged Woman! He sank back at the memory of her community art class in Willapa just a year ago. A gale off the Pacific rattled the wood stove, and puffs of smoke rose on the downdrafts as the motley group drew on paper. All the while, AM rhythmically pounded with a mallet the metal backs and legs of chairs she had tied together. Father Jonathan and some of his older friends hummed church hymns. By the end of the afternoon, the shape of a female creature emerged which she stuffed with sponges, foil, driftwood, a baby doll, whatever washed up on the beach. She told Reade she planned to wrap it in a clear skin of plastic and weld a metal cap at the base: she wanted it to fly from the pole in front of the gas station where Pegasus stood.

"Do you know how to weld?" Reade had asked AM.

"Can you teach me?"

"I can," he said. He didn't want to leave her side, but his neighbor, Aunt Doris, and her friend called Shell Lady were waiting in the cab of his truck for a ride home.

Reade sipped his tea, studying Charlie Kim sitting across from him. "Did you buy The Winged Woman from Honey Dearborn?"

"Yes, I did."

"Charlie collects Maggie's work," Robert said. "He is also her biological father and has the birth certificate to prove it."

"I didn't come here to talk about that," Reade said.

"We miss Honey," Charlie said. "Art was the most important thing in her life."

"Besides her son, Frank," Reade said. "He was my neighbor in Willapa."

"Really," said Robert. "We've heard rumors about her wayward son."

Reade couldn't help but compare Charlie Kim's features to AM's. Her skin tone was similar, but his face was fuller in middle age. His hair was straight, unlike hers. Both noses were small, but Charlie's spread across his face. And he wasn't tall like her.

"I met Maggie's mother in the mud at the Woodstock festival," Charlie said. "A few months later she contacted me. She was living in a communal house called Old Red and asked me to father a child, no strings attached. A love child. I ended up staying a week."

Reade waited for him to continue.

"Maggie came to New York at age sixteen to look for me. I was going through my own shit at the time. My partner was sick with AIDS and, trying to protect both of us, Julia told Maggie that her father was dead."

A tug pushed a garbage barge down the East River toward the Atlantic. Only then did it dawn on Reade where he had seen Charlie before. Yes! His handsome angled face was familiar. He was in the raw footage Garden Gate Productions showed them in Willapa when they came to interview AM. Charlie and Robert sat at Honey's deathbed as she looked directly at them. Robert wore his long blond hair straight below his shoulders, a long fitted white tunic, white pants, gloves, and short white boots.

AM was amused when Reade told her that he apologized to Charlie Kim. She wasn't surprised that the Winged Woman ended up in his possession. Charlie was on Saxton's subscription list for Flash News, her first performance piece with Saxton. Charlie owned a complete set: sixty-five photographs of her painted torso, documenting *The New York Times* headlines over two years. Still, it made AM weary to hear Charlie, once again, claim to be her father.

"The story is dead," AM said. "Mother may have had a difficult time conceiving. She may have asked dozens of men to father a love child, but hundreds claim to be my father on the internet. And they call me every word ever used to destroy a woman. Yet I stand."

NINE

MOUNT RAINIER and her sisters greeted Reade as the plane flew over the snow-capped Cascades. His eyes followed the edge of Lake Washington to the Evergreen Floating Bridge and the Arboretum, the land of his conception. He imagined his thirty-year-old mother and fifty-year-old father in bed, the curtains pulled on a summery Saturday night. *It's an act of science as much as lust*, he thought: the winning sperm penetrating the egg, followed by cell division, gills sprouting and morphing, buds becoming arms and legs, fingers and toes. Birth is what got him reading books at age fourteen. Without telling his Ma, he bought an old white mare and tied the horse to the rusty swing set in the backyard. But New Year's Eve firecrackers spooked her and she broke loose. Reade spent the night in the arboretum searching for a white horse in a white fog. His mother took one look at the mare the next morning and told him to call a vet.

NINE

The mare was pregnant. As it happened, he was alone in his cousin's field when she gave birth. Like Georgie Saxton Pierce, the first foal died. The second got up on its wobbly legs and found his mother.

The car Reade reserved at the airport was waiting for him; the new bus system to the car rental lot was surprisingly efficient. Seattle's abundantly wet green hillsides next to Interstate-5 begged him to breathe deeply. Crossing the congested Duwamish River, he saw from the West Seattle bridge that the old elevated Route 99 was half torn down. He felt the urge to stroll through Pike Place Market, sip a cup of orange spice tea, and admire the beautiful fresh pink salmon. But he was only moments from Billie! Many of the small Craftsman-style homes from the forties were renovated with private gardens and fences with an Asian feel, but not the Smith-Bordeaux bungalow. Pulling into the driveway, he noted that nothing had changed since they bought it. They had barely lived in it.

Becky greeted Reade at the door with Billie in her arms. At four months, he was chubby with brown hair and hazel eyes. He stared at Reade a moment, then buried his face in Becky's neck. With few words, the fledgling family laid down together for what felt like a sad last family nap.

"Let's walk down to Alki Beach," Reade suggested when Billie began to whimper.

The weather was merely damp and foggy, no longer drizzling. They bundled Billie into a little blue cotton striped snowsuit, and Reade carried him on his chest down the long steps to the beach. The bramble on the left had become a homeless encampment with more than fifty tents, some straight from REI, others built of tarps tied together with rope. They didn't see a soul, but voices from within the tents were audible, and Reade imagined people huddled in sleeping bags to keep warm. Toward the bottom stairs, they passed stinky piles of human shit and take-out garbage. When the WALK signal turned, they scurried across Alki Avenue to the sandy beach with the view of downtown Seattle.

"I've never seen that homeless encampment," Reade said.

Becky shrugged. "We should put the house up for sale before the neighborhood goes to hell."

"I read West Seattle is now California North."

"We'll get a good price, then," she said.

"We're getting divorced," Reade said. "That's the reason to sell. Neither of us lives here."

"Look, I'm twenty-five years old," Becky said. Her words were paced and threatening. "You're twelve years ahead of me, Reade Bordeaux. I'm still a kid running away from things. Now I feel like I have to run away from being a mother like I ran away to the military when I married you."

He put his hand on her back, hoping to calm her so they could have a conversation. "Don't call it running away," Reade said. "Life has chapters and escapades, first runs and reruns. It's not a straight line. If you could have anything, what would you want?"

She laughed. Her long hair was lighter than he remembered, more blonde than red, and her skin freckled as though she'd been vacationing in the sun. "I want a home run," she said.

"Seriously," he said.

Becky hurried ahead, then turned and yelled: "My parents didn't teach me to dream."

"Then use your imagination," he said, catching up to her. "You're a superhero to me and Billie. You can do anything."

"I'm a better actress than you know. That's why the military fits. I've got a script. It's about following rules. No imagination is necessary. I'm a Commissioned Second Lieutenant so I guess I'm good at it, or maybe better at it than anything else I've tried, and I've been accepted into a physical therapy program in Texas starting this summer."

"Congratulations," Reade said. "I'm happy for you."

Pebbles rolled in with the waves of Puget Sound as they sat on a damp bench. There didn't seem to be anything else to say, and yet Billie's whole life needed to be figured out. He unzipped Billie from the front carrier. His plump pink cheeks and dark snowman eyes made them smile as he wrapped his fist around Becky's outstretched finger.

"Mom offered to raise Billie for five hundred a

week," Becky said. "When he's school age, dad will raise him down at the beach."

"Over my dead body!" Reade said. He stood, walked away, then came back to face her. "The paternity test was positive. I want full custody. Our attorneys will hammer out your visitation rights."

It was Reade's ex-mother-in-law, Lydia, who handed Billie off to him the next day. He added the words gold-digger after her name on the Bully List. He wondered if the five-hundred bucks a week was proposed when she advised Becky to keep the pregnancy.

"What are you worried about?" Lydia asked, standing next to the car. Her cigarette smoke billowed as Reade buckled Billie into the car seat. "Becky's an officer in the U.S. Army," she said. "Meyer needed you. Never Becky."

Reade felt euphoric pulling out of Lydia's driveway with Billie buckled into the back seat. Surely, this is an abundance of love. Reade wondered if his father ever felt this way about him. He must have, he decided, but assumed he'd never know for sure.

TEN

THE CLOTH WALL, AM's third performance of the season, ran Tuesday through Sunday for two more weeks. It was the scariest thing Reade had ever seen. Eight open human mouths appeared through holes cut in a cloth wall, with bright red lips lifted in a snarl, the black-dyed tongues wagged in unison, flashing fluorescent white teeth. Strange noises erupted from these mouths, reactions to AM's readings from various documents. The American Constitution elicited long ribbons of whoops and smiles and song, but readings of racist U.S. policies, such as the 1882 Chinese Act barring immigration, brought snarling and choking sounds. Ferocious gnashing of teeth started with the reading of the 1924 Native American Act which barred voting. The Japanese policy from 1942-45, interning people of Japanese descent, conjured deep moans that worked their way into high-pitched screams. Ferocious lip-licking, snake-like hisses, and barks filled the warehouse when AM read from The American Plan, a policy put in place in 1910 declaring that any woman suspected of sexually transmitted disease or any woman standing on a street corner with a man she wasn't related to could be arrested. The audience followed suit, moaning, cursing, booing, and crying. It was a visceral zoological experience. The last subject of slavery—the foundation America was built on—the literal buying and selling of humans, and the slaughter of Native people—the stealing of their land and natural resources—brought mayhem. Teeth from those eight mouths ripped through the red curtain, and humans dressed as red flames broke through the wall and pounced, fraying the fabric. Entwined in the curtain, the humans moved together as one great throbbing wound—wobbling, tripping, tied, and bound—until they fell prostrate on the floor.

Each day by noon, Billie and Reade headed out on a walk, often toward Brooklyn Bridge Park with its berms built as a water barrier to keep the next hurricane from washing away the Brooklyn-Queens Expressway. Billie, traveling in a backpack, pushed off on the bar with his feet in excitement as they crossed the bridge itself. He was excited by the noises of bikes thumping over the wooden path, the ferryboat horns, the zing of cars, and the chatter of colorful tourists. His little fingers reached overhead toward the cables of the bridge. On Wall Street, they touched George Washington's hand at Federal Hall, knelt in Trinity Church on Broadway, and visited the American Indian Museum at Bowling Green. Billie slept to the drumming and chanting until they settled on a bench of the Staten Island Ferry when his fusses prompted a change of diaper and food.

The line at the warehouse was only half a block when Reade returned, only one hour before closing time. He noticed an older man with a goatee, wearing an inappropriate straw hat for the cold weather, sitting in the driver's seat of a black SUV intently watching the crowd. He didn't notice as Reade clicked a photo of him to include in his Bully List.

Each evening AM walked upstairs dead tired and without much of a voice. She got down on her knees, held Billie's perfect tiny fingers and toes in her hands, and talked to him about her day using complete sentences. Propped on the bureau next to the framed black-and-white photograph of AM, Georgie, and Saxton was a family snapshot Reade brought back from Seattle: Becky, Billie, and Reade. AM and Reade found themselves standing side by side, gazing at the two family pictures, squeezing each other. Words were not exchanged. Neither family existed any longer. Early the next morning, Saxton arrived with a tripod and lights. AM was still in bed. Billie and Reade climbed in next to her, leaning against the headboard. She wore a little white T-shirt; Reade was bare-chested, as was Billie. The photography session over, Reade dressed Billie for the day's outing.

"One more shot," Saxton said. "Over here." He

pointed to the spot of sun in front of the old heavy red velvet theater curtain they pulled across the windows at night. Saxton smoothed his black vest over his striped shirt and combed his hair over his brow, while AM slipped on a lace overcoat and took Billie in her arms. Through the lens, Reade noted the soft East River light on their faces. The picture was beautiful, but Reade wanted to blurt out that it was yet another fake. That is until he caught himself and bit his tongue. The pretending was a sort of healing, a way of imagining Georgie Saxton Pierce.

Lulu had formal photographs taken at a lavish party she and Kermit held one Sunday afternoon to celebrate Billie's arrival. Invitations were sent to over a hundred friends and relatives. A reception line was formed to greet the guests. AM had last seen most of the guests at Georgie's funeral, exotic human shapes, colors, and sizes. It was the adoration. Billie tugged at the brightly-wrapped gifts that piled on the table beside them. Reade turned to AM when a man in a white turban and silver earrings paused and bowed, his hands together, eyes closed.

"Is that your holy man?" he whispered.

"What are you talking about?" AM asked.

"In your sleep, sweet. You said your father is a holy, wholly, holey man. Which kind of holy did you mean?"

Charlie Kim and Robert stood in front of them. AM graciously took their hands and exchanged sweet nothings. Reade was relieved to see Charlie's face bruise-free. He was surprised that Lulu invited them. Her attorneys filed lawsuits against parties distributing fake birth certificates, fake sex videos, and other slanderous stories of AM over the internet. Then again, Charlie Kim was a major collector of AMs. Maybe he truly believed that AM was his daughter. During cake and champagne, Saxton appeared dressed as a ragged jester, barefoot with beads and bells. He double-kissed their cheeks, exuding an odor of sexual escapades, and mesmerized Billie with silly faces. After refreshments were served, they washed Billie's sticky hands and laid him down in Georgie's nursery. Lulu was, once again, a grandmother.

As Reade and AM gathered their things to go home, he said, "Good performance."

"I feel Georgie kicking down the door," she said.

Before they were able to step into the elevator, Lulu's attorney asked AM to come into the library. She formally delivered the good news that the cash from Frank's trunks was real. When she started in on a discussion about the taxes owed on the inheritance, AM interrupted.

"I'm setting up a 501(c)(3) nonprofit, The Honey Dearborn Art Center, with a mission to serve immigrant women and children of Queens, New York. A performance and educational institution. I want the cash deposited under that name. Lulu is working on a list of potential board members and bylaws. Could you draw up the nonprofit partnership agreement for us?"

Meanwhile, Reade's attorney, JT, turned to the thorny issue of custody. Reade left Becky a message that he had selected a realtor to sell the West Seattle bungalow, that he was in touch with a house painter, a radon expert, and a gardener. But Becky had disengaged. Reade had the weird feeling that they would forever fall together as the earth falls around the sun. Against JT's advice, he sent her a check for half of their savings account, mostly consisting of money left from the sale of his mother's house. Even when he saw that Becky had cashed the check, she sent no response. Worse, she missed her first scheduled Skype session with Billie.

ELEVEN

"LET BABY GRIP YOUR POINTER FINGER," said Jim, the swimming instructor. Sitting in the kiddie pool with six adults cradling babies, Jim's chiseled face was relaxed, his muscular body, hairless, including his shaved head. "Rotate baby's arms in circles, one then the other, like a cartwheel, in and out of the water. Keep baby's arms directly in front. Keep them circling. This is the basic stroke in swimming. How many of you consider yourselves good swimmers?"

No one raised their hand. Reade wondered if he was the only one who spoke English.

Jim continued, "Turn baby on her back, holding firmly. Gently glide baby across the top of the water in front of you. Smile. Let baby experience the floating position."

Billie was a champion kicker. He was content

splashing his fat little arms and legs until, swallowing water, he cried.

Jim moved in beside Reade: "What's his name?"

"Billie. I'm his dad, Reade."

"Try putting Billie over your shoulder. Now pat his back. When he calms down, start again in the floating position."

Jim waited for Reade in one of the several chairs outside the pool area. He watched through a big window as a dozen women practiced synchronized swimming in the adult pool like ballroom dancers. Reade emerged from the family changing room with Billie, bundled for cold weather. Jim motioned for him to take a seat.

"Do you like to swim?" he asked Reade.

"I don't know how."

Jim's forehead wrinkled; his lips frowned. "I'm surprised. You seem like a natural."

"I have recurring nightmares about drowning, and last year I very nearly drowned in the Pacific trying to save a friend caught in the current."

"Not knowing how to swim is a disability. It takes a lot of guts for adults to learn. It's a big commitment, but Billie will need years of practice, not just classes. I suggest you join the adult swim class. It's Thursday mornings at ten, just before this Water Baby class. The Y has brilliant daycare. Real professionals."

For Reade, the hardest part of swimming was relaxing into the rhythm of breathing: in through his mouth, turn and dunk his face, blow bubbles out his nose. He seemed to need to relearn it each time he swam. Once he got it down, he was able to make the transition from breaststroke to freestyle. He liked the swim class. He even joined the swim team at James' insistence. Not that he would ever race but to swim laps three times a week in order to build muscle memory and perfect his stroke.

Once an avid surfer, Jim shared a bungalow on 90th Street in Rockaway, two blocks from the ocean. He swam year-round and invited Reade to take a weekly swim in the Atlantic. Not a bed or dish existed in the rental, just some folding chairs, a large garbage can full of empty take-out cartons, a few beers in the fridge, and a lot of equipment. Jim fitted Reade with a bright yellow wetsuit and an orange buoy to wear around his waist. As the sun crawled up the horizon, waves rolled in from the southeast. The current cut close to shore and fanned south. Standing at the water's edge, Jim pointed out the swim lane between two buoys, a half-mile apart. He ran down the basics once again: cup your hands; thrust them deep into the water; take deep breaths; feel the pull against your torso; flex your legs; make small rhythmic kicks; breathe in through your mouth, out through your nose.

The water was relatively shallow, but fishermen, kids, and surfers drowned here every year. As Reade's feet touched the water, he remembered holding his father's hand. A rogue wave hit. Tossed in the foam,

Reade hit bottom and came up screaming. His mother didn't swim, but she dropped her murder mystery under the umbrella and retrieved him from the waves. As a nurse, she saw right away that his shoulder was dislocated. By the time Pa dragged forth, his Ma had manipulated his shoulder back in place, and his pain vanished. After that, his shoulder dislocated easily. His mother scolded him for doing it on purpose and suggested he share his comics at school instead. But dislocating his shoulder kept the bullies entertained.

"Why did you quit surfing?" Reade asked Jim one day as they waded into the waves.

"A neighborhood friend used to climb on my shoulders while I surfed. It was great fun until one day she hit the water wrong. I thought her floating was a stunt. Even as they loaded her into the ambulance, all she cared about was her jewelry she marked with a feather in the sand. Paralyzed from the waist down, it took five years for her to decide to live. One day she bought a van, hired a medic/driver, and continued with her acting career. She became a regular on the soaps."

TWELVE

BILLIE'S CRY woke Reade at 2:15 in the morning. He got up to warm a bottle. After testing the milk on his wrist, he leaned back in the rocker and stuck the nipple in Billie's mouth. Only then did Reade smell smoke.

He punched 911 on his phone, woke AM, and pulled on a pair of jeans. Sticking his head out the window, he saw a conflagration at the south end of the warehouse, orange and blue flames and billowing smoke. He wrapped AM and Billie in a blanket and draped the diaper bag over her shoulder. They fled the building and joined a small group of people at the back of a weedy lot across the street.

"FIRE! FIRE!" Reade yelled as he ran back up the stairs. He felt like an idiot not knowing who, if anyone, was sleeping in the warehouse. Alberto, of all people, and another guy scrambled down the stairs. Reade found six others he'd never seen before curled up in the raw space on the fourth floor.

"FIRE! GET OUT! NOW! OUT," he yelled.

There were no safety rules posted, no extinguishers, or even a certificate of occupancy. Four more people stood on the roof gazing down at the gas station when an explosion knocked them all off their feet, its heat singeing their brows and eyelashes. Herding them toward the metal stairway on the outside of the building, he yelled, "DON'T TOUCH THE RAILING, IT'S HOT! GO! GO!"

The sirens silenced as the trucks pulled to a stop in front of the building. Firemen swarmed the street, some scrambled to the roof dragging a hose. A tow truck cleared the street of parked cars, and a man with a bandaged arm stood by an ambulance. Police moved AM and the small group of onlookers a block farther, beyond the shredded ailanthus tree, toward the East River. Reade found AM and Billie wide-eyed. He wrapped his arms around them. Together, they stared at the mound of smoking rubble, all that existed of the old gas station.

"Do we have insurance?" Reade asked.

"We do."

"Good. I hope they catch the arsonist. The fire chief said there'd be an investigation."

"Arsonist?" AM questioned Reade.

Alberto gave Anna Magdalena the key to his Williamsburg apartment. "Use the apartment for as long as you need it."

"Thanks, Alberto," she said. His generous act woke her. "Text the volunteers that the performance is canceled. And call Viv. She'll be devastated. I don't want to speak to anyone."

Three blocks from the fire, Billie peeked out from beneath his blanket. The night was cold. Silhouettes of firemen on the warehouse roof looked surreal. Steam rose from their arcing hose. Reade was concerned about the Granet, Frank's journals, and the remaining cash under the bed. He pulled off his jacket and covered AM's head as they passed a cameraman and journalist interviewing a young bearded bicyclist. Neighbors huddled on their porches, staring toward the warehouse. One woman nodded to another across the yard as Reade and AM passed.

"I didn't know they had a baby," she said.

Reade opened the passenger door of his truck for AM. As she got in, he noticed a man on the roof two blocks beyond the Honey Dearborn Art Center. He stood like "Mr. Clean" on the TV ad when Reade was a kid: bald, muscled, his hands on his hips, a cigar between his teeth. Reade closed AM's door and snapped a photo of him. As he got into the driver's seat, he kept the suspicious man on the roof to himself. They were safe: they had diapers, formula, wheels, and shelter.

As Reade started the truck, the street light shined on Billie sucking at AM's breast, her naked upper torso marbled in the blue smoky air. She closed her eyes and leaned back into the seat, her mouth open in a silent scream. Reade hesitated. He didn't want to disturb whatever it was she was feeling. Billie dropped off to sleep, and her milk spouted like a fountain from each breast. Reade cupped his hand to catch the ambrosia.

"I'm a milk mom," she said. "Proof I'm mammalian."

"It tastes like melon...or café au lait," Reade said. He dabbed Billie's wet face and neck with his T-shirt and moved him to the car seat in the back. At a stoplight a few blocks away, he saw that AM's breasts were actually blotchy red. He touched one. It was hot and hard.

"It's painful," she said. "After Georgie died, hot wet towels helped. And pumping my milk. Lulu found an agency for me to donate it."

Reade remembered an article he read about scientists tracking the Y cells from male babies, cells that actually continued to live in their mother's organs and tissues her whole life. He imagined Georgie alive in AM; Billie's cells in Becky; and his own in his mother. *Maybe*, he thought, *it was his own dying cells that he felt when Ma died.*

The Honey Dearborn Art Center closed before its scheduled public opening. AM and Reade were dependent on Lulu, Viv, AM's no-nonsense publicist Jen, and even more so on Alberto as news of the fire spread. Notes and gifts were left inside the gate at the Center. AM's face was blasted over the internet along with Honey and her "crazy son" Frank, described as AM's lover, which made AM laugh. Even Reade's name headlined, Reade who never had any online presence. One tweet labeled him a cowboy and spun a story about lassoing AM out west and hiding her underground for a year. Someone wrote about Frank Dearborn as "Frankenstein," Saxton as a werewolf, and the Honey Dearborn Art Center as Anti-American. Even Charlie Kim posted a photo of "his family": AM and Reade pushing Billie in the stroller down a street in Williamsburg.

At last, Reade understood Charlie Kim's lashing out for what it was: entertainment and self-promotion, to be part of a story. It had nothing to do with his punch or AM calling him a fake father. Her silence spurred Charlie on. Reade spent hours with the police detectives assessing the smoke damage to the Honey Dearborn Art Center, while Alberto intuited AM's every need. Not only did he stay in touch with her gallerist and publicist and volunteers, but he also loaned Reade his moped so he could dart around the city undetected. Alberto kept the refrigerator filled, picked up and dropped off laundry, and dealt with Gallery A. The Honey Dearborn Art Center board of directors voted to hire Reade as Director of Operations, in charge of safety and renovations, with an annual salary of $60,000.

THIRTEEN

LULU OFFERED Reade and AM a loft on Beach Street in Manhattan. AM didn't want another disruption, but once they moved in, they both appreciated the ample space, the fresh paint on the walls, and the anonymity. They got used to the big old windows rattling as trucks sped over the cobblestones toward the West Side Highway. Reade enjoyed long walks through the nearby neighborhoods of Greenwich Village, Chinatown, and Tribeca while AM focused on Billie, even ignoring the Honey Dearborn Art Center. Billie now clapped his hands, traveled on all fours, and showed four teeth when he smiled. Between her desk and his crib was a big square of soft carpet where they played. Reade shopped, cooked, and fed the family. Whenever possible, he got them dressed and out for a walk along the Hudson. As the loft had no tub, they filled a large plastic boat on the kitchen floor, big enough for all kinds of imaginative dramas with toys and bubbles and splashing.

AM and Reade curled up together on the sofa when Billie was down for the night, and he gave her the progress report: Lulu's bridge loan got the renovation going as they waited for the insurance payments to kick in. Thankfully, the art restorer assessed the Granet as having little more than smoke damage when he dropped it off on 36th Street. And the monkey money? Most of it was safe in the storage locker. He washed the remaining smoky hundred-dollar bills that were under the bed—about $25,000—on the light cycle of the washing machine and dried them on cool. Frank's journals smelled moldy and smoky, and Reade suggested that he photocopy them before AM attempted to read them. The ruins of the gas station had been scraped into dumpsters and hauled away. Several people in the neighborhood voiced relief that the eyesore was gone. The yard around the triangular warehouse had been cleared, and Reade was excited about creating a small sculpture garden. Lulu introduced him to a landscape architect, Yoshiko, who believed that gardens tell stories and promote harmony.

"She is going to teach me to rake pebbles into an ocean," Reade said.

AM nodded and smiled.

"There isn't much Lulu can't handle," Reade continued. "She comes up with multiple solutions, like transforming me and the landscape at the same time."

Saxton was on the rug with AM and Billie when Reade came home to Beach Street one afternoon, the stuffed animals in a round-up. Billie was medicine for them, just as Billie had been briefly for Reade and Becky. Half-nibbled veggies, crackers, cups of tea, and an empty baby bottle littered the floor. *All good*, Reade thought until he spotted the pistol strapped to Saxton's ankle. It was eerie the way Saxton irritated him. Reade learned to expect the worst from him, just as he had from Frank Dearborn. When Saxton got up to kiss AM and Billie goodbye, he made a quick pirouette and kissed Reade on his lips. No man had ever done that. Saxton smiled in triumph.

"Next time, leave your gun at home," Reade called down the stairwell. He waited to hear the front door squeak shut before going back inside. From the kitchen window, he watched Saxton cross Beach Street and head north along the Hudson. He set Ella Fitzgerald on Spotify to calm himself as he poured milk into a clean bottle and screwed the nipple in place. Glancing out the window again, he marveled at the dog walker with a half-dozen dogs wearing coats and booties. AM joined Reade on the couch as Billie settled in with his bottle.

"Is Saxton's gun fake, like his eye patch?" Reade asked.

"Saxton is a lesson in tolerance. I used to be just as infuriating. It took you, Reade, and a year of Willapa to change me."

"I don't want guns around Billie. No guns in the

house. I buried my father's entire gun collection along with Candy when I put her down."

"You put Candy down?"

"Yep. When you ghosted me. Before coming to New York. She was dying of starvation. Her teeth were ground down and her belly bloated. It's a natural death for a horse, but I couldn't bear it. You were there the day Bubba dropped her off, remember? When he claimed that Candy was born in my pasture."

"Bubba with the hand-sewn nose."

"I brushed Candy and told her stories of all the happy children she carried on her back. Pa's Smith & Wesson is what I used. One bullet behind her ear. She shuddered and fell, and I nudged her into the pit with the backhoe. Before covering her over, I soaked Pop's gun collection in saltwater and laid them alongside her. All nine of them."

AM's spell broke after Saxton's visit. Reade wondered if Lulu had sent him for this purpose or if Saxton knew intuitively that AM needed his nudge. Or maybe hearing about Candy's death got her moving. Whichever, Reade celebrated as he watched her iron-like will kick into motion. She hired Elah as a regular babysitter and set up lunch dates to meet the board candidates Lulu had vetted.

The used pick-up Reade bought with Frank's cash ran well, and he quickly learned to navigate traffic like a New Yorker. At one of the millions of stoplights between Beach Street and Queens Boulevard, his phone beeped. Reade exited the Brooklyn-Queens Expressway and pulled up in front of a hydrant: Alberto sent a video of a pedestrian turning down a hundred-dollar bill from someone wearing a monkey suit. Others on the sidewalk ignored the bill, too, but a young woman pushing a stroller tucked a C-note into her pocket. Alberto said that more than $5,000 was given away by monkeys in Mott Haven, South Bronx, Coney Island, East New York, and East Harlem. This pop-up performance fulfilled the sixth and last of AM's grant requirements for the season. Viv was happy with the press. Excited recipients of the gifts told reporters of buying diapers, school supplies, paying bills, and splurging on clothes for a night out. Just as Reade guessed, a crowd of people lined the sidewalk around the Center by the time he pulled up to unload his Home Depot supplies. He lifted his empty hands, shook his head, and smiled.

"I like Beach Street," he said to AM. "Maybe we shouldn't move back to the warehouse."

"Reade, the Honey Dearborn Art Center is our home. It's where we work. We have a state-of-the-art kitchen in the community room now, thanks to you, and a Shinto garden soon. We can skip the formal opening, but fall classes are full. The teaching artists are lined up. Training starts in July. It will be good for Billie to be around kids. I need to be there."

Elah was stretched out on the rug with Billie counting his fingers out loud while AM lingered over a cup of tea. Reade expected her to be absorbed in her work, but instead, she suggested they borrow the bicycles in the vestibule and ride to Red Hook, a Brooklyn neighborhood Reade had not yet visited.

AM maneuvered a silver men's bike through Tribeca's small streets. Reade followed on a red hybrid. A wind kicked up the waves at the East River beneath them as they climbed the wooden slope of the gothic Brooklyn Bridge, dodging tourists, pausing for selfies. They coasted down the other side, wound through the small cobblestone streets of DUMBO to Brooklyn Bridge Park, and then along the bike path on Columbia Street, past the shipping cranes to Van Brunt Street. AM turned down Dikeman to Conover and a block south, stopping in front of the little, green house Saxton owned. It was rented now, since renovations after Hurricane Sandy. A three-story apartment building stood next to it, and the rest of the block was surrounded by razor wire and metal fencing that secured a school bus parking lot. The house was 20 feet by 20 feet, covered in a pattern of round and rectangle asphalt shingles. It had a flat roof, a wrought iron fence out front, and an alley that led to the backyard where a horse shed once stood.

"I lived here the summer I was pregnant with Georgie," she said. "Purple wisteria vines twisted up the brick houses on Dikeman Street. Puerto Rican, Polish, Irish, and Italian neighbors sat on folding chairs on the sidewalk. Spanish music blasted through the neighborhood. Artists scavenged building materials and furniture from dumpsters. There was always free parking and on weekends, neighbors gathered at Sunny's Bar for music and poetry."

They continued down Coffey Street to the pier in New York Harbor and hunkered out of the wind just in time to see a gleaming white Queen Elizabeth II emerge like an apartment building from Buttermilk Channel. It was so close, its wake spilled over the deck and the smell of creosote rose from the blackened pilings. The lone fisherman got swamped, packed up his gear, and left as rays of sun popped out between the bulbous gray clouds, tinting the harbor the greenish copper color of the Statue of Liberty. They felt like they were back on the Willapa beach in one of the driftwood windbreaks. Reade pulled off AM's wet sneaker and tucked her foot into his coat pocket. Worn out from Billie's middle of the night awakenings since the fire, they drifted off to sleep huddled on the pier, only to be woken by a squall of driving rain and wind. Grabbing their stuff, they pushed the bikes toward a stone doorway of the Civil War warehouse across the street. Slumped down on their butts, soaked and shivery, AM's long arms and legs balled up like a wet spider on Reade's lap. He covered her with his jacket and put in an SOS text to Alberto.

They looked like they were sitting under a waterfall. Slowly, they warmed in the heat of their own breath. AM's arms and legs began to unfold. The sheet of rain turned to a white curtain of hail, closing off the entry. They had unprotected sex in their own private cave, disrupted only by a pack of wild dogs pushing into their space, lashing, yelping, tails whipping. As their barking subsided, they listened to the choppy sea slap against the pier. When Reade next looked out, Alberto was parked across the street, loading their bikes into the back of the van. He winked as they zipped their clothes and climbed into the steamy front seat. Alberto had shared stories with Reade of sex before AIDS and later, in need of spiritual guidance, how he converted to Catholicism as he was sure he would be the next to die.

FOURTEEN

SOMETHING CRUNCHED under Reade's feet on the cellar steps. When he pulled the string of the light bulb, the entire floor moved: insects, two inches in length, with antennas and articulated brown armor swarmed the place. One crashed into the side of his head. He grabbed it for a closer look: it had wings! He had never seen a water bug. The exterminator he contacted indicated that they must have been smoked out of the old gas station and conveniently, their new home was only a few feet away. He suggested that they keep the light on and spread scented dryer sheets around until he had a chance to schedule them in. Reade alerted the staff of a three-day evacuation of the building.

"I don't want to find any water bugs in our fridge," Reade teased Alberto.

"I eat only organically raised, dry roasted grasshoppers and crickets. Nothing off the street."

Reade was happy to be officially in charge of operations at the Honey Dearborn Art Center. After the dead insects were commercially vacuumed and the entire building sprayed, he opened the upstairs windows, rented a dozen industrial fans, and brewed a big pot of Seattle's market spice tea to sweeten the air. He also removed the prankster "tag" by painting over the entire front door and stoop in black lacquer paint. He changed the hardware, making the front door usable again. The first floor was gutted. Studs and sheetrock walls create a playroom, nursery, and three classrooms. He built a proper second-floor living space for the family with its own kitchen. Fire extinguishers and signage were placed throughout the building, and a certificate of occupancy was in hand by the end of May. That same week he planted a row of arborvitae along the fence to give the garden some privacy from the street.

AM's gallerist, Viv, suggested an October exhibition of her artist Shanika Williams and showed Reade and AM photographs of her sculpture: large chunks of glass infused with subtle color, thick and crusty, or smooth mammalian-like curves. Viv was photographed standing next to each piece to show its size. Some were waist-high, others as high as her shoulder.

"Beautiful, eh?" Viv said. Reade gave a thumbs up. "We'll go together to make the final selection."

Billie became a fixture on AM's hip as she sorted the classroom deliveries: African drums, calligraphy ink, brushes and paper, a dozen digital cameras with chargers, batteries, and laptops. Reade washed down dishes and appliances, table and chairs, Billie's changing table, and restocked the cupboards with dry goods and spices. Lulu sent Billie's gifts, still stacked in the nursery from her party. Reade picked up the bed, sofa, plastic boat, and linens from Beach Street and had a washer and dryer installed. AM was right. The warehouse felt like home. He enjoyed sorting and folding clean laundry and putting things away.

Helen Apaccuchi's soup was simmering in the kitchen when a limousine pulled up in front of the Center. Out popped Ann Spears, a fashion branding social media guru, and her entourage. She had been vetted by Lulu as a potential board member, and AM settled into the long dining table with her.

"What is that unusual smell?" Ann asked.

"A family soup recipe." She opened her phone to read from the Center's weekly menu. "Ingredients include dried tilapia, mushrooms, onion, ginger, garlic, cocoyam leaves, fufu, and cassava."

"Ama," Billie whimpered. He was teething again. AM settled him sideways on her lap and lifted her shirt to nurse.

Ann leaned in. "I read that his birth mother is in the Army!"

AM nodded, dismissing the comment.

"I don't understand how you can nurse if you aren't his biological mother."

"It takes patience," AM said. She was prepared to launch into a speech about wet nurses throughout history if Ann questioned her further. Luckily, Helen came over and set the table with coffee and biscuits. AM thanked her and began peppering Ann with questions about her fashion business, her Eurocentric travels, and her philanthropic success at her daughter's private school. By the time Billie had finished his snack, she had decided on another way for Ann to help rather than joining the board.

"Lulu described your lovely apartment as big enough to hold a hundred guests. How about hosting a cultivation event for us?"

"Yes, I could do that," she said, brushing crumbs from her lap. "When are you thinking?"

"A Tuesday night in early November?"

"I'll look at my calendar and let you know."

"That's really kind," AM replied, picking up her phone again. She texted Daisy and asked her to give Ann a tour of the classrooms. When Daisy peeked her head into the lunchroom, AM waved her over and made the introduction.

"Daisy, is the music class in session?"

Daisy lifted a finger to her ear. "I hear the chorus warming up."

"Excellent," AM said.

Ann looked at Daisy, a young round-faced woman

with smooth dark skin and large dimples. "Where are you from?" Anne asked.

"Ghana."

"How did you get the name Daisy? You speak such beautiful English."

"English is my first language. Daisy is my favorite flower and a family nickname." Then she turned to AM. "Are you aware that a photographer has set up a tripod in the hall?"

AM looked to Ann who was applying orange lipstick as she gazed into a compact.

"I'd like a few shots of us out by that big piece of art in the hallway," said Ann.

"I'm sorry," AM said. "I thought we made it clear: no photographs."

"Oh, no. This is not for social media. Just for my personal files."

"Please tell your photographer to put the camera away," AM said. "It's been so nice to meet you. I'll send Alberto over to the music room. He'll be organizing the fundraiser with you."

A messier photo opportunity occurred one evening when Reade met up with AM, Viv, and some collectors at a fancy French restaurant in midtown after a performance by a 90-year-old jazz singer at Birdland. Just as the main course was served, he felt something bump against his leg and a small boy jumped out from beneath the table, gripping a cloth bag with several stolen wallets. The boy screamed as the waiter grabbed the bag and put the tiny thief out on the sidewalk. The scene seemed to Reade like something out of a movie. Heads turned and a young man passing their table recognized AM. Flashes went off before she could hide her face. Reade excused himself. On the sidewalk, he saw the boy jump into the passenger side of an SUV. As it zoomed off, he unrolled the window and stuck out his tongue—that's the shot Reade got for his Bully File. He was frustrated. It was hard to be vigilant when everyone on the street had a camera. AM went out less after that and never alone. Like a tag team, Alberto dropped her off and Reade met her. Or Alberto dropped them both off and they took a cab home.

FIFTEEN

MANNY CALLED to let Reade know Granet's *Choir of the Capuchin Church in Rome* was ready for pick up. As the elevator opened, Manny hurried to greet Reade. He was wiry, strong, and wore a clean apron, his hair tied in a ponytail. His eyes were bright, the kind the old masters painted. Handing Reade some typed pages, he drew his attention to the Granet and compared it to a six-by-eight color photograph he took the day Reade dropped it off.

"This flaking," he said, pointing to the lower middle of the Granet photograph. "We secured this spot with eight percent sturgeon glue. After removing the surface dirt and dust from the entire painting, we vacuumed and brushed the reverse and removed the canvas from the stretcher. We applied a cellulose poultice to soften it and dried it under pressure." Manny compared the top left of the photograph to the painting. "This was rewoven with a few linen threads and re-adhered. Belgian linen was added to the perimeter of the canvas. Splits and old nail holes in the stretcher were repaired with wooden inserts. Varnish and discolored overpainting were reduced and thin layers of mastic varnish were applied. To protect the paint surface, I used gouache and watercolor. Final retouching was done with resin colors. The frame was cleaned and, lastly, I attached an archival backing to protect the canvas and provide some environmental stability."

The old processes reminded Reade of the early conversation he had with AM about mixing paint with horse piss and cobwebs. Upon opening the bill, Reade was delighted that Manny's estimate was spot on. "Thank you," Reade said.

Manny took a final photograph for his files and secured the painting in thick brown paper and tape. He swiped Reade's debit card and they said goodbye. On his way out, Reade paused in the lobby to call Kermit. He wanted him to see the restored painting before taking it to Queens.

The director of the Israel Museum of Art had just left Kermit's office. Construction on the new wing of the museum, which Kermit donated, was nearing completion. A final selection of European paintings and drawings of biblical subjects had been decided upon, and a tentative opening date was selected for next spring. Kermit solemnly reminded Reade that the wing would be dedicated to the memory of his parents who died in the Holocaust.

Kermit examined the surface of the Granet with a magnifying glass. "It looks very good, Reade," he said. "It is not over-cleaned. This is a great fear among collectors and museum directors, for good reason. Even a masterpiece cannot hold its value if repainted or layers of paint are destroyed."

Reade directed Kermit to the new details that appeared: the grain of wood in the wainscoting lining the chapel; the sunlight on the priest's hands at the center of the painting; and the twenty-six bearded monks around the perimeter, their brown hooded robes now stood out from the background. The whole choir of monks breathed—their foreheads wrinkled, bald heads shined. They seemed to shift from foot to foot through long hours of prayer. Two monks squatted in conversation in the corner, another knelt in pain, and a third slumped over a pew, eyes toward heaven as if begging forgiveness. And lit from behind, the altar boys' ears pinked, hairs of a cowlick gleamed, and the edges of their lace blouses were bright as the flames of the tall candles they carried.

"Look," Reade said. "The scripture text is red. I hadn't noticed that before. And see here how Manny repaired the spot where layers of paint had flaked on the lower right side? He also plastered the broken portions of the frame."

"Look at the painting within the painting at the top

of the chapel," Kermit said. "It is now clear that this is Jesus ascending to Heaven, not Mary. Both have blue and red robes, and both have long hair, but look at this face in the magnifying glass!"

Reade was startled. "Facial hair."

"Yes," he continued. "Jesus wears a beard. This is very good, Reade. Well done!"

Kermit then took Reade aside to show him a Govert Flinck painting, *Rebecca at the Well*. "It is a beautiful painting, Reade, with excellent provenance. It was in a private collection in Amsterdam for three generations before ending up in the hands of a shipping magnate in Maine. You see the servant offering jewels to Rebecca if she will marry Abraham? Look at her face. She wants the jewels but isn't so happy about the old man."

Kermit's cheeks creased into dozens of lines as he smiled. "You should buy this painting. It is an important painting. For you, $36,000."

Reade laughed. He wanted to remind Kermit that he has a six-month-old baby. How could he afford this? His new position at the Honey Dearborn Art Center brought in only $60,000 a year. He was in the middle of a divorce. But Reade saw that Kermit was serious and he nodded. "It's beautiful."

"You are a smart man, Reade. From exporting, I became an art dealer. I hired world experts from the best universities as consultants. You will, too."

"I'll let you know when my Seattle house sells," he

said. At the door with the Granet securely rewrapped, he turned to Kermit. "Where's Jules?"

Kermit had been energetic when Reade arrived, so dapper in his double-breasted suit and pocket watch, his thick silvery-red hair slicked back. Now he now swayed on his feet, drained of energy. "Jules is in the hospital with pneumonia. It's the second time this year. His son flew in yesterday to help Janine look after him."

"So sorry to hear," Reade responded. "Jules is such a kind man."

"Lulu comes in twice a week to help me with correspondence, but Jules is my right arm. He is very special."

"Please call if you need me for anything," Reade said.

Julian Manfred Hagel died before Reade could send a note or visit him at the hospital. Reade met his widow, Janine, a lively French woman in her late eighties who once owned a toy manufacturing company. The funeral at Riverside Memorial Chapel on the west side was bustling with what seemed like dozens of funerals taking place simultaneously in the one building. Their group of sixteen was escorted from a waiting room to a side room and on into the chapel when the funeral in front of them emptied out through a side door. A Rabbi prayed in Hebrew, concluding with the Kaddish, the ancient prayer for the dead. Reade wanted to hear Jules get up and tell his story one last time. He wanted to know who his parents were and exactly how he survived the Holocaust as a boy wandering from Poland to Belgium. But no one in the small group stood to bear witness.

Janine's face was covered in a black mantilla that fell over the shoulders of her black dress. Reade imagined her as a young girl praying to die a saint like many of the Catholic girls in his school: lost in the maze of prayer and the saturated colors of stained glass; the overwhelming smell of incense; the marble folds of the statues; the priest drinking Christ's blood from a gold chalice; and learning to swallow the host, Christ's flesh, without letting it touch their teeth. Jules had said that he met Janine when he was sixteen. It was not only Jules' excellent French that saved his life, the French language enabled him to properly woo Janine after the war.

"I'm Reade, Anna Magdalena's husband," he said, taking Janine's hand. Her sad gray-haired son held Janine by the elbow. "I'm sorry for your loss. I enjoyed every moment I spent with Jules."

Lulu, Kermit, AM, and Reade found themselves standing alone on the sidewalk in the middle of the afternoon. They walked up Broadway to a nearly empty diner. Lulu dabbed her eyes, and together the four of them huddled and sipped coffee, mourning in silence. Reade became aware of the fact that AM, Lulu, and Kermit had mourned together before. Baby Georgie Saxton Pierce was again in their thoughts.

SIXTEEN

READE WAS DELIGHTED to celebrate AM's fortieth birthday with a picnic on Overlook Mountain in her hometown of Woodstock. On the chilly last day in April, they drove north through the Hudson River towns, scenic landscapes like *The Little Red Lighthouse Beneath the Great Gray Bridge*, which AM said was a children's book. She pointed out the Palisades, a mile-thick rock covering most of New Jersey, and the forbidding razor wire on the fence of Sing Sing prison. A lone boat sailed on the wide, steel-gray water at the Indian Point nuclear power plant. They passed a small suspension bridge, old brick factories with rows and rows of skylights next to the tracks, and an empty barge pushing past West Point, a fortress at a strategic corkscrew in the river. AM gave a great sigh when the worn Catskill Mountains appeared like rounded elbows and knees of elephants across the Hudson.

Their journey ended in a tiny cabin on the Millstream which wound through the town of Woodstock. The one room was barely bigger than the bouncy bed the three of them snuggled into. At four in the morning, birds broke into song on a bush outside their window.

AM covered her head with a pillow. "They sound electric."

"Acoustic," Reade said as he turned over.

They put Billie in the backpack and strolled to a coffee shop for muffins and yogurt. AM pointed to her childhood home, a small wooden house nestled in the woods among a dozen others. She shared bits and pieces of her complicated household growing up. Her charges—half-siblings, twins Mia and Mick—nine years younger. She was called Maggie then—the 3Ms is how Julia, their mother, referred to her children. The 3Ms was also the name of her women's jazz trio. Neighbor kids ran in and out of their house while her mother made ends meet. Hungry men eyed AM, the fathers of her sibling's friends, men her mother brought home, men who seemed to have free run of the house. But AM kept her distance and gave them no encouragement. Her mother was proud that AM could take care of herself. She earned a brown belt in an after-school Taekwondo class in sixth grade.

"Maggie! It's me, Miriam," a woman yelled. She was stopped in traffic on the town green.

"Hi, Miriam," AM replied. She leaned in, her hand

on the roof of the car. "How are you? How's the program?"

"Going well," she said. "Who is this little one?"

"Billie," AM said. "And this is my partner, Reade."

Miriam was a bright-eyed, middle-aged woman with dark curls. "Are you still living in Manhattan? I don't see you on Facebook anymore."

A driver honked at Miriam.

"Whoever heard of honking in Woodstock?" Miriam said. She rolled her eyes and drove off.

"She saved my ass twice," AM said. "Miriam arranged for some small part-time jobs and mentorships—one at the Woodstock School of Art and one with a costume designer in Kingston. Later, when my mother moved to Los Angeles, she helped me get the fellowship with Ginger in New York City when I was seventeen. Westbeth was the first artist building in the city, and it became my home for two years. I had a bed in a corner behind a screen. Sometimes I joined the dancers. Mostly, I took photographs of their routines, cooked, and did chores for Ginger as well as the poets and painters and writers in the building."

AM chirped like the morning birds. She had never opened up to Reade about her childhood before. As they drove through the lush green backroads with small wooden houses, she talked about her high school friends who gathered at Magic Meadow on McDaniel Road for the full moon.

"That's where I learned the thrill of performance,"

she said. "My friend Steve was into drawing with fire. He used flammable foam on big rocks and one night, he set up a ring of fire and we took turns jumping through it. Philippe Petit lived outside of town—the guy who walked a tightrope between the Twin Towers. Sometimes we hid in the woods and watched him practice walking a wire strung between his two barns."

"Where are your friends now?"

"Stevie died in a car crash on Glasco Turnpike—so sad. It seems like one high school student was sacrificed on these winding roads each year. We grew up together in a communal house called Old Red until I was twelve. He was a brother to me. My friend Carol works for the United Nations—I don't know where she's posted right now. She moves around a lot."

They drove up the steep mountainside switchbacks with houses strewn here and there with prayer flags and parked across from a huge Tibetan Buddhist monastery with a gold spire. Billie fell asleep chewing on a cracker in the backpack as they walked. It was an old dirt road, steep and rocky. Signs warned hikers to stay on the path and watch for rattlesnakes. Mountain laurel bloomed in the woods, and they quickly warmed. Only one lively hiker strode past on their way up, an older man who smiled at them on the switchbacks. After a mile and a half, the trail flattened somewhat. The eerie remains of a concrete lodge appeared, a reminder that Overlook, with its stunning views, was a tourist destination a hundred years ago. The trail continued beyond this, but AM pointed toward a picnic table. Reade took off the backpack and set Billie down.

"You go first," she nodded toward the fire tower. "Go ahead. The view is fantastic."

She opened her coat and sat to nurse Billie.

"You've been up?"

"Every birthday that I can remember."

Reade climbed like a cat, holding to the thin black metal railing, circling up and around to the top without pausing. As far as he could see, green waves danced with the curvaceous sliver of the Hudson River. Small lakes nestled in the Catskills to the west and to the east the blue Berkshires reached into white cumulus clouds.

"Happy Birthday," Reade said, joining her at the table. "It is May Day. Noon. The time of your birth, right?"

"Thank you, Ree Dee, for making it happen."

The man who passed them on the trail sat on a nearby log. He wore a knit hat and sipped from a thermos. Without any words, he lifted his drink to them in a toast. The stranger's sparkling eyes did not divert from the little family. He walked over to them with an open brown paper bag.

Reade reached in and took a dried fig. "Thanks."

Black suspenders held up the man's dark wool pants. Reade noticed his scarred and chapped hands. AM withdrew a dried apricot from his paper bag. They silently nibbled fruit as the man retreated.

A spark of sun warmed them. Deciduous trees

swayed in the dampness. Reade cut bread and cheese and apples they bought from the city. They gazed at the landscape, but his eyes turned to AM. She looked beatific nursing in the open air.

Back in the city, Gallery A sent tickets for the opening night of *Akhnaten* as a birthday gift, and AM screamed with glee. "Philip Glass!"

Reade had no idea who Philip Glass was but found *Akhnaten* online and listened as Alberto laid out their evening clothes he selected from the costume warehouse. Reade noted that there were very few words in the opera—it was mostly meditative chanting and drumming—as AM pulled a fluffy red dress over her head. Except for its color, a deep mustard yellow, Reade's outfit was a conventional three-piece suit with a white shirt and black string tie. He laughed at the black shoes, however. They sported unusual big black buttons, something George Washington might have worn, with buttons instead of a buckle.

"I read that Akhnaten and Nefertiti marry," Reade said. "Pharaohs often married their sister or brother. Brothers are Gods," Reade continued. "Sisters are revolutionaries."

AM's eyebrows arched in a smile.

Alberto interrupted, "Anthony Roth Costanzo plays Akhnaten. He's naked throughout the performance, except for his coronation. His body is waxed before each performance and his voice will pierce you, like Anna Magdalena Pierce."

Afterward, Reade read to Alberto the notes he wrote while listening to the opera: "Drum drill. Unbinding of a mummy. Ken-doll naked. Harmonizing voices and horns. Staccato pulse. Ephemeral vocals. A golden pate. Big raccoon eyes. Hoop buckling. Layered lace. Leather gauze. Doll's heads swim in slow motion. She with the animal pelt. Voice. Voice. Voice. Crown rise. High balls. Pins spin. Step. Dance. Song. Prayer. Adoration. Sun Pageantry. Brilliance. One God. Pins spin and whizz through the air. Sound flows into the image. Balls attack. Chaos. Pin battle. Death ritual. Binding. Burial. The end is like a Shakespearian play with a whole new story of the boy, King Tut."

Alberto gave him a thumbs up.

SEVENTEEN

AS SCHEDULED, Becky arrived in New York to pick up Billie at the beginning of her summer semester. It was a twenty-four-hour emotional nightmare. Reade and AM met her at the JFK Marriott with Billie and his carefully-packed luggage. Becky immediately dumped it out on the bed and, in a whirlwind, began winnowing it down. The three of them watched her from the doorway until Becky grew weary and pulled Billie from Reade's shoulder. They dropped into a chair. Becky trotted out his little rubber giraffe from her coat pocket, which he stuck in his mouth. Becky shut her eyes. AM and Reade took off their coats and began repacking.

"Take the backpack," Reade begged. "Billie loves it. And his snowsuit, please. The beach can be cold, even in summer. And these are Billie's five favorite books. They take up practically no room."

"Mom has books at her house," Becky responded.

It was as if Becky thought all books were equal. Her plan to divide Billie's next two months between her mother's house in Seattle and her dad's in Willapa was equally flawed. Reade wanted to trust her but cringed at the idea of Lydia babysitting Billie. What if Billie disrupts her card game? What if ash falls from her extra-long cigarette while she's changing his diaper? The situation with Meyer was even worse. Becky planned to stay in his moldy house, and hiring a housecleaner wasn't going to make it kid-friendly. She also planned to bring her dad home during her stay, but no way could she care for an Alzheimer's patient and a ten-month-old. Reade remembered the rainy night Meyer showed up at his farm, soaked and shivery. His ghostly gray eyes made no sense. He didn't know where he was. No words formed in his mouth. Reade gave him dry clothes and soup and made a bed for him on the couch, a place Meyer slept more and more often. The next day Reade brought Meyer back to his house and stocked his fridge. Checking on him two days later, Reade found the front end of Meyer's car smashed with tufts of hair and dried gut stuck in the grill, the windshield cracked into a spidery mess. Worse, he got a call from Sheriff Fox to pick Meyer up at the station: he had been arrested for breaking and entering. Weekenders, owners of a beach house a few blocks from his own, found him sleeping in their bed.

"Reade," Sheriff Fox said, "get your father-in-law to a doctor. Next time I'll lock him up."

AM had weaned Billie, or so she thought. But after Billie's departure, she slathered her nipples with ointment and bound them with cloth. Still, the nipples festered and cracked. Worse, she took a vow of silence. She danced, made love to Reade, and sometimes whispered in her sleep, but standard communication at the Honey Dearborn Art Center became slips of paper or notes posted on doors. Vivian, Lulu, and the board of directors were not only tolerant but adamant that AM have the privacy she needed during this difficult time. Yet AM pulled off the week-long professional development beautifully: her nods, smiles, and bows had the warmth of words as she greeted teachers and staff and went about her business. Alberto conducted his warm-up exercises and his daily lecture on transformative community action; Daisy told stories of growing up in her rural village in Ghana as she served the teachers home-made soup and bread for lunch; AM assisted the art teacher in the sculpture workshop making figureheads for the bows of imaginary ships. She tore pieces of cardboard and newsprint, twisted paper, and mixed the wheat paste as the teaching artist demonstrated folding and taping cardboard, creating facial features, and how to apply strips of papiér maché to smooth the shape. AM hung the figureheads on the wall in the main room: a bearded magician with big eyebrows and a pointed hat; a woman with hands together in prayer; a swan diver leading with her breasts; a three-headed monster; a dolphin; and a golden, sharp-horned bull, like the one at Bowling Green in the Financial District.

The Capuchin Monks took lifelong vows. Gandhi had regular silent Mondays. Bucky Fuller held a two-year moratorium on speech but knowing this didn't help Reade. At wit's end, he stopped by an animal rescue shelter on Queens Boulevard and picked Rusty out of the many barking dogs. Rusty was a medium-size Lab mix with a short brown coat and one white toe. His left eye had a congenital deformity, a reddish-brown lump in the white of his eye near the cornea. Rusty made AM smile even as he slinked along the walls and pooped in the hallway at night.

"Maybe you could sing to him," Reade said. "I'm not asking for words, but at least hum the songs you sang to Billie, for instance? I need to hear your voice as much as Rusty."

AM preferred her sequestered life at the Honey Dearborn Art Center since taking her vow which, by the way, silenced Reade, too. He was tired of hearing only his voice. As they ate their dinners of steamed vegetables and soba noodles on the roof, they watched from folding chairs the dazzling tableau of Manhattan skyscrapers burn in the sunset across the East River. They looked at art books together. The Leonard Baskin woodcuts Kermit gave to them equaled the best of the abstract expressionists, Reade thought. He tried to staunch the flow of their emptiness for Billie by reading aloud from AM's collection of literary works written in prisons: Cervantes, *Don Quixote*; Jean Genet's, *Our Lady of the Flowers*, about the extraordinary topic of murder and masturbation in the Paris cemetery; Gandhi's *The Story of my Experiments with Truth;* and O. Henry, with his ridiculous plots twisting and turning. She smiled, rolled her eyes, and stamped her feet when wowed, or she drew little pictures, forcing Reade to think visually. Sometimes, which delighted Reade, AM mouthed swear words.

Whenever he was desperate, Reade pulled a small notebook from his back pocket. She understood that this meant he was begging for communion. She wrote "14 Days" and drew a fat-faced Billie Buddha. He made a list of all of his upcoming chores: broom cleaning the West Seattle house, which sold for $10,000 over the asking price; check on the Willapa farm; figure out what to do about Buckeye; and secure custody of Billie. Then he added his departure date for Seattle in ten days. He hated to leave her. He drew himself as a stick figure in a cloud of tears, arms out front, cape flying behind, and AM in a big empty bed below. She added a smile to the female figure and drew a picture of Reade flying back east with Billie in his arms. Once again, Reade found himself wishing for a good, old-fashioned nor'easter to break her vow, like the lullabye—*when the wind blows the bow will break.*

Viv turned down VIP dinners and cultural events requesting AM's presence as she obviously could not socialize. This spared Reade hours of watching her charms from across the table. While he enjoyed the way she wove relief into the endings of her sometimes-shocking stories, he was never seated next to her: no squeezing her thigh under the table or whispering in her ear; she was literally "bought" for those two or three hours. Sometimes collectors pulled Reade aside to ask personal questions. He learned to say something authentic. A tidbit that made them laugh was enough to satisfy them.

AM walked Rusty to Socrates Sculpture Park where he swam for a stick at the edge of the East River. She shampooed him and vacuumed his hair that shed everywhere. He seemed to help her insomnia but not Reade's. As they lay entwined in the half-dark city, he propped open the unwieldy *History of Western Art* against one shoulder, using the other to angle the streetlight onto its pages. In year one thousand, when the world didn't end as people expected, a spiritual rebound occurred. There was a cultural push and pull: while churches filled with new creations of art, the crusaders pillaged and killed from the Holy Land, across Europe, to England.

Reade continued swimming laps in the Atlantic with Jim each week. Rising up and over waves between the buoys, he cupped his fingers, pulled water against his chest, stretched his torso and lungs, and kept his legs parallel and ankles loose. This built muscles. After a few laps, the synchronizing of stroke and breath became meditative. Staring through goggles into the green water, he saw again the face of the stranger on Overlook Mountain: the man with no words; the man who shared dried fruit from a brown paper bag. And he added this strange man who had taken an intense interest in them to his Bully List.

One night his Ma appeared at the end of their bed. He tried to touch her but couldn't. Her clothes and skin, even her brown hair, were ghostly white; otherwise, she looked healthy and energetic, her flesh firm. Like AM, she did not speak but watching her gestures and facial expressions, he gleaned her thoughts. For instance, he told her about his move to New York: a city of brick, metal, asphalt, and glass crammed with people from around the world, and he could tell his Ma was proud. He told her he witnessed a woman get hit by a livery cab as she crossed the street. Ma nodded as if to say, yes: I taught you how to cross the street when you were a boy! He told her about swimming at Rockaway, and the strange nirvana inside the curl of a wave he felt sometimes, just like in AM's drawing. Is that what death feels like, he asked? Was he drowning?

He felt Ma's warmth. She was so patient with him growing up and even now, standing at the end of his bed. He told her about all the small observations he kept to himself: "You! Don't look at me! Do you hear?" yelled a man in the subway. "Do you? Huh? Today is not the day, do you hear me? Not a good day to look at me."

He told her about the breeze he felt when a nun in a long black robe sat on the stool next to him at a Shake

Shack. She's hungry, he thought, but her hawk-eye landed on his phone sitting on the counter. When he stuffed it into his jeans, she walked out the door.

He told her about the dollar he gave to the Latino trio with cowboy hats on the subway, harmonizing the popular Spanish songs Pa used to like; the dental hygienist who talked to him like he was a child: "Have you been a good boy?" she asked. "Open up now and let me see those little babies." All the while her electric tool dug into his gums.

He mentioned the young man in a white apron masturbating in the stairwell of a restaurant, desperate for privacy, unable to restrain himself. And the guy in an elevator with a muddy chlorinated mop bucket, playing a shoot-out scene on his phone, over and over gunfire and screams. The man's tears rolled down his cheeks, his fingers unable to disconnect from the violence. And about the waiter in the coffee shop who, when Reade ordered a second cup of tea, said: "My girlfriend's first husband made her use the same tea bag, day after day after day, until on the fortieth day she divorced him."

His Ma began to sway and fade. Wait, he called out to her in the dream. Let me tell you about Anna Magdalena. He wanted his Ma to love her as he did. Remember Frank Dearborn? His mother left AM a warehouse in New York. He told her about AM's controversial performance pieces and about Kermit, how he was tutoring him on the old masters. He told her how they turned the warehouse into an art center for immigrant women and children. His Ma nodded approval. He told her how brave these women were, escaping a culture that didn't allow them to drive, vote, hold jobs, get an education, or even eat bananas because that was considered sexually provocative. He related that one woman was taught that short skirts cause earthquakes! How women are considered property. How a woman without a husband, father, or brother to rule over her is forced to beg or become a prostitute to feed her children, or was forced to sell her daughters instead of watching them starve. And these women as girls vowed to their fathers that they would remain a virgin until they marry. Even now, living in the U.S., they are unable to break that promise. Ma nodded. Reade remembered her work with women in the Seattle jails. Violence against women happens in America, too, she seemed to say. Women throughout history have been treated like slaves.

Waning now, flickering like a candle, Reade was surprised that his mother didn't seem to see AM in bed next to him. He told her he sold their Seattle house and that he bought the old Willapa farm on the beach. He told her he married Becky Smith, Meyer's daughter. Meyer was okay but Becky's mother, Lydia, never did like him, he said. And just as he and Becky divorced, she got pregnant and from sadness came great joy. I have a nine-month-old son, Billie Bordeaux! AM is helping me raise him. But Becky has him in Seattle now, and AM took a vow of silence in protest. She walks around with long pieces of fabric wound around her body like a church statue. He told his Ma that he hung a three-foot photo of Billie in their loft, like a giant Buddha, and AM carves holes along the edge of the sheetrock with a knife and pushes little notes into the cracks. It's her wailing wall.

Ma was agitated now, her fists clenched. It was an image so startling that it woke Reade: take care of your son, his Ma seemed to say. No one can raise him better than you.

EIGHTEEN

STROLLING ROOM to room through the Seattle bungalow, Reade noted the realtor's touches: a bouquet of dried flowers in the dining room; a bowl of oranges on the kitchen table; the immaculately smoothed bedspread with bright yellow pillows against the headboard. A rack of never-worn dresses hung in the closet, bought by Becky's mother; a few of Reade's work shirts, jeans, and a pair of sneakers: these were their only personal effects in the bedroom. Packing the dishes, pots and pans, silverware, and numerous unused wedding gifts into boxes, he remembered reading about the giant 600-pound octopus living under a rock at Alki Beach, with arms 30-feet long and a nervous system as complex as a human's; how her little suction cups latched on to taste you. If you were a smoker, she might squirt water at you, or disappear in a cloud of black ink, or squeeze into a hole the size of a fist; if she thinks you're delicious, she'll wrap an arm or two around you.

Reade made a list of the IKEA furniture to donate: sofa, coffee table, side chair, kitchen table and chairs, and bedside tables. Luckily, the bathroom cabinet and the refrigerator-freezer had been taken care of by the cleaning company he hired. From the garage, he loaded the rental van with things to take to the beach: fly fishing gear, gardening clippers, grass seed, hoses, sprinkler, a used lawnmower, hammock, and outdoor chairs and table. What to do with the snowboard? He hadn't used it in many winters. From the front step, he gazed at the view of the snow-covered Olympics and left messages for JT, his attorney; the realtor; the Church of Our Lady of the Lake where he planned to drop off his donations; and lastly, the one he dreaded.

"Lydia, this is Reade Bordeaux," he said. "I haven't heard from Becky. I assume she doesn't want anything in the West Seattle house. I'm donating it all. I'll be at your house to pick up Billie on Friday around dinner time. Let's say six o'clock. We have a redeye to New York and need to be at the airport by eight. That's the day after tomorrow. Unless I hear differently, I'll see you then."

The drive to the beach was automatic, even in a downpour, the wipers at full speed. Traffic subsided once he turned west onto 101 at Olympia, and twenty minutes beyond, after passing the eerie 30-year-old half-built Satsop nuclear power plant, the rain let up. Turning south again at the Mendocino shortcut, he noted that the egret nest at the top of a telephone pole looked occupied. He felt at home on the narrow two-lanes through old-growth Douglas fir. AM felt strangely closer with each mile: crossing the Quillayute River that flows into Willapa Bay and rounding the inlets, he remembered her wish on the island. Maybe they became each other after all, with their lives so entwined.

Buckeye was kicking a circle in the pasture as Reade drove up to the farm. He wished Frank Dearborn still lived across the street. He wished Frank would chew him out from his porch, all irritated and anxious, the way he got when Buckeye stirred up dust in the pasture. Reade spotted the giant yellow cat sitting on the fence post—the same cat that licked Buckeye's ear last visit—the cat that started showing up after the goat died. Reade saddled Buckeye and rode him out through the pasture into the small evergreens and up over the dunes. The surf exploded against the beach. Mountains of foam had built up along the sand and, picked up by the wind, bounced like balls along the beach. He rode into it, tasting its flecks of salty froth, cawing and flapping his arms more like a gull than a forty-year-old man.

Three bundled figures emerged in the landscape: it was the famous beach cleaning trio wrapped in coats and hats, scarves and rubber boots, carrying plastic garbage bags and walking sticks. They moved in unison across the sloping beach, their heads bobbing like incoming waves. The woman with a keen pair of eyes nearest Reade was Jeff's Aunt Doris, his next-door neighbor. She spotted a plastic straw ten yards away and bent to pick it up.

Reade reigned Buckeye in. "How goes it, Aunt Doris?"

She beckoned with her finger, and he slid to the ground. Up close, beneath the pointed knit cap, Aunt Doris was bearded. Her eyes were bright ultramarine, the color of Japanese glass floats Reade found on the beach as a kid.

"My car is due for an oil change. Have you got the time?"

"Sure. I could do it tomorrow morning. If Jeff's around, I'll teach him how since your oil really should be changed every 10,000 miles, not just when I'm available."

"Thank you for hiring Jeff to look after your place, Reade. He's doing an excellent job. I keep an eye on him. He thinks the world of you." Aunt Doris begged him close again with her finger. "I'm moving to Arizona to be with my sister in the fall. I have college money for Jeff. Maybe you could talk to him about it. He never was interested in college and now that he has a girlfriend, I don't have much influence."

At age twenty, Jeff had morphed into a self-aware man with enhanced listening skills and a two-day growth on his face. His Jimi Hendrix hair was cut short, and he carried a new muscular upper torso. As a certified volunteer member of the rescue squad, he worked out most mornings and told Reade with pride about the dramatic rescue he made dangling from a helicopter in a wetsuit to save a fisherman. Bonnie Rainwater, his girlfriend, worked with him at the station. She was a no-nonsense type with pretty eyes and long black hair. She tenderly stroked Jeff's hand as they sat on the old leather couch in Reade's living room. He had guessed she was a few years older than him but no, they graduated from high school the same year. Their first conversation, however, only occurred during Jeff's training.

The farm looked in good shape. The old house was tidy. Nostalgia set in at dinner as Reade ate potatoes, thick carrots, and fat beets from the garden. Jeff had taken up beekeeping and showed off his white outfit, explaining the details of his new hobby, like how to use the smoke and the importance of remaining calm. Bees, he found, were really sweet little puppies once he got over his fear of their sting. He had four hives in the apple orchard. Attentive to Reade's culinary preferences, the meal was capped with a piece of apple pie. Afterward, Jeff made show-and-tell of a pile of flotsam he and Bonnie picked off the beach. Some had vertical Japanese lettering, probably from the Tsunami that hit Japan a few years prior. A storefront in town was collecting it to return to Japan.

"I cleared Mrs. Baxter's ghost from the house," said Jeff.

"Oh, yeah?" Reade remembered his Ma at the foot of his bed. He was still trying to decide if she was a ghost or a dream. "How'd you do it?" Reade asked.

"We smoked it out with sweetgrass. I didn't mind the ghost weeping, but her laughing creeped me out. We didn't want to sleep in the house until she was gone, and the space heater wasn't warming the tower very well. Now we sleep in the guest room on the first floor. Is that okay? Bonnie stays over most nights." Jeff blushed. "No smoking cigarettes," he added. "I kicked the habit. Bonnie doesn't smoke either."

Mrs. Baxter's ghost was local lore, and Reade guessed it was the reason Becky never liked to sleep in the farmhouse. Apparently, Mrs. Baxter used the first floor of the house as a manger, complete with horses and chickens. He never saw evidence of that or her ghost, but he liked the new rumor that the Baxter ghost had vanished.

"Sounds good," Reade said. "I ran into Aunt Doris on the beach. She said she's selling the house and has a college fund for you, Jeff."

Jeff and Bonnie looked at each other. "We do want to go to college, just not right now," she said.

"How about I give you a fifty bucks a month raise if you stay on until June? I should know by then what I plan to do with the farm. Maybe then you'll be ready for college."

The night Frank died came back to Reade when he went up to bed. He had dropped AM off at her studio after they watched the news at the Depot Diner. He wasn't sleepy and built a bonfire out by the garden and stared at Frank's house, expecting him to pull up in front. The next morning at dawn, Reade woke to a banging on his kitchen door. Opening his eyes, he was surprised to discover AM curled up in the chair next to his bed wrapped in a blanket. He was so excited he ignored the pounding and bent over her, intent on stealing a quick kiss, a lick, or a bite. But where? One small morsel of ear peeked out beneath the blanket, one elbow, and then he saw her foot. Even as the pounding downstairs became more persistent, he got down on his knees and sucked the cold round bit of her little toe, sending adrenalin through his veins. He pulled away as the banging downstairs increased. It was Meyer with Reade's hammer and screwdriver from his toolshed wedged deep into the doorjamb. When Meyer saw him, he lifted a fat geoduck from his bucket, its gigantic neck hanging down around his gut. Meyer wanted to play a game of scrabble and stew the geoduck for breakfast. Reade went along with it, all the while expecting AM to descend the staircase nude, something dramatic. Instead, she made bowline knots in Pa's ties that she found in the closet, anchored them to the leg of Reade's bed, and lowered herself out the window.

A phone call from Reade's ex-mother-in-law brought him back to real-time.

"There must be some misunderstanding, Reade. Becky and Billie and Bubba...you know Bubba from the Red Barn? They drove to Texas a week ago. Bubba had some horses to deliver. He was her first beau, and Becky never got over that boy. You know my daughter; she's gotta have it. She told me that you never satisfied her sexually, Reade, so I can't blame her."

Reade drew a deep breath, her words searing his brain. "Give me Becky's Texas address, Lydia."

"She doesn't know where she's going to live. The Army's paying for her to go to school, you know, in Houston. By the way, you owe me $1,000 for babysitting Billie for two weeks. Becky left Billie with me when she went to visit her father, but he's pretty much dead. It must have been Bubba she was seeing."

"Tell her I'm coming after her, Lydia. Tell her to text her address before my plane lands in Houston or my attorney will get the police on the case."

Reade knocked on the door of Meyer's assisted living unit, a sour-smelling house from the 1960s. It was run by a husband and wife. She did the cooking, cleaning, feeding, and laundry; he did the shopping, showering, and yard work. It happened to be all-male residents at the time of Reade's visit, which looked a lot like purgatory. Meyer didn't recognize him even as Reade opened the Monopoly board and set out their two usual markers: the shoe and the car. His forehead was bandaged and when Reade asked the caretaker about it, she said that Meyer had an altercation at the breakfast table and knocked out another man's tooth. Now he was confined to his room.

"Meyer," Reade said. "Remember the three-foot geoduck you dug up last winter? We made damn good chowder. Remember me? I'm Reade. I married your daughter, Becky. Have you seen her lately?"

Nothing registered in his soupy eyes. He stared at the silent TV screen. Reade patted his hand but couldn't get Meyer to look at him.

"Is he drugged?" Reade asked the caretaker on his way out. "I'm his son-in-law. My wife, Becky, talked to you a week or so ago. She said he was fine."

"Let's see," the woman said, checking her book. "Yes, Becky called two weeks ago. Meyer hasn't spoken a word in a couple of months now. It's not surprising your wife didn't tell you. This kind of thing is so hard on families."

Reade then drove to Bubba's Red Barn, jumped the locked gate, peeked through the blinds of his dark trailer, and toured his empty barns. A fresh mound of dirt in the pasture rose larger than Chief Nahcati's grave on the hill above Willapa. It was newly raked and sprinkled with grass seed. Bubba's truck and trailer were gone. Reade guessed he probably took his one or two decent horses and buried the rest.

It appeared that Becky had planned the getaway, and Bubba didn't have the backbone to buck Becky's swagger or her seductive, coppery mane. Emotions congested Reade's head. He felt a bloody nose coming on. He wanted to crawl under the covers with AM, but she was three thousand miles away. He couldn't even talk to her. Instead, he punched Alberto's name into his phone and welcomed his lilting tenor, even if only a voicemail. Reade laid out a quick sketch of his situation to pass to AM. Next, he thought of calling James, his swimming buddy, or even Aunt Doris to chit-chat, but he scratched that. Instead, he sat in the driver's seat of his truck and paid JT by the minute to update him on Becky's U-turn, then drove back to his farm to wait out the night. When JT called back, he informed Reade that Bubba, aka Stanley Shiner, had one living relative, a sister, Teresa Gonzales. He gave Reade her suburban Houston address, once the Shiner family farmhouse. He also provided Reade with the name and address of Becky's Army base, and if need be, he'd contact Houston police to track down Billie. Technically, he said, Billie's been kidnapped.

Dawn rose above the Coastal Range, beaming sunlight through the green Pacific waves. At his mother's favorite bakery, Sheriff Fox and his three cronies were the only customers. Reade nodded to them and thumbed through the rack of tourist postcards next to the cash register while he waited for his coffee: the chainsaw mermaid, a prize-winning sandcastle, Ike the crocodile-man on permanent display at Marshall's Free Museum, and AM's CarPark. He bought the four

CarPark postcards and sipped his coffee in his rental car. He remembered how Honey pulled Frank's Cadillac off the auction block when Reade asked for a donation. Before installing it on Main Street, Reade, AM, and the high school kids took it for a joy ride, south to Oregon's Cannon Beach for ice cream. All six failing high school kids got on board with the CarPark project and ended up graduating.

Before Reade left town, he jotted a note to AM on the back of one of the postcards and dropped it in the blue mailbox on Main Street:

> Becky, Bubba, and Billie left me in the dust.
> I'm flying to Texas, fingers crossed
> Billie Boy and I will be home before you can say
> Blistering Blue Barnacles.

On the tarmac, while waiting for the flight to take off, Reade pulled up his Bully List, noting the dates each photo was taken. He was surprised that there were twelve: Saxton was still number one, but Reade doubted he knew how to shoot a gun–he was a pretender– and deleted him from the list. Number two: "Mr. Clean," the bald, cigar-smoking neighbor Reade photographed the night of the fire, stayed. Number three was Charlie Kim. Reade had confronted him and so he deleted Charlie. A slew of anonymous photographs of suspicious-looking guys on the street or in cars outside the Honey Dearborn Art Center came next. They stayed. Reade removed the guy on Overlook Mountain. He seemed too friendly to pose a threat. Then he added Bubba and Becky. She had turned on him.

NINETEEN

READE WENT through the motions of deplaning, renting a car, and checking into the Holiday Inn. He was exhausted and anxious, but a super bloom of yellow flowers on the flat outskirts of Houston reminded him that Billie was near. He drove past a long line of shopping malls, red stop signs sticking out of dry sandy soil, subdivisions with taupe-colored mailboxes and postage-stamp-size plots of grass. As the streets began to curve, an old white farmhouse set back from the asphalt road stood out as the Francis Shiner homestead. A young woman peeked from behind the curtain as Reade turned into the drive. The front door opened an inch when he knocked, the chain lock still in place. Reade explained his situation as he wiped sweat from his forehead and shoved his driver's license toward her through the crack.

"Becky's not here," she said. "I'm babysitting."

Reade snorted and coughed at the cool air conditioning that seeped out of the unpleasant-smelling living room. Toys scattered across the floor were a game-changer. As if on cue, Billie crawled into his sight.

The girl picked him up and unlocked the chain. Reade grabbed Billie, twirled him above his head, and brought him down for a slimy kiss. He found a paper napkin in his pocket from the plane and wiped Billie's runny nose. Billie's diaper dragged to his knees. Ripping it off, Reade saw an ugly, red-raised rash between his scrotum and thigh. He scrounged through Billie's bag that was open on the sofa, found some ointment, and taped on a new diaper. Down on the floor, father and son rolled a soft blue ball back and forth.

"Who are you?" Reade asked the teenager.

"Renee. Bubba's niece."

A scruffy-faced guy in T-shirt and shorts scurried toward the front door with a backpack, ignoring Reade, who snapped a photo of him. Then Reade turned and snapped pictures of the kitchen and living room. Billie looked up, his pacifier held between his four teeth. Leaning against the sofa, Billie pulled his clothes from his bag and threw them on the floor.

"Who's that?" he asked.

"My boyfriend," said Renee. She stood over the kitchen sink, squeezing soap onto the sponge, and started in on the dishes.

"Shouldn't you be going to school, too? I need to speak to your mother."

"She can't take calls. She's an emergency nurse. She'll be home by six."

"Where's Becky?"

The girl held Reade's gaze. She was in a fix, just doing what she was told, except maybe for the boyfriend. She took her hands out of the water and shook off the suds. Reade wondered how much of his story Renee knew.

"I think Becky and Uncle Bubba went to get married. They left a few days ago."

"You're joking, right?" Reade asked. He laughed loudly. "You mean they're off on their honeymoon? Becky and I just got divorced last week." Reade took a breath, not wanting to spill too much information. He deposited Billie's diaper in the overflowing garbage, tied the bag, and set it outside the front door.

As he washed his hands in the bathroom, he remembered losing his temper as a safety manager at the Seattle Pipefitting Company. A welder who knew better wasn't paying attention and lit his pant leg on fire. His buddy said to Reade: "If you yell at him, the situation will be about your bad temper, not his stupidity, and he'll never learn."

"Renee, I can manage Billie, but I'd like to leave your mother a message so she knows I'm here."

"She's expecting you."

"Oh, yeah?"

Reade focused on Becky and Bubba. He remembered seeing them together only once, the day Becky and AM met. Now Becky blew up their custody plan. How could he ever trust her after this? As he stared at Billie's cherubic little body curled beside him, he was happy to have twenty more years to watch Billie grow.

Reade put in a call to JT.

"Stay put," he said. "Don't let anyone trick you into leaving the premises, with or without Billie."

"Becky doesn't even want to take care of Billie. She doesn't seem to care what's best. So why doesn't she want me to have custody? Does it come down to the fact that she wants me to pay her mother to raise him?"

"It'll be okay, Reade. Becky crossed state lines and broke the custody agreement."

Reade finished the dishes, vacuumed, dusted, and organized the cupboards while looking for something to eat. A warmed can of tomato soup was lunch. Billie didn't like the sharp-tasting tomato but gummed the saltines. After scrubbing the tub, he gave Billie a bath singing their favorite watery tunes. They built a castle on the living room floor using his books and toys. Billie drove his little cars around, crashing the buildings. Only then did Reade realize that tomorrow was Billie's first birthday. Surely, Becky will show up.

"Sorry to bother you, Lulu," Reade said, "but I'm stuck in Houston and afraid I'm in need of a hotshot lawyer. My ex-wife, Becky, ran off with a horse dealer, dropped Billie in Texas, and, I just found out, eloped."

"Where's Billie?"

"I've got him. He's fine. Becky left him with her boyfriend's niece."

"Give me your attorney's name and number, and I'll put mine in touch. You two may have to rise to the occasion."

"What do you mean?"

"It sounds like wedding bells for you and Maggie."

"But I don't think she wants to marry me. I mean, we've never talked about getting married."

Lulu laughed. "Anna Magdalena Pierce is not shy about vows, Reade. You want to be in the strongest position possible when it comes to children, and in this country, most judges prefer parents who are married. Give our bubala a kiss for me, and we'll be in touch."

"What?"

"That darling baby of ours."

Alberto called next. He asked permission to use Reade's comp ticket to see the *Honey Dearborn Story* with AM. "She needs an escort," he said. "I've come up with a good disguise for her—a brown wig, trench coat, baseball hat, baggy jeans, hiking boots, and funky glasses since she can't wear shades in a movie theater."

"Be my guest."

"Have you seen the trailer? It goes like this: On a dark night at the Ilwaco Marina a fishing boat enters; its wake sets all the boats in the marina rocking and bobbing; the camera pans to a sailboat, bumpers squeaking and groaning against the dock; its riggings chime rhythmically; a scream rings out, 'Blue Blistering Barnacles, Reade!'"

"Enjoy the mockumentary," Reade said, wondering if Alberto was familiar with AM's habit of blurting out lines from books during sex.

Alberto chuckled. "Thanks, buddy."

"Wait, I have a favor to ask," Reade said. "It's probably the most personal thing I will ever ask of a friend. And I trust you, Alberto, even if you tease me. You've been through a shitload of medical, political, and legal crap, so I won't describe my crazy situation. But make it straightforward. Be creative. Be your most poetic self. I mean, say lovely things to AM for me."

"What the fuck?"

"I need you to ask AM to marry me. I have to have an answer now. It's an emergency."

He sighed. "Jesus, Reade. I thought someone was holding a gun to your head and you needed ransom money, or you wanted to send me off on some mission impossible."

"It feels like that," Reade said. "Is your answer yes?"

"Yes, man," Alberto said

"Thanks," Reade said. "And please make sure all your romantic words are on MY behalf. No actual lovemaking. You are asking her for ME."

"Will do."

"I await your full report," said Reade.

Late in the night, a very weary JT arrived at the door carrying a paper bag with two large coffees and donuts.

NINETEEN 149

Under the other arm was a fat accordion file. "Lulu has me on retainer," he said. "She hired a private jet at Boeing Airfield to fly me here. Ah!" he said, spotting Billie. "He looks like you, Reade. He has your brown hair and greenish eyes."

"Mine are blue," Reade said. "Billie's eyes are hazel. Becky's are brown. But greenish is good." He pulled Billie up onto his lap and broke open the box. Tearing off a small piece of plain donut for Billie, Reade stuffed the rest into his own mouth—he was sick of eating canned soup and crackers. "Hey, I really appreciate your traipsing down here, JT, but is it necessary?"

"We've got to win, right?" he replied. JT looked at Reade through black-framed glasses. He looked exactly like the kid who gave him the paper route when he was eleven and JT got a job at the gas station. Three years older, JT was impatient with Reade back then and very thorough about teaching him the route. He didn't want his loyal customers complaining to him and had rules he made Reade swear he'd follow: 1. Don't be late. 2. Don't let the paper get wet. 3. Always carry dog treats. 4. Smile when you knock on doors to collect. 5. Carry a lot of change, you'll get better tips.

"Whatever happened to your high school girlfriend?" Reade asked. "With the long blond hair."

He shrugged. "She married Joey, the football star. What about Becky, running off with half-nose? I remember him at your wedding, wrestling some drunk dude in the barn." JT's laugh was a low saxophone squawk, like he sucked air into his lungs, closed his throat, and choked.

"I forgot Bubba was at our wedding. They've been friends since she was twelve."

"Let's get down to business," JT said, looking at his watch. "I have to meet Lulu's attorneys downtown at 1:00. Tell me about life with Becky since Billie's conception."

Billie sucked happily on his bottle in the playpen, his thumb and pointer twirling a brown curl. Reade hoped Billie would never know the story he was about to tell. "Conception took place while Becky was home on leave —one of three afternoons. She returned to South Carolina after that, and I didn't see her until the annunciation, eight months later. But she called from the hospital with a vague illness at some point. I wanted to visit but she said it wasn't necessary—her mom had been there—she just needed rest. It must have had something to do with the pregnancy. Anyway, I was confused when, at eight months, she told me she was pregnant. We were just divorcing."

"What about using contraception?"

"I thought we were."

"Any domestic violence? Drug abuse? Marital affairs?"

"No, nothing like that. I guess I didn't understand what I was getting into when we married–that ROTC meant a military life. That was never going to work for me. You know the rest. The paternity test was positive."

"AM didn't play into the divorce?"

"No, I met AM in October. We spent Saturdays riding my horse on the beach or doing something outdoors. She had taken a one-year vow of celibacy so it was platonic until July first when her vow ended. We had sex once, then she disappeared."

"Why Saturdays?"

"We worked Monday through Friday, and she taught a Sunday art class."

"What's her art like?"

"She's a performance artist. She calls herself an esthetic terrorist. Her mother named her after Anna Magdalena Bach."

"Did you say a terrorist?"

"Yes. Like Bach's wife: uncompromisingly devoted to art."

"Jesus!" he said. "I'll leave THAT out."

"So you and AM were just friends during the last months of your marriage?"

"Yes."

"Why did you move to New York?"

"She inherited a warehouse and asked me to help her turn it into a community center for immigrant women and children of Queens."

"What?"

"Women and children of Queens, New York."

JT glanced at his watch.

"The truth is, I probably fell in love with AM the second time I met her. We were sitting on a log on

Willapa Bay and she took her clothes off and walked into the water. I never felt that way about Becky."

"And you can't swim."

"No, not then. But I swim in the Atlantic almost every week now."

"Okay," he said. JT was done with the chit-chat. "So, are you *sure* you want to get married again? There might be some other way out of this. I mean, I wouldn't want to marry a second time."

He pointed to the signature line on the marriage license.

"How can that be?" Reade demanded. He noticed that AM had already signed. Her swirl of beauty and dignity was like the signatures on the U.S. Constitution.

"It's a copy. I just wanted to show you that AM has signed. The New York lawyers will ask you to sign the real one today."

When JT drove off, Reade strapped Billie into the backpack and they walked toward the old family barn behind a row of poplars. The Texas air felt great after being cooped up in air-conditioning. A mix of yellow, red, and black-speckled chickens greeted them.

Reade slid open the barn door, and the darkness smelled of peat. A stamping and snorting drew them toward two young mares: their coats too thick for Texas. Badly in need of a fan or air-conditioning, a good brushing, and mucked-out stalls, they were also low on water. He thought of Rusty at home in Queens, missing his daily three-mile walk. Hopefully, Daisy and AM were taking him to the dog run. Reade snapped a photo of Bubba's truck parked behind the barn, including its Washington plates, and sent them on to JT.

"Is your Mama planning to return, or what?" Reade asked Billie. "If only you could talk. I bet you got an earful from Bubba and Becky on your drive to Texas."

TWENTY

THE SUN DIDN'T GO DOWN until 9:00 in Houston, but Billie and Reade were exhausted. Reade added bubbles to Billie's bathwater and sculpted him into a snowman. Their laughing and splashing as the bubbles melted were interrupted by a pounding on the front door. Reade wrapped Billie in a towel and headed to the living room.

"Uncle Alberto!" Reade exclaimed, clearly surprised to see him standing there.

"Happy Birthday, Billie!"

Pulling Alberto into the living room, the three of them hugged. Billie squirmed out of the towel, hit the floor, and bounced up and over to the couch.

"You're walking, Billie!" Alberto was dressed in western attire: cowboy boots, a plaid shirt rolled to his elbows and tucked into belted jeans. "I dropped my bag at the Holiday Inn," he said. "Lulu said that's where you are staying."

"Technically, yes." Reade taped a diaper on Billie and slipped a shirt over his head. Lifting the cardboard lid of the cake box, he showed Billie the round layer cake, his name spelled out in blue letters.

Alberto looked around the house. "This place looks like a movie set from the 1930s."

"Check out the kitchen. No counters. A free-standing sink with a pump, a wood cookstove, and an icebox," Reade said. "Luckily there's a microwave on the table to heat up the canned soup we've been living on. There's a full-size electric refrigerator in the back room. By the way, did you come all the way to Texas to report on my marriage proposal?"

"AM's answer is yes," Alberto said. "You're good to go."

Reade leaned in, snapping his fingers, impatient for Alberto to spill the story.

"I asked her to lunch at the Russian Tea Room for a change of scenery. It was a straight ask. I made it clear that *you* asked *me* to ask *her* to marry *you*. Lulu had updated AM on your situation. As everything on her part had to be written down, it wasn't the time or place for a detailed conversation. I borrowed a ring from the prop shop, a delicate imitation yellow sapphire encrusted with small fake rubies. I put it on her finger, and the waiter popped champagne. He took this picture of us."

Alberto handed Reade his phone. AM wore a jaunty little black hat over her hair that fanned out from her face, round sunglasses, a black-and-white striped dress with a Peter Pan collar, and fitted see-through sleeves scrunched up to her elbows. Alberto wore black on black. The tablecloth had small plates of food and two full champagne flutes. AM held up her notebook. It said, "I do."

"A nice couple," Reade remarked. He touched the screen to zoom in on AM. Ecstatic to see her again, he imagined her face in an oval frame carved of a single piece of wood, hanging in the Metropolitan Museum of Art.

Alberto lit candles and they sang the birthday song to Billie. Reade snapped more pictures for the moms. Billie dug his hand into the cake as Reade spooned a bite into his mouth. After cleaning him up, he held a cup of water to Billie's mouth.

"Has AM told you how we met?"

"No, I don't think I've heard that story."

"We were on a month-long fellowship at an Etruscan hilltop town in Italy. Six artists. At the time, she was painting at the Art Student League, living with the dance troupe at Westbeth, and dancing at the men's club downtown. I was the kid from Detroit on a gap year before college. We each had our own studio but shared a communal kitchen. Meals were a lot of fun after the never-ending rain and fog. We slept together one night after a big spaghetti dinner with lots of wine—it was playful, or should I say play-acting. A decade passed before we saw each other again. I ran into her at a party—she and Saxton were doing their Flash News performance. She wore a mask, but I could tell it was her."

"Uh-huh," Reade said.

"A few weeks later I got a call from Viv," he continued. "She asked me to schedule an interview. AM had recommended me for a discrete position of bodyguard. AM's art demanded complete freedom. She needed to feel safe to be daring. And she was getting death threats, harassed on streets, and haunted online."

Reade nodded.

"I was hired as AM's personal assistant. That's what I asked to call it. I drove her everywhere, escorted her to events, and walked down the street with her. When she got pregnant with Georgie, she quit the Flash News and took a teaching gig in Brooklyn. She loved working with children. As you know, the pregnancy was fine and baby Georgie brought three perfect days of joy. Then she fell to pieces—we all did—when Georgie died. Eventually, she set out on her road trip. That's when I found Willapa."

"What do you mean?"

"Willapa Bay. The last pristine body of water in the contiguous United States. I suggested the place. She loved it, set up her studio, and took her vows."

"Did you research me, too?"

"After she mentioned you. Just enough to fall in

love. My concern was how you'd behave toward a New York City performance artist who vowed celibacy, among other vows. I thought that might be a problem for a married plumber. But AM has her striptease down."

Reade's hair stood on his arms. Confused, he wondered if Alberto was teasing. Did he belong on the Bully List?

Alberto saw Reade's sudden crazed look, and said: "AM didn't tell me about you until she fell in love."

"Oh, yeah? When was that?"

"Your canoe paddle to the island of the ancient cedars."

Reade found clean sheets in a cupboard for Alberto, and he crashed in one of the upstairs bedrooms. Back on the couch next to Billie's playpen, Reade googled the Etruscan culture of 900 BC. He read about its great wealth and trading partners, the Celts and the Greeks, and that the Etruscan culture fell to the Romans in 400 AD. The remains of the ancient stone cities built on hilltops, once islands in a great ocean, riddled with caves and tunnels, were now crumbling.

Unable to get comfortable, Reade turned over and over. He had a headache from too much sugar. Around three o'clock he got up to find aspirin in a pocket of his bag and heard yet another knock at the door. He switched on the outside light and pulled the curtain aside. Becky stood on the porch. He opened the door with his finger to his lips.

"You made it to your son's birthday," he whispered.

It wasn't Bubba on her arm, but a stranger in a cowboy hat. "Hi, I'm Reade," he said. "And you are?" The man's back was to Reade—he slowly removed his hat as he turned. "Saxton!" Reade exclaimed. "What are you doing here? I mean, make yourself at home while I go throw up." Reade's head was spinning. He couldn't imagine how Becky and Saxton had crossed paths, and he wasn't sure he even wanted to know.

Reade lingered a moment, trying to read Becky's eyes. Her face was heavily made up. She wore false eyelashes! While she bent down to touch Billie asleep in the playpen, Reade ran to the toilet and heaved three times. He flushed, wondering if he could trust Becky for even the five minutes it took to rinse his mouth and wash his face. Saxton was no longer in the living room when he returned.

"Is Billie sick, too?" she asked.

"No," Reade said. "I think the birthday cake upset my stomach, among other things. It's been a tough few days, Becky."

She laid down on the couch; he took the chair across from her. "So, Becky. What's up with your running away to Texas with Billie? And Bubba, for God's sake, Becky! You crossed the line. How can I trust you with Billie ever again? Did you and Bubba really get married?"

She stared straight up at the ceiling. "I married Saxton."

"Oh, you are killing me!" Reade whispered. "He's

AM's ex! You and I were divorced for one week and now we're related again?"

"Bubba chickened out. I think it was Billie. He didn't want to raise your kid."

"Well, good of him. So, why marry? You don't even know Saxton. He's a chameleon! You won't recognize him from one day to the next. Tomorrow he'll be Lord Byron with a big curl hanging over one eye."

"Saxton likes my fatigues," she said. "We toured the base and spent some time at the shooting range. It seems that marrying a sharpshooter has been his life-long dream."

"Okay, Annie Oakley," Reade said. "Maybe he thinks a female sharpshooter will be good protection. Beck, he prefers to sleep with strangers! How can a wife be a stranger?"

"Mom's not always right, but she's never wrong."

"What do you mean?"

"When she said you didn't satisfy me sexually? The truth is, no one person satisfies me. Saxton is the same. We are perfectly happy to have an open marriage."

Reade bit his tongue. Just how many people did she sleep with during their two-year marriage, he wondered. And the story of the female officer raping her, if that's what it was? Why did she tell him about that particular encounter? Then it occurred to him: it was no longer his place to ask such questions.

"Nothing has changed, Becky," Reade said. "I want full custody."

TWENTY

Becky and all her stuff in the back bedroom were gone by dawn. Alberto was gone, too. Was he in on their wedding scheme? Reade watched Billie's little mouth move in a sucking motion and then snuck out onto the front porch to call JT. He wept into the phone.

"Hold on, Reade! Saxton's marrying Becky was not part of the plan," he said. "Saxton flew out to stop Becky from marrying Bubba. Again, Lulu's attorneys are on it. Texas troopers are involved."

"He stopped her from marrying Bubba, alright," Reade said. "And she'll be sitting across the table from me at every family holiday forevermore."

"Reade, she's living in Texas. Besides, you were already tied to her as Billie's father. Pack him up and meet me at the Holiday Inn by 1:00. That's the plan."

Gone were the horses when Reade went out to feed and water them. Gone were the truck and trailer. He cut a banana and poured Cheerios and milk into a bowl, spoon-fed Billie, washed and dressed him in jeans and a t-shirt, even little tiny socks and red sneakers he'd never seen before. He unrolled the window to gulp down the warm wide Texas sky as he drove away from the farmhouse. A pattern of frilly clouds spread as far as he could see. He wanted to throw rocks at the Texas landscape. Rolling his mother's wedding ring around in his pocket, he remembered the day he was sick and his Ma showed him a picture of the Eiffel Tower in Paris. Together they compared it to the tiny complex platinum structure that held her diamond. Becky left the ring next to Billie's bottles and nipples above the kitchen sink, a place he would be sure to find it.

The green Holiday Inn sign sprang up, and before turning onto Airport Boulevard, Reade glanced at Billie through the rear-view mirror, asleep in his car seat, his yellow rubber giraffe in his fist. Lulu greeted them in the lobby and held Billie close.

"I'll dress him," she said. "Your clothes are laid out on your bed. If all goes well, we can make the 6:00 flight back to New York."

"AM?"

"She's in the conference room. The way it's turned out, we could have done this at City Hall in New York."

"Lulu," Reade said. "Saxton and Becky got married!"

"I know, Reade. Be glad. She chose the better man to be Billie's stepfather. But not to worry. We all support your full custody. Saxton, too."

Left. Right. Left. Right. Reade's legs somehow moved down the long hall. After dressing, the shiny black wingtips landed on the sterile hotel carpet as he moved closer to the conference room. He wished he could sit in his Willapa orchard, but here he was in Texas, a white rosebud pinned to his black tux.

Everyone was in place when Reade pushed open the double doors. Men and women, mostly strangers— probably attorneys—filled three short rows of cushioned chairs beneath the acoustic ceiling tiles. The fake art had been taken off the walls and stacked in a corner. The conference table had Lulu's touch—champagne, candles, roses, and a tiered white cake. To one side, a photographer adjusted her tripod. A woman seated to one side played a Bach cello concerto.

"Hey, Reade! I'll be officiating," Alberto said. He was decked out in a red bowtie, slacks, dark blue jacket, and shiny plaid shoes. He showed Reade the words AM had written for the ceremony and he nodded. As he approached the altar, Kermit slowly rose from his front-row seat next to Lulu. On her lap was Billie, dressed in a very tiny tux.

"Mazel tov, Reade," Kermit said.

"I didn't expect to see you here," he said as they shook hands.

"It's a family wedding."

Kermit slipped an envelope into Reade's hand which he placed in his breast pocket. Reade spotted the newlyweds in the back row, Saxton and Becky, as AM walked in. She took Kermit's arm and together they walked down the aisle. Finally, standing next to each other, Reade and AM couldn't stop grinning. She lifted the tulle draped over her head, revealing the same dark wavy hair-do that fanned from her face as in the engagement photo with Alberto. Billie backed off Lulu's lap and waddled over to AM. She picked him up and kissed him. Across her bare midriff, between her sparkly stretchy white shorts and matching short-sleeved top, were the words I DO painted in big block letters, the same lettering she used to sign her art.

Alberto read her vows, a rhyming and repetitious rap poem which ended with the standard question.

"I do," she said out loud.

"A perfect Texas storm!" Reade shouted to the audience. "The wind blows and the VOW BREAKS!"

"And down comes baby," she whispered.

AM pointed to her belly. In pink ink above her I DO was I'M DUE.

"You're due? Is that what you're telling me?"

"I DO and I'M DUE."

Alberto shifted his feet and leaned in. "Let's get married," he said sternly. "We have a plane to catch."

Reade couldn't help but linger one more second. He looked to the ceiling and took a deep breath. He thought again about his father's last words: NOT ENOUGH LOVE. All these years he felt guilty that he didn't love his Pa enough. Or maybe his Pa was referring to the state of the world. But now he decided that his words were a dare. His Pa wanted him to search love out; he shouldn't wait for it or count on it. Reade took AM's hand and for the first time, on this wedding day, he was pleased with his father.

"A revolutionary," AM said.

TWENTY-ONE

READE BOUGHT a ticket for *The Honey Dearborn Story: The Life and Death of Mother and Son,* the last afternoon it played at the Independent Film Center in the Village. He found it entertaining but, at the same time, it was like watching a home movie of his life without him, as if he had never been born. Willapa and New York City, his two homes, were featured as well as people on both coasts he considered family: Honey, tucked into her Park Avenue deathbed, received Saxton, Lulu, Alberto, AM, Elah, and even Charlie Kim and his lover in the white go-go boots, Robert. The audience could not hear what any of the guests said, only Honey's riffs on not wanting to die alone. Her future audience comforted her as she died. She wanted to live forever, like Shakespeare's promise to the Dark Lady *that in black ink you shall still shine bright.* Honey held up photographs of Frank, from a tiny babe to a bean pole with golden ringlets down his back, to a clean-shaven graying man. The later shots were taken by the detectives standing in Reade's rhododendron bush. A short clip of Frank played of him pulling up in front of his house driving his white Cadillac. He gets out, unlocks his front door, and enters his house without a sideways glance. Moments later, Frank has finished his task and now locks his front door, gets back in his car and speeds off. Reade had seen this Charlie Chaplin-like sequence hundreds of times in real life. Frank's section of the documentary ended with his death on the Portland gas station men's room floor, the footage Reade and AM watched at the Depot Diner, followed by footage of Sheriff Fox badmouthing Frank; Aunt Doris dabbing her eyes with a tissue, and AM in her Willapa studio, her fingers poking a stray curl back into her giant black hive as she talked about Frank's vulnerability and his cars.

In reality, Reade chose not to be filmed by Garden Gate. He did not want to publicly talk about his neighbor. Instead, he offered the film crew his farmhouse for the month of June and moved on to his boss's sailboat in the Ilwaco marina. Reade's name appeared after the credits in the thank-you column.

As he headed down into the subway, the vision of Honey's last small, graceful gestures stuck with him: Honey opening her mouth for the nurse to administer medication on her tongue; A Black minister making the sign of the cross and anointing her forehead; a group of veiled women at her bedside saying the rosary; Honey's gnarly hands and diamond-clad fingers periodically reaching into the air as she admired her red nails; the way she lifted one leg and then the other, almost as if she were curious about death creeping into her body feet first. She submitted to a sponge bath, her eighty-year-old skin and bones naked before the camera. Just as Reade breathed a sigh of relief that Honey was dead, she reached out and slapped a nurse who smoothed her hair. A sudden flurry of beeping machinery brought nurses scurrying into the room. A doctor checked her pulse, and that was it.

The film continued to roll in Reade's head for days. He questioned the mysterious workings of the world, like the warehouse Honey gifted to AM, Frank's monkey money, and even his good luck at having moved Frank's trunks into storage before the fire. And then there was Lulu's love and respect, shining on them, and Billie, and the little revolutionary in AM's belly. Even baby Georgie, Rusty, and Buckeye came to mind when he tallied his good luck.

Reade met up with Yoshiko and Shanika William, the glass artist at her studio. It was in a vast Bronx warehouse that looked like an iceberg had crashed into it. Filled with so many large chunks of glass, they seemed in danger of melting in the summer heat. Yoshiko selected three sculptures for the garden, roughly three-by-five-foot rectangles, with some distressed markings, a mixture of colors, clear and foamy white to milky yellow or sea green. A week later a forklift rotated the sculptures in the Shinto garden, and the security straps were taken away. Natural light penetrated their interiors giving them a monolithic feel like they had broken off a mountain top or streamed in from outer space. Shanika was pleased with the installation. After she said goodbye, Reade followed Yoshiko's lead: they pushed seven yards of small round gray and yellowish pebbles evenly across the garden floor with long wooden rakes. Once distributed, she showed him the design she wanted and they combed the stones in concentric curving ripples between paths, sculptures, the crooked pine, and the young plum tree.

"This is the ocean," she said. "The garden must be raked daily. Raking brings harmony."

Reade still didn't know what she meant, but he agreed to rake fifteen minutes a day. Manhattan skyscrapers stood in the background instead of the Japanese mountains he'd seen in Yoshiko's garden books. Like a blind man, he hoped to eventually see the seventy-two seasons and eighteen sub-seasons she talked about. If the garden had a traditional pool with multi-colored carp or a stream of flowing water, it might be easier for him, but that was not in the budget. Instead, he had to pay attention to the visiting birds, and measure the rain in the shallows of the sculptures and the snowfall on the pine and plum branches to determine the seasons.

"No weeding or mowing," Reade said. "But we need

a bigger gate. If goodness enters through the center and humans are supposed to step to the side. And what about a dragon to keep away fire? I like the idea of dragons evolving from fish. Maybe we need a wooden fish."

"We can talk about that next week," Yoshiko said. "But keep in mind, Reade, the flow of goodness doesn't depend on the size of the gate. It is about awareness. Abstraction engages the imagination more than representational images."

Jim and Reade were alone in the Atlantic except for three Russian women dipping in the shallow waves, their middle-aged bodies clad in flowery bikinis. The Atlantic was chilly, choppy, thick, almost muddy. Jim's wife bought him a wetsuit that matched his bright orange swim cap for better visibility in the water, but his powerful strokes and kicks still made keeping up with him a challenge for Reade. Each time he entered the ocean, he was tossed in the waves like a little boy. He resisted putting his face in the water and swam sidestroke until his neck ached. Only then did he switch to freestyle. By the time he reached the first buoy, he had a good stride. His nightmare of Becky drowning had subsided as he had hoped since learning to swim, but opening his eyes underwater, he still saw her face. Becky Smith Bordeaux Rose. How botanical her name sounded. Did she even take Saxton's name? Oh, yeah, he remembered that she dropped Bordeaux. She's Becky Smith Rose. Becky and Saxton, the polyamorous pair.

Becky studied as Saxton soaked up the rituals of Taps and Reveille. Was Becky kidding herself by thinking a baby would have saved their marriage? Did AM encourage Saxton to marry Becky, or was it Alberto or Lulu's idea? Of course, Lulu was right: Saxton was a better choice than Bubba; Saxton kept Billie close, and with Billie now Saxton's step-son, Lulu was now a bona fide grandmother. After the first mile, Reade tired and headed toward the beach. Still a fledgling swimmer, he thought of Leonard Baskin's print with that title: a heron stands on one skinny leg at the shore.

It began to rain as he waited for Jim on the beach. The drops were large and dimpled the sand. As he opened his mouth to catch the fresh rain water, he remembered a favorite image from the Garden Gate film: the cinematographer had somehow captured the bright fog and slow wet sun of Willapa, which turned each hair of Buckeye's brown coat into a tiny rainbow.

TWENTY-TWO

HUNDREDS of small online donations had arrived at The Honey Dearborn Art Center since the fire. City, state, and federal grants were up. Anonymous gifts, totaling more than $52,000, came in from as far away as China. AM's vow of silence had lasted seventy-two days, the length of Billie's absence. As the September heat waned, AM's second performance season began with The Book Project. Participants of all ages lined up at dawn and were greeted by volunteers with clipboards and pens. Forms needed to be filled out and turned in. The thirty available desks filled quickly. The screen page explained the Twenty-Four Hour Write to Freedom philosophy: *the blank page is an opportunity to practice freedom. Every human has a personal story to tell, and in sharing these stories, we discover that all human beings have a unique voice and these voices are all equal. We all have the innate tools necessary for self-expression: the five senses, imagination, emotion, and memory. Past, present, and future are within. We are infinite. Stories can heal the world.*

In the evenings AM scrolled through the computer reading aloud excerpts from The Book Project as she began turning excerpts into a vocal performance. One participant described how he never really had a home, never had been loved, and never loved anyone. Another wrote that she attended the best schools around the world and until lately was oblivious of anyone's pain but her own. Most wrote detailed stories of loneliness, their efforts to scrape together rent, of illness, abuse, homelessness, and anger. She pulled words from the air to circle ideas that excited her: Protean. Esperanto. Conqueror. Praxis. Immaculate. Rogue. Oppressed. Creator. Ontology. Radiance. Anima. Amorphous. Incarnation. Festooning. Repair. Void. Uncommon.

While Lulu continued to take Kermit's dictation, Reade scheduled two days a week at the gallery, researching paintings and organizing files. He welcomed visitors as Jules had done, positioned paintings beneath the spotlight, always on the alert for Kermit's sales pitch. At the last auction of the season, Reade bid on a beautiful painting attributed to Ludovico Carracci titled *Magdalena Penitente*. Like his own Magdalena, she was thoughtful, engaged and sensuous! He was so excited, the auctioneer's words pounded in his head like horse hooves on dry hard ground and, desperate to not be overlooked, Reade halfway jumped from his seat with each new bid. This drew unwanted attention. His face reddened. But when the gavel came down, he had succeeded in securing the painting for just under thirty thousand dollars. Afterwards, he sat tight and watched the sophisticated bidders through to the end. Several introduced themselves when he rose to go, handing him their business cards. His name meant nothing to them, of course, and they knew better than to ask who he was representing. The stack of business cards Reade placed on Kermit's desk amused him.

"I need you to deliver a painting to my friend Luuk van Hoop in Amsterdam," Kermit said. "Amsterdam is a beautiful city. You should take a few days to study the paintings at the Rijksmuseum and the Rembrandt House. And be sure to visit the Anne Frank House."

Kermit pulled a small photograph from an envelope. It was of a young, red-haired woman. Hand-written on the back was a name and date: *Greta Fleur, 1938.* "She gave this to me the day I sailed for America," Kermit said. "My sister was eighteen years old, living with our parents, and studying engineering. She was in love with a gentile, Thomas Rhines. Thomas joined the resistance and died in a death march." Kermit wiped his face with a kerchief. "I hired experts to search for Greta after the war. They scoured newspapers, death camp lists, and synagogues across Europe, South America, Canada, Japan, China, and Israel. I will be eighty in February and one day I will be dead. But the search for my sister must continue. All I ask is that she knows I never forgot her."

He returned the photo to its envelope. "Please keep this."

Kermit's wedding gift was an around-the-world honeymoon ticket, good for one year. At dinner one night, Lulu spoke up, "I would like to take care of Billie while you honeymoon. Elah has agreed to help. Perhaps Saxton could fly in and spend time with Billie. We'll take Rusty, too. I always love a full house."

"Sweet," AM said.

"But I have to insist that there are no guns in the house," Reade said. "I've talked to Saxton about this already. Becky carries, too. I can't say what they do in their own house. But in my house, I don't want guns."

"The Jews were doomed when the Germans took our guns away. We had no way to defend ourselves."

"I'm not taking them away," Reade said.

Lulu squeezed Reade's hand. "I understand. I promise no guns in the house. Neither pirates nor cowboys, neither my son nor your ex-wife will harm Billie."

But AM's pregnancy at age forty-and-a-half was a risk. Her vitals needed to be checked weekly. Georgie's inexplicable death weighed on everyone. So far, blood pressure, temperature, hydration, vitamins, nutrition, urine, and weight gain were all fine. AM was, however, experiencing some tingling in her hands and feet and some dizziness which her nurse felt could be the beginnings of early gestational diabetes. Travel was not recommended. The honeymoon was postponed until after Revie's birth. Revie was what they called their unborn daughter. It was short for revolutionary which, in AM's imagination, is the role of all women. As Reade and AM bantered about what her real name would be, the nickname made Reade smile: like a car's engine, he imagined her full of life.

Reade progressed with his fifteen minutes of Shinto raking each day. He meditated on many things, including ghosting his Bully List for good. This propelled him to visit the warehouse of "Mr. Clean," two blocks from the Honey Dearborn Art Center. He knocked on the door at 6:00 a.m., the time he knew fabricators began their day. A lean, young man opened the door wearing a leather apron. An earring dangled from one ear. Peering through the door, Reade saw some interesting chairs with clean lines made of wood and metal.

"I'm looking for the owner of the building," he said.

"To lease space?"

"No, I'm a neighbor, two blocks south. The Honey Dearborn Art Center. Are these your designs?"

The guy nodded. He seemed distracted. Disinterested. Maybe even disrespectful. The whirling sound of machines and a familiar smell of grinding rubber gaskets flooded Reade's nose. "I used to weld pipe fittings for water systems out in Seattle. My name's Reade Bordeaux."

"Gregory," he said. His feet shifted. He took a sip of coffee. "What's up over there? I see people line up and buses dropping off little kids and women with headscarves."

"We have art classes for women and kids until 3:00 Monday through Friday, and performances on the weekend."

"What about the tent on the roof?"

"Temporary storage," Reade said. It was the first thing that came to him. "What goes on upstairs here?"

"The landlord warehouses Turkish rugs he sells at flea markets. This is his card. Omer Ahmet. He's a decent guy."

"The big guy with the bald head?"

"That's him."

"I'd like you to stop by the Center some afternoon. I'm usually around after 3:00. We need a couple of outdoor benches for the garden." Reade pointed to a chair with legs that curved at the ground like feet without toes. "I like that one."

Gregory looked Reade in the eye for the first time. His facial expressions went through acrobatics. He didn't expect a job to come in over the transom. Standing taller now, he nodded and he gave Reade his business card.

As for the honeymoon, Reade and AM celebrated nightly in the old circus tent of heavy blue canvas erected on the fenced roof of the Honey Dearborn Art Center. Alberto bought it online and hired professionals to secure its twenty-foot metal structure with a dance floor. They tied the wide doorway flaps open so the city lights splashed against the back wall. Evenings, Reade and AM carried their glasses of iced mint tea up the inner stairwell. AM danced for Reade, a mix of her childhood ballet, modern, and striptease. Twirling him onto his feet, he began with the ballroom lessons he took with Becky in preparation for their wedding, which morphed into the swim, the twist, and a kind of horseplay before doing his own version of a striptease. After, they cooled each other with the ice from the mint tea before relaxing on the pillows at the back of the love shack.

TWENTY-THREE

THE SCHIPHOL AIRPORT was situated in the shockingly flat green landscape of Holland. It was early morning when the bus dropped Reade at his hotel on Museumstraat, near the Rijksmuseum. His room was small and clean, the walls hung with prints from the Dutch Golden Age. After a shower, he sank into the thick cotton sheets and woke up starving. He bought bread and a quarter pound of yellow cheese and sat in a small park, sipping coffee in the drizzle. Satiated, he rented a bike from a shop across the street and rode in concentric circles: past the flower market packed with shoppers, various arched bridges, and the slow-moving dark water of the canals lined with houseboats. Pausing at a storefront, he watched a woman sitting provocatively in an overstuffed chair filing her nails, her face clownish with make-up. It was the famous Red-Light District he had read about. In the next storefront, a woman wore only a shawl and stockings, her nipples erect in the cold as she blew smoke through her nose. When she noticed him pushing the bike, she curled her finger, daring him to enter. Other storefronts were empty midday but set up with similar boudoir furnishings. He peddled on through the autumn-spiced air of late afternoon to the sounds of ringing bicycle bells, cyclists signaling hand turns, bikes with mothers or fathers, a kid straddling the handlebars, and one or two holding on in back.

At Prinsengracht, he crossed a small plaza toward a metal sculpture of Anne Frank, hands behind her back, her chin lifted skyward. Someone had placed two fresh flowers, pink and red, at her feet. On the corner was her father's warehouse, a museum since 1957, the Frank family hiding place during the war. Reade's mother had assigned *The Diary of a Young Girl* when she homeschooled him, and he remembered they discussed the book for weeks. She used it as a sex primer for him, pointing out Anne's changing body, her desires, and Peter's male anatomy lesson with the cat. They tried to solve the mystery of how she accomplished in two years what other writers accomplish in a lifetime. His mother explained that war accelerates life: as a young nurse in training, there had been a shortage of doctors at her Seattle hospital as most of them had enlisted. She dared Reade to see what he could accomplish in two years.

"I'm not a writer," he said.

"Neither was Anne," replied his mother.

The Westerkerk Church bells chimed, the sound that comforted Anne while in hiding until melted down for bombs. Reade pulled up his e-ticket on his phone and followed the procession of tourists up the stairs and through the famous bookcase, a perfect entrance to a writer's house. Otto, Edith, and Margot's room was visible first. Past the bathroom was Anne and Fritz Pfeffer's small room with the two narrow beds a foot apart, and the desk. Pfeffer didn't take Anne's writing seriously, and Otto had to intervene so that Anne could work in peace a few afternoons a week. The kitchen doubled as Mr. and Mrs. van Pels's bedroom. It contained the woodstove where Anne mourned the loss of her grandmother's fountain pen, accidentally thrown away with the potato peels. Like all other visitors, Reade climbed the ladder from Peter's small room to the attic and was surprised by the life-size paper cut-out of Otto Frank, the lone survivor of the Secret Annex. His sad face told the whole story. As he said on the video downstairs in the museum, he never would have known his daughter if he hadn't read her diary. Back on the bicycle, Reade figured that Otto had his own secret Bully List as he tried to figure out who betrayed his family.

After a nap in his hotel room, he removed Kermit's small painting packed in a carry-on bag. He wanted to see what he was handing off to the van Hoops. Carefully unwrapping the brown paper, he was delighted by the simple still-life with a branch of blossoms, red and green grapes, and an enameled pitcher on a table in a dark greenish background. He googled the signature, A. Vollon, and found a French painter, Antoine Vollon, who died in 1900, revered for his realistic perfection. *An exquisite gift from Kermit to his friend,* Reade thought, as he rewrapped it. Maintaining its crisp edges, he slipped it back into its cloth bag. The rain stopped and he was glad to walk the one and a quarter kilometers according to his GPS, just under a mile, to the van Hoop house. It was one in a row of red brick homes, only two windows in width, three stories. Each of van Hoop's seven windows bloomed with red flowers; its door was painted greenish-black, the color of the background of the Vollon still-life, a color many doors were painted in Amsterdam.

Dressed in a three-piece brown woolen suit, Mr. van Hoop greeted Reade. His wife, Mila, was regal, her hair twisted into a French roll the way his Ma wore hers. Mila's skirt draped to her knees. She wore a white blouse, and a sweater with tiny pink roses covering her thin shoulders, and her shoes were sturdy black. The van Hoops were kind, as Kermit promised.

"Call me Luuk," he said, taking the cloth bag from Reade. "Would you like a glass of sherry?"

"No, thank you. I'm fine."

"Then allow me to show you my picture gallery."

His still-life collection lined his long hallway and the six small rooms on the ground floor. Upon entering each dark room, the paintings sparkled like platters of rubies and gold; but upon closer inspection, juicy oysters glistened on the shell, sliced lemon, grapes, and half melons filled with black seeds. At the dinner table, a breeze stirred the garden outside the window. Flower heads swayed on their long stems as Mila set out a turret of soup, a platter of meat and greens, and potatoes bubbling with butter and cheese.

"Flowers are Mila's passion," said Luuk.

"And I would guess cooking, as well. This is a beautiful meal," Reade said.

Her finale, a lemon quark cake in the shape of a crown, was dotted on top with glazed blueberries and served on a traditional blue-and-white patterned platter. Lemon rind spiced the soft sponge cake.

"Do you mind if I take a picture?" Reade asked before she cut into it. "What is quark?"

Luuk nodded to Mila and they spoke briefly in Dutch while Reade pulled out his phone.

"Quark is made from cow's milk," Mila said in a guttural sing-song, full of tongue and elongated consonants, more Dutch than English. It was the first words she had spoken.

Like the van Hoop's house, the Rijksmuseum was also red brick but massive, with towers and turrets and white stone detail around its arching entrance. Inside, Reade gazed upward for two hours. Vermeer's *Milkmaid* in the blue skirt and bonnet poured an unending flow of milk from a pitcher next to chunks of bread, like the miracle of loaves and fish. His *Woman Reading a Letter* was a perfect private moment: she and Vermeer clearly shared a secret. Reade smiled as he continued through the galleries. Tourists surrounded *Night Watchman*, and he moved on to *Mary Magdalene*, dressed in Italian clothing, seductively poised at Jesus's feet. Frans Hals took another approach with his realistic painting of *Merry Family*: it was humble and joyous. The family was oblivious to the painter.

Reade was struck by *Girl in the Large Hat* by Caesar Boetius van Everdingen 1645-1650, a portrait of a woman exceedingly confident in her yellow summer dress. But more than that, it was her red hair and her knowing look. He pulled the photo of Kermit's sister, Greta, from his wallet and compared their rebellious looks. Lining them up as best he could, he took a picture of the two, side by side. Now he understood why Kermit thought there was a chance Greta survived the Holocaust: who would kill Summer?

He wandered through the outdoor market, bought frites with a spicy peanut sauce, something that took getting used to, and washed it down with coffee. Locals filled their cloth shopping bags with vegetables and bundles of flowers. Reade had never seen so many flowers and families and bicycles. Wandering past tables of second-hand items for sale, he came across the blue and white patterned dishes and bought one that looked like Mila's quark cake dish.

Van Gogh's self-portraits at his museum were vibrant with their multitude of colorful brushstrokes.

Reade was surprised by his Japanese influence, and his friends Toulouse-Lautrec, Gauguin, and Seurat. His brushstrokes seemed to make leaves lift in the dry warm grass: he could smell the sun in Van Gogh's fields. Like Anna Magdalena Bach composing and playing with her husband and thirteen children, Vincent gave his whole self to art: he wrote to his brother that painting was like eating bread.

At Rembrandt's House, Reade studied his technique, especially in his later years, the soft visible brushstrokes that caused him to fall from favor, his life ending in bankruptcy. These very same brushstrokes inspired the impressionist movement two centuries later. Reade thought of his father when he saw Rembrandt's bed built into the wall—the bed he slept in with Saskia and, after she died, his housekeeper Hendrickje. Reade's father and brothers slept in bunk beds built into the wall when they were growing up. He remembered hearing that, frightened by thunder one night, their father told them to go back to sleep: it was only God throwing a sack of potatoes down the stairs.

TWENTY-FOUR

THE TRAFFIC of Queens Boulevard disappeared as the cab turned at the East River and stopped in front of the Honey Dearborn Art Center. Reade entered the side door as classes were still in session, and passing through the garden, paused to examine the pebbles after a week away. To his surprise, the curved rows were slightly flattened, as if bird's feet had patted them down on takeoffs and landings, or gravitation pull flattened them as trucks rumbled past. Yoshiko was right that the Shinto message of harmony was a daily practice. It wasn't just the pebbles that would fall into disarray: Reade looked forward to taking up the wooden rake.

Jeff texted while Reade walked Rusty and Billie north through Socrates Park, past oil tankers, a police boat, and four Skidoos driven by boys in wetsuits. He reported that Aunt Doris had fallen down the stairs at her sister's house in New Mexico and had broken her ankle. He and Bonnie had flown in to help after her surgery and during the week they were gone, a meth addict had moved into the tower at the Willapa farm, which was now uninhabitable. Sheriff Fox dragged the guy off the top balcony after acting like he planned to jump. Jeff wanted to know if he should board it up.

"Clean it up as best you can and see if there is someone you might know in the Coast Guard or the University of Washington Research Center who might rent it for cheap, like $200 a month, just to get someone in there," Reade asked.

"I'll ask around," Jeff said. "But the drugs on the peninsula are destroying the place."

"Like any small-town America," Reade said.

"Bonnie and I applied for an early decision to the University of New Mexico in Albuquerque. We'll move in with Aunt Doris now that her sister is in a nursing home."

Yikes. Reade couldn't keep the farm without Jeff or someone like him, and there was no one like Jeff. He paid him to live there and take care of the place. The house needed scraping and a couple of coats of white paint. The old kitchen floor needed replacing. The upstairs bathroom leaked and needed gutting. The house should be insulated, the cellar sealed, and the oil furnace replaced with something green. And what the heck could he do with Buckeye?

He and AM finally met up, but she was ensconced in the third-floor loft with two assistants, an industrial sewing machine, reams of cloth spread on tables, patterns, drawings, cans of paint, and a box of large wooden alphabet stamps she found in the warehouse. In a corner was a stack of large curved shapes of linoleum to print a dozen unique, six-foot images of women from history.

And the board had a new hire: Dov, a thirty-five-year-old formerly Orthodox Jewish man, was the new development officer. His job was to write government grants. Reade introduced himself over a cup of coffee. Listening to Dov describe the adjustment it took to walk down the sidewalks of New York, buy groceries, learn to cook, and use the internet shocked Reade. Dov couldn't believe Chinatown existed, for instance, only a mile as the crow flies from the street where he was born. He had met his wife in a photography program to support people leaving their religious communities. She attended Cooper Union, became a teaching artist, and now worked in a public school in Bedford-Stuyvesant. Only when his wife began taking him to museums did he understand that some cultural stories, like his own, aren't told in New York City.

The board was negotiating a two-year contract for Alberto to step up as executive director on January first, finally allowing AM the sole position of artistic director. Alberto had already taken over many of the daily executive director tasks, such as maintaining partnerships, speaking engagements, and the annual budget. A sticking point was that he requested the position include an apartment, a precedent set by AM's living space at the Center. The board wanted to hear from Reade about the possibility of building a second living loft at the Center, the least expensive alternative.

Reade grabbed Alberto on his way into the building and they headed up to the fourth floor. The industrial stairs were wide and newly painted, with safety signage, and a window at each landing. The fourth floor opened into a vast raw space with uninsulated walls stripped down to the wiring, even a couple of broken windows, and the same bathroom as on the other floors, with three non-functioning toilets, sinks, and a single open shower stall.

"What about if we split the space in half? You take the front with the river view. On the eastern side, we build five small offices, each with a window, for the program director, grant writer, operation manager, executive director, and volunteer coordinator. We'd need to turn the bathroom into two—one for your living space and one for public use. At the top of the stairs, there's room for a conference table, a couch, a couple of chairs, and a small kitchenette for staff."

Alberto stared out the western windows, the fenced-off no-man's-land at the edge of the East River, the shaggy tree branches covered with vines and wind-torn plastic bags. Behind that, the Queensboro Bridge, Roosevelt Island, and turning northward, the Rikers Island prison complex with highways and bridges lacing the blue sky. He turned to look Reade in the eye.

TWENTY-FOUR

Only then did Reade sense that something was wrong: Alberto wasn't dressed in his normal snappy clothes but in jeans that didn't fit and sneakers. Not even his usual haircut.

"I'll make a sketch," Reade said. "The apartment will be about fifteen hundred square feet. Talk it over with Ronnie." He couldn't guess Alberto's problem. Was it the four-flight walk-up? "I have to carve out some bedroom space in our loft for the kids on the second floor, and right now the third floor is occupied by AM. It's the fourth floor that needs renovation, Alberto. It's good for the Center and good for you. Look, saving on rent, plus a few years as executive director, you'll be ready to take on the world. Your loft could be available as soon as March if Lulu gets her architect involved."

"Ronnie and I broke up after twelve years. He locked me out of the apartment. I thought he was my life partner."

"I'm sorry to hear that," Reade said. "What happened?"

"He fell in love with Jose, the dramaturg. I heard rumors, sure, but shrugged them off. When I saw them together at a club, I began dating the hottest guy I could find and posting photos on Instagram."

"So where are you living? At you Williamsburg apartment?

"No, that's rented. I'm on my sister's couch."

"Let's take a look at the third floor," Reade said. They paused on the landing as Reade fumbled for his key. Opening the door, AM's work in progress looked basically like a big mess. "Maybe she could make room for you temporarily. What about this corner? We could fit a bed and dresser in this nook."

"I don't have furniture."

"We can get you a bed. But you'd have to stay out during the afternoons so AM can work. Otherwise, the place is insulated with new wallboard. It just needs painting. The bathroom is functional. You could use the Center's kitchen in the mornings before classes, and on evenings and weekends. I'd have to clear it with the board, though, as well as the fourth-floor plans. But I don't see a problem."

Alberto breathed a sigh of thanks. "Oh, by the way, Che Guevara dropped by, left you an envelope. It's with your mail. He said you asked him about making benches for the garden."

"That's Gregory," Reade said.

TWENTY-FIVE

A LUCKY YELLOW sun shone brightly by noon on the day of Shanika William's opening. As the first guest artist to exhibit at the Honey Dearborn Art Center, there was a good buzz. Everyone knew it was a lot to ask the art world to come to Queens on a cold Saturday, especially with the subway thirteen blocks away. But the event was scheduled to end by 5:00, enabling guests to hurry back to Manhattan for evening engagements. At 3:30, Lulu tapped her glass, introduced herself as chair of the board, and commended the team for a successful first year of bringing the arts to new immigrant families. And she announced Anna Magdalena's exhibit, Imaculatta, opening in the fall at Gallery A in New York and traveling to Cleveland, Chicago, Minneapolis, Portland, and Los Angeles.

Shanika took the microphone and told her story as an artist beginning with drawing, working in clay, moving to wood carving, and then to experimenting with glass. She was honored to have her work exhibited in the garden designed by Yoshiko Eto. "Each time I see it under the sky of New York City, the light fractures its colors and shapes, reflecting a new world. Bring your friends and see for yourself the transformations that take place."

Tiny Daisy snaked through the crowd to the podium. Always cold, she wore jeans, a down jacket, and a pink hat with a snowball on top. "I came to Queens from Ghana as an immigrant in the fourth grade. Today, as program director, I visit my elementary school and many other schools in Queens to invite mothers and children to attend our free classes five days a week. My favorite part of each day is lunchtime because we cook family recipes from Ghana, Somalia, Afghanistan, Turkey, and many other countries. Let's give a round of applause for our dedicated families and teaching artists."

Anna Magdalena and Alberto, with a velvet purple crown upon his head, stepped through the crowd. AM took the microphone and told a story of a mother and her two young daughters fleeing Syria and the dangerous two years on the road, the good luck and good people and organizations offering food and shelter every step of their way. Now, after finally arriving in New York, they were reunited with family and have a home, school, and a community. As Reade listened, he was surprised to notice that she wore black leggings, boots, and a ragged black sweatshirt, as she did in Willapa. And her face was painted a simple blue with her red initials, like Frank's face the day he died. Only then did he realize that they would all have to dress themselves from now on: Alberto's theater warehouse privileges had been revoked.

The garden crowd flowed onto the sidewalk and, at the same time, some people pushed through the gate to get closer. AM spoke for five minutes, about Honey Dearborn, the women and children, and the team. Alberto pointed to the volunteers wearing the purple crowns, ready to accept donations for the education programs. He lifted his crown from his head and bowed deeply. That was when Reade saw "Mr. Clean" standing inside the warehouse, scanning the crowd through the window. Reade thrust a peace sign into the air which Alberto spotted as he rose from his bow. It was their signal. He reciprocated and the crowd thrust their peace signs skyward, along with cameras and phones. AM vanished up the side stairs as Reade made his way through the excited audience. He caught sight of Shanika with her long dreadlocks, running her hand over Gregory's smooth bench. Next to her, Gregory looked like Che after all, with his black curls falling over the white collar of his shirt. They walked to her sculpture, the one Yoshiko called turtle. Now it was Gregory who reached out to touch its edges.

Alberto, inside the Center, swayed to the drummers and guitar players sitting on the floor. "Mr. Clean,"

Gregory's boss, did have a shiny head. He balanced a full plate of small bites in one hand and a paper cup of wine in the other, but he was not the powerful "Mr. Clean" Reade had imagined the night of the fire.

"Hi, I'm Reade, the operations manager," he said. "Your tenant, Gregory, told me you owned the warehouse down the block."

His head unfolded from his neck, surveying the table spread with food. "I do. Omer Ahmet is my name. I like this spicy mango salad, and the salmon with avocado is excellent." Then he added: "This is breakfast for me. I'm an insomniac and rather than keep my wife up all night, I come down here to work in my warehouse. I see you fixed the building. It looks very good."

"Thanks," Reade said. "Gregory mentioned you sell at the flea markets. Which one is best?"

"I sell all over—Long Island, downtown Brooklyn, Dumbo, Chelsea. Upper West Side. Jersey. It depends on what I'm selling."

Alberto gave Reade a silent growl out of the right side of his lip, revealing an eye tooth. A trained actor rids himself of personal habits in order to take on unique physical characteristics. Reade guessed that some actors, like Alberto, retain these quirks and make them their own. Alberto's lip curl—so uncharacteristic of him—clearly conveyed his annoyance with Reade's distrust of Omer Ahmet. And Alberto wasn't going to let Reade off easy.

"Remember," Reade said in anticipation. "I'm the

one who got you a rent-free loft. And bed, pillows, blankets, sheets, a bedside table, and a lamp. I built walls around your bed and hung a door."

"I'm going to tickle you, Reade. First chance I get," Alberto said. "When you least expect it. So watch out."

TWENTY-SIX

SAXTON AND BECKY were coming off two nights in the honeymoon suite at the Plaza Hotel, just a few blocks south of the Central Park Zoo where Reade, AM, and Billie awaited them. The Delacorte clock tower chimed and the bronze animals circled as tiny snowflakes dropped from the hazy blue sky. Barking sea lions, sunning themselves on their island, scooted across the rocks and dove into the pool as their handler arrived for the two o'clock feeding. Billie jumped up and down in the backpack. AM looked like a hybrid sea lion in a black down coat with the hood pulled tight around her face.

It was Saxton's New York swagger, the bowler hat, and an unlit cigar that Reade noticed first. But Becky completely stymied him with her princess wave, her little navy-blue hat perched on her head at an angle instead of something warm, her strawberry hair tightly wound. Did Saxton shop for her clothes? Did she want to look like a flight attendant? Reade relaxed somewhat when Becky gave Billie a hug and kiss. As Saxton drew close, Billie turned his head and got a kiss on his ear. Reade laughed.

"A good morning to you, Reade," Saxton said.

The penguin house offered warmth even as the Antarctic diorama looked chilly. The hundred or so penguins, waddling up and down the rocks with wings spread, elicited squeals from children at the glass window. AM gagged at the sour smell and bolted back out through the door as soon as she entered. Reade followed and stood next to her as she threw up in the nearest bush.

"I hate seeing animals inside buildings," AM said. She spat and wiped her mouth on the back of her glove. "I'll meet you at the monkeys."

"M-o-n-k-e-y," Reade said, elongating the moment. Since her vow of silence ended, AM spoke but she preferred gestures, glints, and even telepathy, to dialog. It was an out-of-context moment, remembering Frank Dearborn: his monkey costumes and m-o-n-k-e-y money. Frank probably visited the Central Park Zoo a million times as a boy. Reade tried to picture him—skinny, tall for his age, blonde, freckled.

"I don't want to sell my farm," Reade said.

AM nodded. "We can live in two places."

As they walked their separate ways, Reade tried to figure it out: turn the farm into a west coast extension of the Honey Dearborn Art Center? An artist residency? But that would blow their privacy, the very thing they craved most. Reentering the penguin house, Reade was happy to find Becky still holding Billie, his hand patting the window as the penguins huddled. Louder than the penguins and children was Saxton. He leaned on the roller bag, one foot on the bench, and addressed a small group of parents and children.

"That was the day the rhino gored the zookeeper," he said. "The spotted hyenas ran out of the zoo and into the park, chasing a man all the way down to First Avenue with their big claws and sharp teeth."

"How old are you?" asked a little girl, holding her mother's hand.

"I'm a grown-up," Saxton said. "This happened a long time ago. The hyenas were asserting their natural desire to run free. It's in their DNA."

Reade enticed Billie from the penguins with some crackers and motioned for Becky to sit with him on a bench near the door. He wanted to hear about her new married life, about Saxton living on the Army base, and their stay at the Plaza Hotel. But these were strange times. He forced himself to tread lightly. He wanted to trust her as Billie did, content in the crook of her arm. He was grateful for a moment away from Saxton.

"How's your program going?" Reade asked.

She shrugged. "I like it, but there's so much

memorization. In one semester, we learned the names of the bones, joints, and ligaments; muscles, tendons, fascias; the nervous system and sensory organs; the heart, arteries, veins, and the lymphatic system. It wasn't fun. Saxton tired of the fatigues and left for Las Vegas. We're just meeting up now."

"I see," Reade said. He smirked at her words, *tired of fatigues*. "What happened to Bubba? Is he back at the Red Barn in Willapa?"

"He's selling it." She stroked Billie's fat cheek. "Dad died. Did you hear?"

"No, I'm sorry. When?"

"August fourth. In his sleep. I wish he could have met Billie. He left his house to me. Bubba is living there for the time being."

"It needs a lot of work," Reade said. "The mold is terrible. You probably need to cut some of those trees growing around it." Then he caught himself. He wasn't her husband. He was off-topic. "Meyer didn't remember who I was when I visited him before chasing you down to Texas."

She wrinkled her nose and sniffled. "My mistake," she said."That took some smoothing over on my attorney's part," she said. "The U.S. Army doesn't like to duke it out with the law."

It meant something to Reade that she admitted her error. And even if she never changed, he realized that he should not whittle Becky down to the marrow. Praise is what she needed. Bubba was always clearly important to her, especially now that Meyer was dead. Still, Lulu was right: if Becky married Bubba, Reade would probably spend the next twenty years chasing her down. Or he'd stop making the effort, and Billie would never know his mother.

TWENTY-SEVEN

THEY ATE Mila's quark cake, which Reade baked as his Hanukkah offering. Lulu praised its delicate consistency and lemon flavor. For Reade, it brought back Mila's lace-edged tulips and purple pansies, the flowers in the still-life paintings, and her garden outside the dining room window. But he was distracted by Saxton's continued discussion of zoo animals with the Rose family. For the first time, it occurred to Reade that Saxton and Frank might have known each other growing up in the Manhattan art world, for Honey and Lulu must have known each other.

"Do you remember Pattycake?" asked Saxton's Aunt Joan. She threw her pointed chin into the room. "The first baby gorilla born in captivity."

"I loved her more when the zookeepers realized their mistake and renamed her Sonny Jim," he said.

"You cried when they moved him to the Boston Zoo!" she exclaimed.

"What about the grizzlies, Betty and Veronica?" his Uncle Abe said. "They scared you so bad you never wanted to leave New York City."

"And look at me now, living in Texas!" Saxton said. He pulled Becky by her hand, interrupting her conversation with Alberto. She wore a tight, long white dress made of faux rabbit fur, her reddish hair falling down her back. Alberto looked surprisingly handsome, too, with his hair slicked down in waves to his shoulders. Reade was dressed in the auction suit Alberto picked out for him, which took some getting used to wearing. He enjoyed listening to Daisy and Elah chatting with Dov, as Dov's shy wife nervously twisted her finger around her blond ponytail.

"Hello, little man," said one of Lulu's artists, squatting to Billie's height. "I think we've met before. I know your Mommy, AM."

"Ama!" Billie said, dropping his dreidel to search the room, his fingers wiggling impatiently. Reade scooped him up before he created a scene with the two moms, which they had avoided thus far. He needed a diaper change. AM heard Billie's call and carried him into the nursery.

Looking formidable, like a grand Rembrandt self-portrait, Kermit approached Reade. He steered him by the elbow into the next room, filled floor to ceiling with beautiful old books. A small desk faced the sculptural trees of Central Park. In the middle of the room stood the large, Black male sculpture that Reade remembered seeing at the Yom Kippur dinner. Like Lincoln at the memorial, this Black man held his head high, his hands curved around the arms of the chair.

"If you are interested in selling your Granet, I may have a buyer."

"I thought there wasn't a market for church interiors," Reade said.

"You might be able to get two or three times what you paid for it. It just so happens that a gentleman called wanting a painting I already sold, so I mentioned your Granet. I told him of Granet's search across Europe for a monastery like the one he knew as a boy which had been destroyed in the war, and that seventeen kings and queens commissioned copies of the painting. I suggested that he visit the Metropolitan Museum to see Granet's large *Capuchin Church*. We can discuss the offer when you are in the office next week."

"I'll sell for triple the purchase price on one condition. You sell me the Govert Flinck for thirty-six."

"*Rebecca at the Well*," said Kermit. His tired face lifted. He took off his bifocals and rubbed his eyes. "Yes. That was my offer. You didn't turn it down, which was good because you know what happens when someone turns my picture down."

Reade nodded. "The price goes up."

The subject of the painting was Isaac's marriage proposal, conveyed to Rebecca by a servant. Reade wondered if AM had Rebecca's expression of delight and terror when Alberto approached her about marrying him, but he would never know. Like Rebecca, AM got the marriage and jewels—in her case, Billie.

Reade gave Kermit the book he bought at the Rijksmuseum, and they turned the pages together. Kermit mumbled over the images, enjoying himself. At the page with Everdingen's *Girl in the Large Hat*, Reade opened his phone to show Kermit the photograph he took of Greta and the *Girl*, side by side.

"It's called Summer," Reade said. "Everdingen also painted Winter, but that wasn't Greta. She was Summer. She has an unforgettable aura."

"Remarkable," Lulu said, who had wandered into the room. She cooed and hummed, comparing the two images. AM joined them, also, with Billie draped over her shoulder. Kermit cleared his throat and pulled a handkerchief from his pocket. All four of them took a moment to imagine Greta as a young woman and who she might have become.

"If this had been painted in the 1950s rather than the 1650s, I would believe that my sister had lived through the war."

That night, undressing in the streetlight before getting into bed, AM gazed at her naked figure in the full-length mirror, massaging her rounding belly. Reade showed her the photograph of the Ghent Altarpiece in the *History of Art*. AM angled her body as Eve did for the painter and silently compared her fertile sloping abdomen. Van Eyck's model of Eve and AM shared a natal knowledge, something the male gaze could never know.

AM pointed to the book. "Notice van Eyck's Eve does not cover herself with the fig leaf like Adam. She has no shame. No guilt. No anger. Not about sex. Not about eating forbidden fruit. Not even as God forces them from the walled garden. That shows true knowledge. They were gaining their freedom."

A call from Kermit the following week moved Reade to take *The Choir of the Capuchin Church in Rome* off their loft wall and wrap it. He arrived early at Kermit's gallery for the appointment with Mr. Roth. Reade looked forward to watching Kermit make the deal, but after Roth's meticulous inspection of the painting, he merely handed Reade a check for $40,000.

"Manny is the best restorer in the city," Mr. Roth said.

"Did you get a chance to see the *Capuchin Church* in the Metropolitan?" Reade asked.

"Yes, I did," he said. "It is very similar—larger, of course—but this painting is more beautiful. And available. Let's keep in touch." The three men shook hands. "I have other appointments today. I'll be back tomorrow at two to pick it up."

"Of course," Kermit said.

Reade and Kermit then examined Govert Flinck's *Rebecca at the Well*. It was as beautiful as the first time Reade laid eyes on it. Like the *Capuchin Church*, he had found a thread of his own life in Flinck's painting. But Reade couldn't afford to fall in love with this purchase. He had growing financial responsibilities. Old master paintings are extravagant investments, like sports cars, or a house built over a waterfall. He had learned his lesson with the Granet: to own an old master is to promise the world its safekeeping. He had to insure it and pay for proper storage. Reade assumed he had no wiggle room, financially. None that he knew of as he and AM still had never discussed their finances.

"How much will you charge me to store the Flinck?" Reade asked, handing Kermit a check for $36,000.

"I will bundle storage and insurance," he said. "As long as you store your painting with my art, it is covered under my insurance. The first year, or any part of the year, storage is $1,200. Each year it doubles."

"I guess that is an incentive to sell," Reade said. He wrote a second check to cover the first year. "Do you know of any museums I should approach right now?"

"Not at this time. Let me think about it, Reade." He removed his glasses and pushed his chair back. Using his hands as leverage against the desk, he pushed himself to a standing position, walked to the couch, and laid down. Adjusting a small pillow beneath his head, he stretched his legs and shut his eyes.

Reade tiptoed out of the room and went home. He tried to nap but stewed about finances and a baby due any day, when the ghost of Jules greeted Reade. His glasses set low on his nose, his chin tucked into his neck,

Jules blinked. He looked directly into Reade's eyes, just as he had when he was alive.

Reade asked, "Why didn't Kermit include *Rebecca at the Well* in his donation to the Israel Museum? It's a biblical picture."

"This picture is in America now after generations in Europe and has never publicly been viewed here. It creates an opportunity for an American Museum."

Reade took Jules' words as instruction. He made an A list of museums, which included the Metropolitan and The National Gallery. Museums with minor Dutch collections, such as The Johnson Collection in Philadelphia, the Toledo Museum of Art, the Chicago Art Institute, and the Cincinnati Taft Museum made the B list. *Rebecca at the Well* was not an expensive picture, even if Flinck was a painter of the Dutch Golden Age and Rembrandt's best student. Reade sent a brief letter of introduction to the director of the Metropolitan suggesting that with its prestigious collection of Vermeer and Rembrandt, he should do the honor of introducing *Rebecca at the Well* to an American audience. He included a photograph and proposed that they arrange to view the painting at the Kermit Fleur Gallery.

When Reade didn't get an answer, he made a call and was passed to Merilla Leviseur in acquisitions. "Mr. Bordeaux, are you working with Kermit Fleur?"

"I've stepped in since the death of his assistant. But this picture is for sale independent of him."

"Jules was very kind," she said reverently. "I met Jules and his wife, Janine, only once. She is charming."

"Yes, I met her and their son at the funeral," Reade said. "Jules is greatly missed."

"Is your family from Bordeaux, Reade? I ask because of your name. I am from Bordeaux."

"I assume my ancestors were from Bordeaux at some point. They came to America with Lafayette, but I don't know more than that. I'd love to walk the Pont de pierre Bridge over the river that flows one way in the morning and the other in the afternoon." Knowing he could ramble on if not careful, he changed the subject. "I just sold a picture by Granet that you are likely familiar with, *The Choir of the Capuchin Church*. Of course, mine was one quarter the size of the Metropolitan's."

"Pictures of churches are not usually my favorite, but the square of light coming through the back window is Nature herself. I don't see it as religious."

"Yes. Natural, not supernatural," Reade said. "And I find *Rebecca at the Well* to be modern in its own way also, even if it is a Biblical subject. Rebecca, not her father, weighs the jewels in exchange for her hand to the old man. Marriage is *her* business transaction."

"Speaking of marriage, and forgive me for asking," she said, "but please clarify your family tree so I can correctly explain who you are to the director. You recently married Anna Magdalena Pierce, did you not?"

"Yes, last summer," Reade said, realizing that he had dug himself into a hole. "And let me clarify: we married for love." He blushed deeply, but over the phone, Merilla Leviseur would never know. Still, it was awkward. Too personal. Not a perfect pitch, he thought.

"Of course, Mr. Bordeaux. It has been great to chat with you. May I ask your price for the Flinck?"

"Fifty-four thousand. I'd like to arrange a viewing at the Kermit Fleur Gallery, just around the corner on 84th and Park."

That Merilla Leviseur knew "the family" seemed coincidental, but Reade should have realized the significance of Kermit's donations to the Metropolitan over the years. Perhaps he should have consulted Kermit prior to the call. If no interest was forthcoming, he decided to continue on the path Jules indicated. If still no success, he'll go back to Amsterdam. Surely the Dutch will buy a painting from The Golden Age. He considered again Merilla's interest in him as another family member getting into the picture business. Perhaps it was AM she was keen on, or Lulu Rose who had an extensive collection of modern art by women. Merilla promised to get back to him the following week when the director returned from Europe, which was as much as he could hope for.

TWENTY-EIGHT

"YOU ARE MY SUNSHINE," Reade sang to the rhythm of Buckeye's hoofs beating the wet sand. It was Billie's first visit to Willapa. Still on New York time, they were up early on the gray morning. All they could see were low clouds touching the wet wintery Pacific beach. Sand rolled in with the waves and settled as smooth as a blackboard with deposits of kelp, logs, crab shells, a two-by-four, or a piece of frayed yellow rope becoming one with the sand. As they approached the North Head Lighthouse, the pungent smell of the salty Pacific gave way to the stench of death. A whale carcass sprawled forty feet across the beach in front of them. Fishing gear tangled in its fin was a mere ornamental trinket, not the cause of death. Its speckled torso quickly narrowed, long and lean, to a gigantic curvaceous tail, flat against the sand. The baleen bristles visible in its mouth turned up as if smiling. Flies danced over its skin. Reade read in *The Willapa News* that gray whales were dying of malnutrition as their Aleutian feeding waters were overfished. Thirty-four had washed up along the west coast this year. A sad warning for all mammals.

"It's a whale, Billie. Look at its big mouth." Reade opened his own to demonstrate. "It scoops up fish as it swims, presses the water out with its tongue, then swallows the yummy dinner."

Back at the farm, Billie galloped in and out of the tall fronds of pampas grass, loving his new freedom as Reade brushed down Buckeye. Bonnie's Appaloosa, Butter, with its white rump sauntered over for a nose rub. Reade introduced Billie to the prickly monkey tree in the front paddock. He pulled a carrot from last year's garden, washed it off at the outdoor spigot, and chomped down. Then came Billie's favorite activity: Reade set him on his lap and they swung between two tall evergreens. The squeaky chain reminded Reade of waking Saturday mornings to AM swinging during their year in Willapa: she pumped so high her bottom lifted off the seat.

Winter was a dangerous time of year for commercial fishermen. Their lights could be seen after dark a half-mile offshore. When Bonnie left for the night shift at the Coast Guard station, Billie fell asleep on the couch. Sipping tea by the fireplace, Reade thanked Jeff for his excellent care in maintaining the property, including fence repairs and keeping the old tractor running.

"I saw Becky at Meyer's funeral," said Jeff. "Bubba was with her."

Reade nodded. "Yeah, they ran off to Texas together, but surprise, surprise. Becky married AM's former boyfriend, Saxton."

"What?"

"Saxton's family is dear to AM, and they've adopted me. And now Becky. So it's all good for Billie."

Jeff grinned and shook his head. "Someone from Lincoln City bought the Red Barn."

"That's news," Reade said. "I wonder what Bubba will do with himself. Becky said he's living in Meyer's house." Reade swallowed a hot gulp of tea. "Do you know what you want to study at college?"

"I've been learning to code online. I might go in that direction. Bonnie wants to be a doctor."

"You've found an ambitious woman," Reade said.

"Isn't that what Becky is doing?"

"Originally, but she decided on physical therapy instead."

The next morning, Reade held Billie's hand as they walked through town, past a barbershop, a gas station, and a couple of real estate offices. They entered Marsh's Free Museum, a store that sold shells and trinkets, Japanese glass floats, hats, and sweatshirts. Billie shied from the main tourist attraction, a "shrunken lizard man". They played the funky old pinball machine in the back of the store and lunched on grilled cheese sandwiches at the diner across the street. In the afternoon, they drove over to the dock and bought two dozen oysters. Reade snapped a picture of Billie standing in front of AM's empty studio before driving up cemetery hill to say hello to Chief Nahcati.

On the way back to the farm, Reade told Billie the story about the day he ate half a slug. "Yuck!" Reade said. He looked at Billie in the rearview mirror. "And I put the other half in my pocket! I was probably your age. Your grandmother had to clean the slime out of my mouth and rinse it with salt water. Ooie! Not a good idea. You'll never eat a slug. Right, Billie?"

Reade found his shears hanging in the garden house where he left them. He wiggled his fingers into his leather work gloves and clapped his hands to soften them after months of sitting on a shelf. As he wheelbarrowed aged manure to the south slope, he remembered Jeff's photograph of the orchard's white bloom last year. The trees were due to flower again in six weeks—time for pruning. He cut dead branches and spindly growth at their center to encourage apple production and trimmed the dead-looking branches with rough bark and fruiting spurs growing too close together. After weeding around each tree, he spread a couple of shovels of compost and tamped it down. Dusk was falling when he noticed a tear in the metal wire fence and mended it, weaving and twisting the broken ends together.

Returning to town the next day, Reade stopped by a realtor's office on Main Street and spoke with the person sitting at a desk. Her name stood prominently in a plastic holder: Nancy Johnson. She had long hair and wore a heart-shaped locket over her sweater. Reade's mother had one like that with his father's photo inside that she kept in her jewelry box.

"Hi, I'm Reade Bordeaux," he said. "I'm wondering if you could answer a few questions. What's the rental market like in Willapa?"

She motioned for him to take a seat. "Rentals are three-quarters booked for this summer right now."

"What about year-round rentals?"

She shook her head. "Very few people want to live here off-season. Californians buy ocean property for family reunions and vacations and hire managers to rent them during clamming season and holidays. I'm one of the exceptions. I came from San Francisco to visit my mother who retired here from Spokane, and I never left."

"Californians are buying in Seattle, too," Reade said. "I just sold a house in West Seattle. What about meth and opioids? My tenant was gone for a week, and someone moved into the tower on my farm and trashed it."

"It's like anywhere else in America." She paused, not wanting to discuss the drug problems plaguing the town.

"My sentiments, exactly," he said. "My neighbor two doors down with the same size property sold a couple of years ago for $600,000 after being on the market for two years. Mine has a barn and a pond, an orchard, an old farmhouse, and a cottage."

"Sales have picked up since then." She smiled. "I know your place with the little duck pond. It's a romantic property."

He took her business card from a stack on her desk. "Well, thanks, Nancy. You've been helpful. I'll be in touch."

Reade stayed up late listing chores that needed to be done, like painting the fences, pruning rhododendrons, rebuilding the garden shed, and doing something with the nasty kitchen floor, all while glancing at AM's white goat head that was hanging above the fireplace mantel. It no longer glowed but still gave him a warm remembrance of the day he met AM.

At 2:46 in the morning, the town siren blasted. Jeff ran upstairs and burst through Reade's bedroom door. "It's a 6.5 earthquake somewhere offshore with the possibility of a tsunami hitting the coast in forty-five minutes," he reported. Moments later, a truck with a loudspeaker drove by the house blaring, "Move to the designated safety ground at the North Head Lighthouse."

Geologists discovered evidence of tsunamis rolling right over the Willapa Peninsula at least four times in recent history, the last being three hundred years ago. It was the same story now: the Cascadia plate was moving under the Continental plate.

"I'm loading the horses into the trailer," Jeff said. "Bonnie will drive your truck."

"We'll head out now, then," Reade said. "Our flight is at two this afternoon. In any case, the road might wash out with a high tide. I don't want to miss my flight."

Billie was sleeping sideways on the bed, his head damp with curls, his thumb stuck in his mouth. Reade changed his diaper and dressed him, packed his stuff, and secured him into his car seat in the rental. Back upstairs, he tossed his personal items into the suitcase, trying to think clearly. He had built a secret compartment in the living room wall to hide his Pa's guns, which he had already disposed of, but there was another small box with his coin collection, his Ma's pearls, the locket, and other odds and ends. He ditched a pair of sneakers and a jacket in order to fit the box in his suitcase, as well as his mother's fifteen-pound cast iron pan and lid. He grabbed a baby bottle, filled it with milk, and took the box of saltines. He chowed down the last piece of apple pie. At the last minute, ran back into the living room for AM's papiér maché goat head.

In the quiet landscape, he waited at the one stoplight as it changed from red to green. He imagined a wall of cold Pacific surging through the small bungalows, the gas station, the Depot Diner, Sid's Grocery, and slamming into the slope of the coastal range. Willapa will be an empty sand dune again one day. The seventy-five-year-old breakwater at the mouth of the Columbia

River, built to deepen the entrance for ship navigation, had caused an accretion of land of nearly half a mile along the southern peninsula. This was of no consequence in the face of a tidal wave. The blast of water will push the sand back up the Columbia River and make mulch of his farmhouse.

TWENTY-NINE

AM BLED FOR THREE DAYS. Drops turned to a heavy flow of dark red with clotting, which she saved for the nurse to examine. The experience scared AM into following Nurse Angie's orders to stay on bed rest. Angie stopped by every week now. After Daisy picked up Billie for the morning class, AM and Reade had a few hours to themselves. She worked from bed wearing one of his t-shirts, a pair of leggings, and a big Kotex between her legs in case of bleeding; he worked on his computer at the kitchen table to keep an eye on her. The March wind made a racket, sometimes whistling, as shadows of bare winter trees flashed across the sunlit walls. He refilled her glass of lemon water and brought her toast or a dish of custard. When she got up to pee, he accompanied her. *No more bloody sheets* was their mantra.

Earbuds blocked the tedious, high-pitched sound of

electric screwdrivers as wallboard was hung on the fourth floor. "Hallelujah," AM sang over and over, oblivious of the noise. But she was frequently interrupted by texts from her assistants on the third floor and usually called back to advise them on printing the large cloth designs. For AM, the trickiest part of Immaculata was the language. She decided to anchor the words of the historical women in a durable format, the sonnet. Emily Dickinson solved her dilemma of language by including alternative words throughout her poems, allowing the reader to switch, so that each poem contained many variations. But AM would be gratified to get one clear meaning across to the public. She was convinced that after Revie's birth, her words would gently settle into a final position like puzzle pieces. She planned to print the ink block letters herself, which took immense concentration to execute without error.

Reade laid down beside her on the bed, twisting her unruly curls around his finger. "Everything will be okay."

Internet abuse had spiked since photographs of AM at Shanika's opening circulated. Her painted face, sunglasses, and clothed body did not disguise her. No one could tell she was pregnant, yet somehow, word was out. It was a vicious game these strange vultures had of picking AM apart, like Captain Kidd, whose dead body hung in London until his bones were clean. There was a long history of women forced to remain shut up and unseen to avoid ridicule. The namecalling, the threats against her and the Honey Dearborn Art Center, and the anti-immigrant slurs were nerve-racking for Reade. Alberto suggested that he follow AM's lead and stay off the internet completely. Gallery A and Lulu's attorneys had an ongoing investigation. Because of the fire last year, still listed as an unsolved arson, the police took the threats seriously. Her followers understood, too, that slander was not an aesthetic or artistic attack, but something darker, hard to put a finger on. A pornography ring spewed footage of a fake naked AM, as if she were purposefully luring men, women, and children into her clutches. The board hired round-the-clock guards for the Center—a male guard from dusk until dawn seven days a week and a female day guard, Monday through Friday—in keeping with the Center's privacy policy for the women.

Alberto moved into his room on the third floor of the Honey Dearborn Art Center by late January. As promised, it had a window, dresser, double bed, nightstand with a lamp, some hooks to hang clothing, and a door. But it was cold as the new walls cut off heat from the rest of the floor. Reade bought him a comforter and a portable heater and crossed his fingers that the old boiler in the cellar kept chugging. A storm dumped three feet of white snow on the ground, and from the window, the city looked like the heart-shaped cake Reade's Ma used to bake on Valentine's day, covered in thick, boiled, sugary-white frosting that turned crunchy, like frozen snow, by the second day.

TWENTY-NINE

As Executive Director, Alberto was up and out early each morning to the shared nonprofit space near Union Square. In the evenings, he kept Reade abreast of his fundraising calls, conversations with board members, the headway he and Dov were making on grants, the payroll tax issues, the budget, and all the miscellaneous tasks AM no longer shared. Reade sometimes woke late in the night to muffled voices and laughter as Alberto and some new lover scurried to the bathroom on the floor above them. These commotions stirred AM, prompting her to talk in her sleep. She had developed a new sensitivity to language during her long vow of silence. Words were delicate, breakable, or poisonous if misused or overused; but in sleep, her words flowed unedited, sometimes relaying conversations she had years ago, like the one with her mother, dying in the California woods north of San Francisco.

"I'm old and I'm greedy, Maggie. I want more life. I want to live just a minute more. Just another day. But my own body failed me. My breasts of all things, Maggie! And there is no one to blame. No one to help me. No medicine to cure me. I'm trapped and in pain. And so sad. It's so disappointing to know the beautiful seasons I will miss, my children and loved ones. But above all, Maggie, I want to be alert and alive until I die. No morphine. No lying around in a coma for weeks. Promise me, Maggie."

Reade turned on his side toward her, his mouth near

her ear, so as to not wake her. "Was your mother in hospice?" he whispered.

"We had a last supper. I pushed her wheelchair through the woods to a place where she could smell the ocean, hear its roar, and see its blue. Legally, she had to administer the deadly dose. She was determined. But the hospice nurse spilled the medication, and mother had to live twenty-four more hours while we waited for another prescription to arrive. She broke down sobbing. I cradled her. She was no more than bones. In the morning, she conjured the strength to deliver the dose and was gone by noon."

"What about your siblings?" Reade asked. "They weren't there?"

"The twins had said goodbye to her before I arrived. They are religious, like their father, and didn't support her assisted suicide."

THIRTY

READE HAD a hunch that Nancy Johnson knew how to position his Willapa "ranch," as she called it, for the California market. She made an appointment with Jeff to tour the property with her photographer on the first sunny day.

"I'll send you comps to support my price point," she said. "$795,000 is a good place to start. You need a bit of paint here and there," she continued. "And absolutely a new kitchen floor. But it's lovely. The daffodils are up and the orchard is blooming."

Yes, Reade's beloved Willapa farm had been spared. No tsunami this time, but he had made up his mind to sell. Finding an upstate property to buy was proving more difficult than purchasing an old master. He was determined to bring Buckeye east, and spring was upon them. He nixed a $500,000 hilltop house in the Catskills near Woodstock that at first sounded enchanting—a mid-century modern house on thirteen acres with heated stone floors and a screened-in porch, a meadow view, an attached studio, and a separate guest house. But Buckeye needed a real pasture, somewhere to run. He moved his search east of the Hudson River to Columbia County, with its rolling hills that sold for $9,000 an acre without any improvements. As he wiped the dew from Shanika's sculpture and looked into the depths of the clear yellow glass, he nixed a wreck he found in Hillsdale for $600,000, a farm with twenty-two beautiful acres on a dead-end road with an old barn, a pond, and a big nondescript house that looked in worse shape than his Willapa farmhouse when he bought it. He needed a place clean enough for a newborn and safe enough to run not only Buckeye, but Billie.

Lulu, Reade's fairy godmother as he had come to think of her, called with a phone number of a friend of a friend, selling a twenty-two-acre horse farm in Columbia County. She suggested he take a look right away and offered to bring lunch and spend the afternoon with AM who was still on bed rest, uncomfortable, and unable to work in her ninth month. Reade decided against taking Billie with him—too many hours of driving—and arranged for Elah to pick him up after his morning classes. A springtime drive sounded bucolic and inviting, but two hours into the trip, the Taconic State Parkway was almost barren: the drive was like going back in time. Fully leafed trees in the city were barely budding when he reached the exit. Still, he was smitten, driving down the meandering dirt road lined with giant black walnut and filbert trees, past hills dotted with new modern houses. Bright forsythia and quince grew stream-side along the old white farmhouses in the small valleys. He recognized the three-rail fence from an emailed photograph and noted the pasture with two small run-in barns. Turning through the open gate, he rounded a rock outcropping to the left and pulled up in front of a low L-shaped barn with two large top windows and side dormers. A child's pink bicycle leaned against the building. A strong, fair woman came out of the barn, set her pitchfork aside, and approached the truck as Reade turned off the engine.

"Katrine," she said, introducing herself. "I'm sorry. My husband, Dan, is delivering a young stallion north of here, but I will show you around. Come in."

The barn, built fifteen years ago, was solid with stalls for twenty horses that Katrine mucked twice a day. Six beautiful black or brown horses greeted them; one with a curly dark mane streaked gold; and another, with a long blond mane falling over his eyes, nuzzled Katrine's shoulder as they passed.

"This horse is thirteen," she said, rubbing its white mottled nose. "We call him Hoover because he eats everything. But he's not well; we have to watch him." Moving down the line, she stopped in front of a brown beauty. "This boy is twenty-seven! I rub ointment on his belly every night or his eczema acts up and the flies don't leave him alone." Then she reached out to a handsome black horse stamping his hoof against the rail. "He was castrated two days ago and is anxious to be back in the pasture with the other geldings."

She led Reade up a wide stairway to a vacant one-bedroom apartment with a wood stove, small kitchen, and bath, and next to the apartment, two large empty storage rooms with dormers that could be turned into bedrooms. Back out front, they climbed into her all-terrain vehicle and toured the riding paths to the back pasture that was divided into three fields with electric fencing and another large run-in barn. A flock of goldfinch lifted off the field, swooping up in small consecutive arcs, landing in a grove of trees. A dozen mares, two with foals, ran alongside the vehicle to the top of the gently sloping hill where Katrine slowed to take in the long view of fields surrounded by woods. She pointed to a pond and the creek running west along the property line. Continuing on the riding trail as it looped back, Reade saw the main barn from the side, noting a covered patio and, beyond, another small paddock. They passed a lone black stallion in the front field again as she pointed to an oval training ring.

Katrine pushed the vehicle into full throttle and they zoomed over a bridge and up to the top of a long hill where she killed the engine. The Catskill Mountains loomed, not lumpy like the herd of napping gray elephants Reade had seen with AM on their drive to

Woodstock, but majestic. In the near distance, brilliant green hilltops popped out of gray woodlands.

"Dan and I grew up in a small town in Montana," she said. "In the summertime, everyone gathered after work at the stables to groom their horses and socialize. Our lives have always centered on horses. Up here is where we are building our retirement home. You can see the foundation we poured last year. The builders are starting to frame next week. Of course, we'll keep a few horses for the grandchildren." She leaned back against the window and stretched her arm on the back of the driver's seat. "You said on the phone that you are selling your farm out west. How many horses do you have?"

"Only one at the moment. And a family—my wife, Anna Magdalena, a one-and-a-half-year-old son and a daughter, due in a few weeks."

"Oh, me, too," she said. "I have a son and daughter and two grandchildren."

Before driving back to the city, Reade stopped at a diner for lunch. Waiting for his bowl of chili, he went through the photos on his phone that he'd taken of the farm, and studied one of Katrine in the driver's seat of her all-terrain vehicle. She was strong, calm, hardworking, and straightforward. *AM will like her*, he thought. Selling the lower twenty-two acres for $900,000 wasn't Katrine's only concern: she was handpicking her neighbors. He hoped they were in luck with Lulu's friend's recommendation. Flipping through the photos again, he noted the white dogwood, purple-tinged lilac, old oak trees, and portions of old stone walls that lay just beyond the riding path. How romantic to sleep above the barn on a snowy night, warmed by horses below. He opened his email to look again at the survey Katrine sent after their first phone call, marking the acreage for sale and noted the privacy of back pasture by the pond and thick woods. They could one day build a simple energy-efficient house and turn one of the large run-in barns into a studio for AM.

"Ree Dee, I would like to bring Hum-Hum to live with us in the sweet spot," AM said when he told her about Katrine and showed her photographs of the property.

"Hum-Hum?"

She slid down under the covers. "The wholly holy one," she said. AM's voice was muffled beneath the sheets. Reade peeked a look at her. She was smiling.

"The holy wall has crumbled," Reade said, crawling under the covers with her. He didn't want to blurt out the word "father" but at last, the secret story of her birth father was beginning to unfold. His name was Hum-Hum. That was a start. And she wanted them all to live together. So now it was up to Reade to figure out how to make it happen. Selling his Willapa farm might take months. He could get a mortgage on it to buy the upstate farm, but he had to make it happen soon. He placed his hand on her taut, bulging belly, like the shell of an egg, strong and delicate, the shape of Katrine's hill.

"Did you have a nice time with Lulu this afternoon?" Reade asked.

"She did everything I asked, including helping me to the bathroom and reading my favorite Shakespeare sonnets aloud."

"Have you eaten?"

"I'm nauseous, as usual. And cold. Make me warm, please."

He spread a second blanket over the bed, tucking it around her shoulders. AM shivered intermittently, like the flank of a horse, ridding itself of flies. He called Elah to ask if she could keep Billie until the evening.

THIRTY-ONE

RANDOM PERSONAL ITEMS began mysteriously turning up in odd locations around the Center: Daisy found a toothbrush in the kitchen dish drainer as she prepped for the morning cook; stinking wet muddy sneakers, cutoffs, and t-shirt were found among AM's fabric in the third-floor loft—something Billie was capable of now that he liked to run around naked—but these were adult clothes. The weirdest and most damning was an earring of Celtic design that usually dangled just below Gregory's left ear lobe, found in a bowl among AM's rings in her top dresser drawer. When Reade handed the stuff to Alberto, he made a positive identification.

"Do you trust him?" Reade asked.

"Trust him to do what?"

"What's right? Does Gregory have a key to the Center?"

"No." Alberto's body froze mid-word, his hand reaching toward Reade, lips parted. "Fuck," he finally said. "Gregory stopped by my office last week to borrow my key, said he forgot his notebook in my room. He gave it back but may have made a copy." Guilt crept into Alberto's voice. "I should also mention something else. Smoking weed with him a few days ago down by the river, he was talking crazy shit about last year in Lover's Lane."

"What's that?"

"The path through the brush to the side door of the old gas station. On a dare, some guy seared his hair." Alberto paused. "His shirt caught fire. The guy ripped it off and threw it through the broken window of the garage."

"So the fire could have been an accident!" Reade said. "What a relief!" As soon as he said that, AM's words rang clear: most human beings are decent; a few are truly bad and need to be feared.

Alberto's face became pained. "Gregory didn't seem to understand what he was telling me. He's a nice kid."

"He's probably near thirty years old, Alberto. Not a kid. Look, I'll call a locksmith to change the keys and instruct the guards not to allow him in the building. Tell him you're back together with Ronnie. In the meantime, the Honey Dearborn Art Center is going to be as supportive of Gregory as always. I hear from Lulu that her friend commissioned six chairs."

Alberto's tragic mask cracked. "I'm going back to

Ronnie! I love Ronnie! I'll convince him to take me back. You are brilliant, Reade."

The weather turned strangely tropical as Alberto attempted to seduce Ronnie. Even humid, with gusts of thirty miles an hour. This was not typical of a New York spring. Dark, overbearing clouds buried the Statue of Liberty and lower Manhattan in gray masses that rolled toward Queens hour after hour but dissipated before arriving. People dashed across streets with umbrellas as thunder rumbled, like trucks shaking not only the elevated Brooklyn-Queens Expressway but the very bedrock of the city. People on the street felt like they could be struck by lightning or hail at any second. But only a sprinkle fell without muddying the dusty streets. Pedestrians covered their eyes with their hands and pursed their lips against the grit. Finally, in the dark of the second night, the storm broke. In a gentle rain, Alberto moved back into Ronnie's Elizabeth Street penthouse.

"I secured a corporate underwriter for the gala dinner at the Bridge Cafe," Alberto said to Reade. Billie was with them. They were having a late lunch at a spot near Alberto's office. "My buddy is playing samba funk —he's donating the night—and the gala committee agreed at the ticket price of $5,000 a plate. We'll make our goal if sell a hundred seats. Twenty-five will have to be outdoors, but I think we can manage that. A performance under the Brooklyn Bridge is free and open to the public; cocktails and the award ceremony at the Café for guests from 5:00 and dinner from 6:00 to 7:30. So far, thirty-five checks have come in, but we need a hundred. Lulu and the board are making calls. I got the permits. What am I forgetting?"

"The women and children?"

"Never. They are part of the award ceremony, singing and dancing. The art they donated will be exhibited outside the Bridge Cafe. Sales go directly into Daisy's program budget. The children will each receive a backpack of art supplies to take home. We need a gift for the women. Lulu is in charge of that."

"And Ronnie?" Reade said, changing the subject. He grabbed the check from the waiter.

"You gave me the brew that is true."

Reade smiled. They had bonded over that old Danny Kaye movie, *The Court Jester*, when they first met.

On the warm June evening of the gala, Alberto Dia and his beloved, cigar-smoking, Ronnie Solis, presided in matching tuxedos over the festivities. With access to the theater warehouse reinstated, Alberto dressed AM in a loose silk jumper with small circular cut-outs. The cloth of the outfit matched her skin tone. Her hair was pulled into a round puffy ponytail and her face painted in a bouquet of flowers. She blended with the ceremonial clothing from Afghanistan, Ghana, Southern Sudan, Nigeria, Somalia, Syria, the Republic of Congo, and Yemen. Holding hands with the children, the women sang a lullaby—first in English, then Arabic and French. The simple sweet sound was palpable. Boats on the East River tied up at the park, and those aboard applauded along with the dinner guests, the staff, and the general public. The Write To Freedom step-dancing group followed. Words selected from the 24-hour writings were called out in sync with dance moves. The performers were practiced and the audience stomped the grassy knoll. The public segment ended with "America the Beautiful" directed by Daisy, her body bending and bowing with open arms as the voices, slow and drawn, quivered in their throats. The tension in the hot air verged on breaking point as if the Brooklyn Bridge cables overhead might snap. But as the song ended, a balm settled over the crowd.

AM and Reade stayed through happy hour, talking with guests about the authentic artistic processes used in the exhibition—calligraphy, block-printing, and watercolor. Saxton showed up in a Hawaiian shirt, plaid shorts, loafers with no socks, his hair dyed gray—which hung over his eyes like a shaggy horse mane—a shocking juxtaposition to his clean-shaven baby face. He lip-kissed everyone, which Reade had learned to tolerate. He stole Billie out of his arms, and the two glided through the warm gardens, with greetings to Lulu's friends and introductions to strangers.

"You never stop loving them, no matter who they grow up to be," Lulu said. "There will always be surprises."

Reade suspected Lulu's insight was as close to explaining her grown son as she would ever come. Why should she say more? Like Honey Dearborn, she had an extraordinary capacity to love. Her message stuck like a signal flag in Reade's brain.

THIRTY-TWO

RUSTY WHIMPERED at Reade's bedside and, getting up, he found AM on the bathroom floor, breathing but unconscious. She appeared to have slipped in the amniotic fluid, which Rusty licked as if trying to be helpful. There was no sign of blood, no noticeable scrape or bump, but AM was unconscious! Her heartbeat matched his, luckily. Dialing Nurse Angie, he slipped a pillow under her head. Angie called an ambulance as he dressed and gathered clean towels, a pan of water, and scissors in case he had to deliver the baby himself. He massaged AM's belly, hoping to feel Revie's kick, but no. It was the words of his swimming instructor, Jim, that calmed him: *Do not panic, cup your hands and pull the water toward you.* He dialed Alberto, whom he had dearly missed since he moved back in with Ronnie.

"I need you," Reade said. "AM fell. I'm waiting for the ambulance."

"On my way," Alberto said.

"Junior's on guard tonight," Reade added hastily. "I'll ask him to stay upstairs with Billie if the ambulance arrives before you get here."

Reade was spooked seeing AM on the floor, just like Frank on the men's room floor. But she was not Frank, he told himself. Her water broke. She fell. Rusty began to howl as a siren drew close. The medics bounded up the stairs with their equipment. The female medic checked AM's vitals and asked for more pillows to elevate her legs. She felt for the baby, listening through the stethoscope. The other medic started her on oxygen and IV fluids.

"She's nine months pregnant?" asked the medic.

"Yes. How is she?"

"How long has she been unconscious?"

"I can't say for sure. Maybe twenty-five or thirty minutes. I think her water broke and she slipped. Is she going to be okay?"

"Her age?"

"Forty."

"She's stable. The baby's heartbeat is strong. It looks like you're going to be a father tonight." She smiled, trying to reassure him.

The city seemed strangely dark looking through the rear window of the ambulance. AM's face was calm, her limp hand warm. The medic kept a hand on AM's lower belly, as if holding the baby in, and her other on AM's wrist, monitoring her pulse. They arrived at NYU Langone on 33rd Street in nineteen minutes, and AM was whisked away on a stretcher. Nurse Angie met Reade in the lobby. She had become a trusted friend over the past months during AM's weekly check-ups. Guiding Reade up the elevator to the tenth floor, she made small talk. She was taking care of him now, even standing beside him at the desk as he filled out AM's paperwork. When his name was called, Angie was not allowed into the maternity ward but said she'd remain in the waiting room.

"You have a healthy baby girl," the doctor said as he dried his hands, his mask hanging around his neck.

"How's Anna Magdalena?"

"She's stable but unconscious. There is no brain bleed but we're going to do a scan." He paused. "Then it's a waiting game. But you'll be able to see her as soon as we finish stitching her up."

His daughter was placed in his arms, all seven-pounds-and-four-ounces. She had Reade's chubby cheeks, AM's ample black curly hair beneath her little cap, and AM's adorable flower petal nostrils. The rest of her was swaddled in a pink and blue striped blanket.

Her lips sucked busily. She made a perfect first yawn. Reade studied her serious human ears, like the soft curves of a nautilus shell. She squinted and blinked, yawned again, and her dark eyes opened, full of curiosity. Reade's tear dropped onto her smooth cheek, which he wiped away with his impossibly giant thumb. He remembered her brother's first nights at Becky's mother's house, studying Billie's round little face by moonlight.

You are my sunshine, Reade sang as he rocked her in his arms in front of the nursery window, admiring all the newborns tucked into tiny glass beds. A chair was brought out into the hall for him, and he was offered a tissue. He described her brother Billie, her dog Rusty, the little children at the Center that she would play with, the bridges and tunnels of New York City, and its tall buildings. Doctors and nurses exited AM's room wearing their scrubs, and Reade was ushered in.

"Anna Magdalena Pierce," he said in a strong calm voice. He sat next to her bed. "Our daughter wants to meet her Mama."

In crept Lulu, Kermit, and Saxton, offering adoration. Lulu came straight to Reade, pulled up a chair, and took hold of his hand. A joyous smile wrinkled her face as she studied the sleeping newborn in his arms. Lulu then turned serious attention to AM. Her fingers ran over the contours of AM's face—chin, lips, cheeks, and eyelids.

Standing behind Reade, Kermit rested a hand on Reade's shoulder.

Reade stood and placed the newborn in Kermit's arms. "Meet Greta. She is Summer."

Kermit's eyes widened. His mouth sprouted a grin, and Reade walked him over to a chair by the window.

Kermit exhaled, as if he could finally rest after his decades long search for his sister. Greta was alive. He mumbled a prayer: "Sh'ma Israel Adonai Eloheinu Adonai Echad. Baruch shem k'vod malchuto l'olam va'ed."

Saxton stared at AM from the foot of the bed. Impatient, he tapped his fingers on his pant legs. He began to pace, his hands locked on his hips, the sleeves of his white frilly blouse rolled as if prepared for work.

A strand of hair fell from the nurse's brown bun. She briskly checked the catheter line, the oxygen tubes, and the IV dangling from AM's hand. She smoothed the top sheet over AM, like a sarcophagus at the Metropolitan Museum, and went back to monitor the machines. Reade could not make sense of the squiggles and so watched the nurse's face as she stared at the screens. Her head swayed. She sucked her upper lip. She placed her palm on her forehead.

"What's wrong?" he asked.

She did not answer.

A harsh whisper exploded from Saxton as he now prevailed over AM:

Whoever hath her wish, though hast thy Will.
And will to boot, and will in overplus;
more than enough am I that vex thee still,
to thy sweet will making addition thus.
Wilt thou, whose will is large and spacious,
not once vouchsafe to hide my will in thine?

> Shall will in others seem right gracious
> and in my will no fair acceptance shine?

Saxton caught his breath. He wiped the spit on his lips with the back of his hand. Small bells on his shoes, previously blending into the hospital noise, chimed impishly. He knelt now, at AM's side, across from his mother, and continued in a voice vindictive, as if AM had wronged him:

> The sea, all water, yet receives rain still,
> and in abundance addeth to his store;
> So thou being rich in will add to thy will
> one will of mine, to make thy large will more.
> Let no unkind, no fair beseechers kill;
> think all but one, and me in that one will.

Saxton pulled back AM's bed covers. He gathered her in his arms. Without lifting her from the bed he tilted her toward the rising sun, gesturing toward the skyscrapers and the strong feminine light. Reade took notice: Saxton ached with love for her. He imagined their tight sexual display years ago in crowded ballrooms, and as he did so, it occurred to him that the family had been here before. Perhaps in this very room, when Georgie slipped into the underworld, and they held AM back.

The nurse's hands fell to her hips. No longer interested in her screen, her eyes were on the family: the grandfather by the window holding the newborn; the lover on one knee; the mother clasping the daughter's hand; and the father of baby Greta Willapa Bordeaux, watching helplessly. The nurse, shocked by Saxton's outpouring, was nonetheless grateful for her patient's recovery. And she smiled.

THIRTY-THREE

EACH MORNING AM asked herself a question, as Bucky Fuller had; and by dusk, she had derived a written answer, as she saw it, from her own imperfect life experience. Each day her question was more difficult. She didn't like small talk or interruptions of unimportant things. Of course, she didn't consider the kids, Rusty, or Reade an interference. She kept the Honey Dearborn work compartmentalized so that it didn't disrupt her artistic thoughts. She and Reade were forging a life together, merely calling out their needs when the urge arose. Selling the Willapa farm was up to him. Reade went ahead with purchases based on his own finances. When the bank's pre-approval came through for the Columbia County farm, Reade called Katrine directly, as there was no realtor. He offered $850,000.

"That means I'll have to leave out my soaking tub," she joked.

"We can't have that," he said. "Eight-six-four is a lucky number. A multiple of eighteen. I raise my offer to $864,000."

When Katrine and Dan called back, they accepted his offer. A title search and a down payment of ten percent were the next steps. They also made the neighborly gesture of offering to board Buckeye if the Willapa farm sold before the upstate closing.

"Sales are about average for May," said Nancy Johnson over the phone in Willapa when Reade called her. "I've shown the farm several times, but no offer yet. I'll let you know."

"Shall we drop the price now rather than waiting until mid-summer?" he asked. "If it's vacant mid-August, I'll have a problem on my hands."

"Californians are savvy, Mr. Bordeaux. They are not afraid to lowball."

Reade called Jeff to ask if he and Bonnie would drive Buckeye to New York. He enticed them with an offer to stay a week and explore New York City.

"Would you be willing to board Butter for a year?" Jeff asked. "We're trying to figure out what to do with her."

"Sure," Reade said. "Horses are like kids—one or two doesn't make much difference. How about we make a trade? I'll pay for your trip across the country with the two horses, and your time will cover a year of boarding Butter."

Again, Reade was disappointed in Becky. It pained him, for Billie's sake, that she chose to vacation in Hawaii with friends instead of visiting her son. She didn't seem to realize that Billie needed her voice, her smell, her touch, no matter how many other people loved him.

"Billie will never know that I changed my mind," she said to Reade. "Besides, Saxton will see him. I don't want to spend my vacation with Lulu."

"Come on," Reade said to her. "You could stay in a hotel."

"Saxton likes staying with his mother," Becky said. "He actually loves his mother."

Poor Becky. Her idea of "mother" was distorted by her own Lydia, a woman only capable of forming relationships with enablers. Meyer loved Becky, but when he and Lydia divorced, she was left in the void of her mother.

"Love is what we are after, Becky," Reade finally said. "That you and Billie love each other. Feel free to stay with us on your next visit to New York if you want."

Reade bought a second crib for Angie's room on the third floor to limit nighttime awakenings of the whole family. If Greta woke hungry, Angie brought her down to AM. If not, she changed her diaper and sang her to sleep.

AM's caesarian stitches were tender and itchy, causing sleeplessness. She hadn't regained her full energy. Still, she pushed hard to finish writing Immaculata, as the poems needed to be stamped on the six-foot cloth panels. With the honeymoon approaching, she'd have to allow her assistants to print it. This meant tutoring them as to how she wanted mistakes to be handled: when to sew a patch over an error; when to put an X through it; and when to leave an error, like an upside-down letter, alone.

"Katrine," Reade said over the phone. "Would it be possible to rent the empty apartment above the barn until closing?"

"Yes," she said. "A thousand a month. Bring sheets for the bed and towels. And sleeping bags if there are more than two of you. We have several cots. Put your horses in the back pasture. We'll move our mares up on the hill."

Jeff and Bonnie were exhausted after their five days of pulling a horse trailer across the country. Each evening they stopped to feed, water, and exercise the horses at the farms Reade had reserved. They were grateful for a long nap in the coolness of the bedroom above the barn but postponed a trip to New York City until their next visit. Buckeye and Butter were frisky, prancing around the field and, after some exercise, settled in and took to grazing and swatting flies, tail to nose, as they did in Willapa. To Reade's surprise, a barn cat appeared. He thought at first that the yellow cat of Willapa had stowed away, but Katrine said, no, she is an old barn cat who hides when strangers show up. Reade poured her a bowl of milk, kindling a friendship.

AM texted, asking if Reade could pick up Hum-Hum in Woodstock and get him settled in the apartment above the barn.

"I need a name," Reade said. "How do I introduce him to Katrine and Dan?"

"As Hum-Hum," she said without hesitation.

"Where do I pick him up?"

"The Zen Mountain Monastery. Drive through Woodstock. Stay on 212 to the town of Mt. Tremper.. It's about a half-mile down the road on the right. A low, wooden building. He'll be waiting for you."

It was a seven-mile drive west to the Rip Van Winkle Bridge over the Hudson River, a curious new road for Reade. He passed a distillery, meditation center, acres of farmland, an old courthouse where Alexander Hamilton once presided, a romantic wedding-cake-looking house with a cupola, and a spooky old Archer Daniels Midland factory. The town of Hudson was once a destination for whale ships. Carcasses were dragged upriver from the Atlantic. The blubber was boiled and made into candles; the bones into stays for men's shirts and women's undergarments. A host of church spires stood tall among the storefronts on Warren Street, once a thriving red-light district. AM told him about the prison industry up and down the Hudson River, but he saw no sign of it. Above town was the castle-like home of painter Frederick Church which overlooked his teacher's farm across the river—Thomas Cole, founder of the Hudson River School.

As AM promised, Hum-Hum sat on a bench in front of the wooden building. Wiry, with a shaved head, he wore baggy brown pants and a shirt of the same rough fabric and sandals. Carrying a paper bag with his belongings, he bowed shyly and climbed into the passenger seat of the truck.

"Thank you for accepting me into your home," he said.

"Well, it isn't much of a home yet. It's an apartment above a horse barn that we are buying from Katrine and Dan. It's a beautiful spot, though, and pretty secluded. You should feel comfortable."

He nodded.

"Do you drive?" Reade asked.

"My license expired four decades ago."

"I can take you to town tomorrow if you want to get a new one. I'll leave my truck for you as we'll be out of town for a while, and you'll need to buy groceries. Have you ever ridden a horse before?"

"No," he said.

"There won't be too much to take care of while we're gone. Just two horses. What do you eat?" Reade asked.

"I'm a vegetarian," he said. "I eat rice, grains, vegetables and fruit. Tea. Water."

Reade relaxed into the landscape as he drove north. He wanted a good look at Hum-Hum, this man who seemed to have awoken in the Catskills like Rip Van

Winkle. Pockets of hollows still held lore—Reade was excited to one day hike the mountains. Hum-Hum seemed curious as they drove into the farm. Reade showed him to the bedroom with new sheets on the bed, pillows, a blanket, and some of his used clothing—two pairs of jeans, four t-shirts, and shorts, socks, a jean jacket, and a baseball cap—just as AM had requested. Hum-Hum set his paper bag down with many nods of thanks. Reade turned on the gas burner and the shower, flushed the toilet, showed him how to use the washing machine and dryer, and left him to go food shopping. Hum-Hum was lying on the bed with his eyes closed, hands folded over his chest, when Reade returned. While making dinner of rice, tofu, spinach, and garlic, Hum-Hum walked the horse trails.

Sitting across from him as they ate, Reade was finally free to study Hum-Hum. He saw a man unbroken. A compassionate man with Greta's eyes and AM's wide face and pointed chin. His scarred hands confirmed Hum-Hum as the stranger who had shared dried fruit on Overlook Mountain; the man AM described in her dream as "the holy one." It was emotional to share a simple meal together. A parent. AM's father. Father and son-in-law. For Reade, it felt like a reunion of a long-lost friend. After dinner, they brushed and watered the horses, and Hum-Hum spoke in halting, thoughtful words, as if each word had a dash between them, or each word was a single note, cresting and falling, always ending on the upbeat.

"I took the monastic vow in Brooklyn in my twenties. In 1979, I helped found the zen monastery at Mount Tremper. I have lived in a spiritual community for fifty years, hiking, composing music, collecting wild edibles, chopping wood, sweeping, raking, and meditating. Three years ago, my abbot was told of my transgression. I broke two monastic rules: number one, a misuse of the senses; and number two, indulgence in sex."

"That was forty years ago," Reade said.

"Yes," Hum-Hum nodded. "Anna Magdalena herself met with the Abbot three years ago to beg compassion on my behalf, that I not be cast out. I was sixty-eight, without money or skills, without worldly possessions. Buddhist life is always subject to impermanence, suffering, and uncertainty. I accept that. It was determined that I could stay. As self-punishment, I have slept on the stone kitchen floor these last three years."

"How did you meet AM's mother, Julia?" Reade asked.

"She was a local organizer who helped raise money for the monastery. After our brief affair, we did not speak to each other for five years. When I overheard two women in the parking lot mention that Julia had a child, I contacted her. I asked if we could meet at the top of Overlook Mountain on Anna Magdalena's birthday. That was the beginning of our secret tradition. When her mother died, she reached out to me. Julia and I were both passionate about music. I played the flute in high school and college. I continued to compose music that is never written or played except in my head."

"AM missed last year's birthday visit. She was in Willapa."

He nodded. "I hiked the mountain and waited as usual. It happened a few times over the years."

Reade wondered if AM knew who ratted on Hum-Hum. She would never tell if she did, except maybe in her sleep. But he was beginning to understand Hum-Hum's influence. Her vows. Her dismissal of small talk. Her love of nature and imagining. Her fearless work ethic. Her goddess qualities.

"I'm happy you've come to live with us," Reade said. "I never really knew my Pa. He died when I was eleven and long before that, he was paralyzed from his neck down after a stroke. I grew up in Seattle. Ma was a nurse. She knit. Read murder mysteries. Cooked. We picked a lot of blueberries together. We spent time in Willapa, the beach where I met AM. I bought a farm and planted an apple orchard. I trained as a plumber and learned to weld." Reade paused and looked over at Hum-Hum, wondering if he should go on. "I was married briefly to Becky, and Billie was born just as we were divorcing. AM's a wonderful mother to him. You met him on her birthday on Overlook when she was nursing. And now we have Greta. Two beautiful grandchildren for you. What about your family?"

"My paternal grandmother was from Spain. She was beautiful, like Anna Magdalena, even in old age. She lived with us in Brooklyn when I was young. I spoke Spanish with her. My grandfather died in WWII so I never knew him."

"What about your mother's side?"

"From Hanoi. Furniture designers. They immigrated in 1955. At the start of the first Indochina war. Everything was taken from them. One of their customers sponsored their immigration."

"How did your parents meet?"

"As a teenager, my father worked in my mother's family furniture factory."

Reade wanted to hear more, but Hum-Hum did not continue. "There's a meditation center about a mile from the farm," he said. "I'll draw you a map. You'll need a cell phone, too, so we can be in touch. We have a busy day tomorrow, and you're going to have to practice driving if you want to get a license."

After a moment of trepidation, Hum-Hum mounted Butter for his first horse ride. Reade adjusted the stirrups, gave Hum-Hum the reins, and Butter trotted off. Reade rode Buckeye. Side by side, they followed the paths around the upper and lower fields as Reade pointed out where they might build a small modern house one day; which run-in barn could be turned into a studio for AM; and that he planned to buy Billie and Greta a pony.

THIRTY-FOUR

MERILLA LEVISEUR from the Metropolitan had not gotten back to Reade. He pressed on with his research and discovered a Govert Flinck expert at the Amsterdam Museum named Tomas Berg. He sent Mr. Berg a letter about *Rebecca at the Well*, asking his advice on placing it in a Dutch museum. To Reade's delight, Tomas called and said he planned to be in New York in a few weeks and they set up a meeting at the Fleur Gallery to view the painting. Never having seen the painting in person, Tomas was excited. Somewhere in that conversation, Tomas explained that he no longer used the phrase Dutch Golden Age, as the seventeenth century did not glitter for everyone. Reade was impressed with this lesson in privilege, and by the end of their forty-five-minute call, they were on a first-name basis. Reade invited Tomas to a home-cooked meal at the Honey Dearborn Art Center after the viewing.

"Excellent," Kermit said upon hearing the news. "I have not met Tomas Berg. but I have visited the Amsterdam Museum many times and know his name."

"Would you advise inviting Merilla Leviseur to the meeting with Tomas?" Reade asked.

"Yes," Kermit said. "Absolutely."

Reade spent an afternoon at the Metropolitan in preparation for the meeting. He studied the four paintings by Govert Flinck, as well as paintings by Caravaggio, Rembrandt, and Rubens. During his late-night readings, he finished Janson's 1,000-page *History of Art, the Western Tradition.* Kermit hired a graduate student named Mark to take over Jules' duties, and on the day of the meeting, it was he who poured coffee and moved the pictures into the spotlight while Reade listened and questioned the guests. The collegial atmosphere in the room surprised and delighted Reade.

"I've read that experts disagree on the number of Rembrandt paintings that exist," Reade said, "but it was Rubens who had the huge workshop. Besides, Rembrandt's drawing skills are so distinctive and visible in a finished painting."

Merilla spoke up. "Yes, *The Reader* at the Clark Museum in Massachusetts is a good example. It's gone back and forth since the twenties—is it, or is it not, a Rembrandt? But to my eye, there is no doubt that *The Reader* is painted by Rembrandt. Even more than his emotional impasto technique, it's the reader's hands so lovingly rendered, as if the book is human almost."

"Scholars agree that *The Return of the Prodigal Son* was Rembrandt's last painting," Tomas said. "He turned a single moment into an eternity. Rembrandt valued immortality over riches; experimentation over repetition."

"Even as he went bankrupt," Kermit said.

"Making art purified him," Tomas continued. "Whether it was sympathy for Jews or intimacy with human flesh, he knew, as collectors and critics didn't, that compassion, even when unpopular—is not the sexiest of human emotions—but is perhaps the rarest, as close to God as humans get."

After coffee was served, Mark shined a light on two beautiful black-and-white prints by Leonard Baskin: Walt Whitman, the lines of his legs strong as the grain of a tree rooted in earth; and a portrait of the painter Lucas van Leyden, with his striking black Dutch hat. These were followed by a Durer engraving in good condition, *Nemesis*, a powerful winged woman. Only after this warm-up did Mark lift the Flinck into the spotlight. Tomas got up from his chair and examined the painting with a magnifying glass.

"A much-painted topic," Tomas said as he sat back down. "The picture tells a happy story. Maybe it reflects Flinck's own happy marriage. Certainly, he married well. Perhaps that is what I'm reading into Rachel's beautiful face as she considers the jewels."

"Yes!" Merilla said. "He married Sophie van der Houven, the heiress of the Dutch East India Company.

But I see the point you made over the phone, Reade: Rachel negotiates her marriage rather than her father, which is modern. It is a powerful message."

Kermit held out his hand to Mark, who distributed copies of the painting's provenance. "It's a beautiful picture," Kermit said.

"Painted in the late 1650s, just before the burgomaster of Amsterdam commissioned twelve canvases," Tomas said. "Flinck, of course, died before finishing those. But his style here is better than his earlier mannered period."

"Maybe he returned to his teacher for inspiration in the end," Reade said.

Merilla placed her hand on Reade's arm. "Sometimes wealth does not cultivate emotional intelligence as well as poverty, or impending death. As Flinck aged, he may have begun to think of his legacy."

"So, I ask," said Tomas. "What is Govert Flinck's place in history? He will remain the best student of Rembrandt, as the Master was not surpassed."

The conversation ended swiftly at the four o'clock hour, leaving Tomas and Reade the opportunity to stop at the Metropolitan before heading out to Queens. He tutored Reade on Flinck's chalk drawings, *Reclining Female Nude* and *A Woman Asleep;* as well as two beautiful small paintings on wood: *The Bearded Man with a Velvet Cap* and *Young Woman as a Shepherdess.*

"Have you ever seen a picture of Govert Flinck?" Tomas asked. Opening his phone, he pulled up a portrait by Abraham Bloteling. He was a fair-haired man with direct eyes and a look of kindness as he gazed over his shoulder at the painter. The painting could have been of Tomas, with similar reddish hair, a short reddish beard, and a trimmed mustache.

"You look related," Reade said.

He laughed. "My wife did some genealogical research. Yes, we are related by way of my great grandmother's father's sister's great aunt's mother's father. You are probably related to him, too, if you go back twelve generations."

AM, Angie and the children, Alberto and Ronnie, Daisy and her uncle, and a handful of teaching artists all welcomed Tomas to the Honey Dearborn Art Center. Together, they toured the classrooms and garden as Reade grilled salmon. He watched Tomas through the open garden door nibble cheese with quince membrillo and sip the white wine Alberto had selected. He pet Rusty as he chatted with Ronnie. Daisy helped set the table and dress the mango salad. She tossed sautéed bits of fruit and spice into the rice. The twelve were congenial, without pretense. The meal felt celebratory, more like a first supper than a last. Even Billie was well-behaved, until he wasn't. At that point, AM and Angie took the children up to bed. Soon the other guests peeled off for home. Tomas, Alberto, Ronnie, and Reade took a tray of cold drinks up to the roof and set the tent cushions in the open air to view Manhattan by night, its lights like thousands of tiny fishing lures in a river of dreams.

"I believe you are right," Tomas said.

"What?" Read asked.

"Historians often discount the internal processes that the artist goes through in making a great work."

On their first phone call, Tomas and Reade discovered that they were born on the same day of the same year. Tomas and his wife, a sculptor, also had a young family. Reade elaborated on his recent visit to the Amsterdam Museum. Then Tomas turned the conversation to American philanthropy. He was intrigued that The Honey Dearborn Art Center confronted issues of racism and anti-immigrant sentiment through art and community. Traditionally, the European governments provided funding for educational programming in schools, but with prejudice against asylum seekers and violence on the rise, it was obvious that European governments were not doing enough to promote a multicultural education for all. It was museums that now struggled to fill a gap.

"Who is Honey Dearborn?" Tomas asked.

"Our benefactor. A prominent New York art dealer whose son happened to be my neighbor in Willapa. Honey Dearborn visited us after her son, Frank, died. AM had befriended Frank at the end of his life. When Honey died, she left this building to AM and enough cash to start the Center." Reade paused. "How did you settle on Govert Flinck as your sweet spot?"

"Sweet spot?" Tomas laughed. "I grew up down the street from the Café de la Nouvelle, an artists' hangout a hundred and fifty years before me. I was intrigued by the group—Degas, Cassatt, Manet, Daumier, Ingres, Toulouse-Lautrec, Louis Lamothe, and his student Jean-Louis Forain, with whom I know you are familiar. And his wife, the painter Jeanne Bosc. Also, their poet friends, Rimbaud and Verlaine, all hung out at the Café. It was actually my research in graduate school that led me to Govert Flinck because not much had been written about him, even as Rembrandt's best student."

"Do you know of museums interested in growing their seventeenth-century Dutch collection?" Reade asked.

"Yeah, yeah," he said. "To be sure."

Reade nodded patiently, waiting for Tomas to fill him in. Tomas was exhausted, and Reade knew to hold that conversation for another day. Alberto and Ronnie offered to drive Tomas to his hotel.

"Tot ziens," Tomas said. The two men shook hands. "Thank you for a wonderful dinner, Reade." After the kitchen mess was cleaned up, Reade looked up the translation: *Tot ziens* means *see you later*. That was better than goodbye.

THIRTY-FIVE

"PHILEAS FOGG," AM said.

This was code for "honeymoon". Kermit's wedding gift was ticking by. Their round-the-world tickets expired on September first.

"We don't have eighty days—or even seventy-two days," Reade said. "Becky's scheduled custody visit is the second week in June. Luckily, Lulu still insists she will take care of Billie and Rusty for the duration."

"I was hoping the four of us might 'nomad' together," AM said. "Rent a house somewhere warm where we could walk to a market, a beach, and cook at home."

"Japan?" Reade suggested. "I'd love to visit the ancient road between Kyoto and Tokyo that inspired Basho's poems and Hiroshige's prints. Although, carrying the kids wouldn't be easy."

"Zeus and Hera's honeymoon on the island of Samos

lasted three hundred years," AM said. Her dark watery eyes pierced him. He braced himself. She was ready to click her heels and make it happen.

"Well, then," he said. "Of course, we've got to bring Billie along. Rusty can stay home with Lulu. He likes his walks in Central Park."

They rented a simple white-washed stone house in a mountain village built on a narrow road leading to the town square. It was a friend of a friend's family home, someone AM knew since her days at the Art Students League. The walls were hung with landscapes and painted portraits of ancestors, men and women with dark hair and eyebrows and deep sunken eyes. It perfectly suited their needs. The kitchen, at the center of the house, led to a stone patio with a small view of the sea between two peaks. From the kitchen, in one direction, was a bathroom and a back door that led to an herb garden and a studio below the house; in the other direction was the front door and three small bedrooms, each with a big shuttered window.

Reade and Anna Magdalena woke to the greetings of the village women echoing *"Kaliméra"* through the narrow road as they hung laundry from their windows. Rena, the caretaker of the house, stopped by to tend the garden and inquire if they wanted milk or fish and bread from the market. After breakfast on the patio, Reade and AM walked with the children through orchards and fields of thyme dotted with small, white-washed houses. A mile down the hill was a crescent-shaped pebbled beach with umbrellas for rent and vendors that sold cold drinks. Billie lifted his chin to keep his head above water as Reade hydroplaned him across the tops of the waves. He dug in the pebbles with a shovel as AM waded with Greta or nursed and read under an umbrella. He played quietly with his little red truck. Just before noon, the village women waded like gulls in the shallows wearing black one-piece swimsuits and white bathing caps snapped under their chins. They worried aloud about their grown children and grandchildren working off-island in Athens until finally, waist-deep, arms held above their heads, they dove together into the clear turquoise sea. Reade swam the mile between the points of the crescent-shaped beach, his eyes open to the sculpted sandy bottom and shadows of passing clouds. Later, when the gray mermaids emerged from behind the rocks in their house dresses, they passed AM and Reade and the children sprawled in the sand.

"Kalispera," the women sang in the afternoon.

"Kalispera." Reade and AM repeated. They packed up the children and followed the women's chatter back up the hill to the village. Lunch on the porch was a fresh platter of feta, cucumbers, olives, tomatoes, and stuffed grape leaves with lemon and olive oil. Billie preferred his usual bread with honey and applesauce—and they all laid down for a nap. Evenings, they grilled fish or chicken with rice and thyme from the garden, and afterward, walked with the children through the village, charmed again to see their mermaids sitting with the old men playing cards, drinking Turkish coffee or ouzo, flirting the way they must have when they were girls and boys tending goats and picking olives.

The villagers nodded, like incoming waves as evening approached. *"Kalinixta."*

Reade and AM imagined the old couples sleeping soundly after sex and, year after year, rising with the sun to tend to chores, healing their aches and pains in the warm salty Aegean, the same idea Reade's mother had when she made him soak his cuts and scrapes in salt water.

"Refugees," said Rena. She held a basket of sandwiches. "Help."

Reade climbed into the rental car with her and drove forty minutes along the rugged southern edge of the island with deep ravines and sharp hills of olive and lemon groves dotted with stands selling honey. They came to the birthplace of Pythagoras, who believed that the numerical movement of heavenly bodies produced music. It was here that Reade first saw tents similar to those of the homeless in Seattle, only these were surrounded by trees stripped of branches, house foundations without windows, roofs, doors, or walls, the wood used for cook fires that smoldered even in the hot summer sun.

"New building," Rena said. She pointed to a concrete foundation where tractors moved earth and trucks of lumber were unloaded.

They continued up the mountainside above the port of Vathi where boatloads of people gathered after the treacherous one-mile crossing from Turkey. Old Army barracks, shipping containers, and tents of tied plastic housed families from Africa and the Middle East crowded together. Children kicked a soccer ball in the rubble. A girl with deep shadows beneath her brown eyes turned to look at Reade, her shirt barely covering her belly and budding breasts. She held a stick and was writing in the dust. He thought of Anne Frank wearing clothes she had outgrown in hiding. A long line of bedraggled, ageless, sexless humans stood in the water line to fill their plastic containers from a single spigot.

"How many asylum seekers?" Reade asked Rena. When she didn't understand, he tried again. "How many people here?"

She held up ten and then five fingers.

"Fifteen."

She shook her head, opened and closed her hands many times, and made circles with both arms.

"Fifteen hundred?" Reade said.

She nodded.

"On Samos?"

As they delivered sandwiches at Mazi, a youth center run by an NGO, a loudspeaker in Greek, English, and Arabic shook everyone to standing attention. Names of asylum seekers selected to take a boat to Ritsona, a camp outside Athens, for processing, were read aloud. For those who remained, the camp was an open-air prison. Adults were forced to carry identification cards stamped in red, which meant that they were not allowed to leave the island. Reade learned from an organizer who spoke English that two thousand children lived on the hill. One-hundred-eighty infants and toddlers. Three-hundred-fifty-one unaccompanied minors. Only forty children attended school. In total, more than fifteen thousand asylum seekers lived in encampments on Samos, caught in the politics of Greek and European governments and the chaos of wars in the Middle East. The European Union had given Greece a billion and a half dollars to aid refugees and to keep them out of the rest of Europe. Yet conditions worsened as their numbers swelled: women became more vulnerable to violence and children ran barefoot through garbage. Protests were organized to fight the inhumane conditions, interrupting Sunday Mass and holidays, and angering some locals. Others, like Rena, were empathetic: they remembered what they learned in school. They, too, were refugees in 350 BC. They were saved by the Spartans, warriors of the Trojan War, who fasted in order to feed the Samian refugees.

Reade reported his findings to AM as she cradled Greta in her elbow at the kitchen sink. With Greta's thigh firmly in her hand, AM squeezed warm soapy water from a washcloth over her belly, legs, and neck. Billie stood on a chair watching as Greta gurgled, her round eyes following his every move. AM noted that her daughter's torso, fingers, toes, and even her tiny nails were longer. Soft dark curls covered her head.

"Your sister is growing up," AM said to Billie.

Billie looked puzzled. "No!" he laughed. "She's a baby!"

"You were a baby once, too," AM said. "I bathed you in a sink just like this."

Billie shook his head and laughed. He jumped down off the chair and drove his little red truck across the floor. AM diapered Greta, slipped a nightie over her head, and sat down to nurse. From the kitchen table, Reade conjured Hans Memling's exquisite *Madonna and Child* from 1792 at the Metropolitan Museum. When Greta fell asleep, AM laid her in her crib, brewed a pot of local mountain tea she picked from the roadside, and retreated to the studio.

"Story," Billie begged.

Reade told him about the little boy he'd seen kicking his soccer ball over the rocky terrain between smoking fires, but Billie wiggled his fingers. He wanted to hear the story of the octopus at Alki beach in Seattle. Billie gave Reade a piece of imaginary seaweed. Reade pretended he was a fish and ate it.

"What a helpful octopus you are, Billie," Reade said in a pretend little voice. "You are so kind to little fish."

"More," Billie begged.

Reade retrieved *Aesop's Fables* from the Samos section of the bookshelf and carried Billie from the kitchen to his bed. He read the introduction to himself before starting in on the first story and summarized it for Billie. "Aesop was brought to Samos as a slave from Africa. But Aesop told such good stories, the people of Samos set him free."

After the morning swim, AM drove Rena and the basket of sandwiches to the overcrowded reception center with six hundred beds. Rena introduced AM to the many local volunteers who brought sandwiches daily and to the school teacher and the mayor of the town of Samos: both spoke some English. At AM's request, Rena found a Palestinian translator named Giglia who spoke French, Arabic, and English. Together, they met with groups of women living in tents and shipping containers. She handed out blank journals and pens, envelopes, and paper and set up pen pals with the women at the Honey Dearborn Art Center. AM took notes about their concerns and made lists of things they needed. She called Alberto and Lulu who agreed to help with donations of medical and sanitary and stationery supplies; baby products, liquid laundry detergent; books, clothing, and blankets; flashlights, batteries, and tents. Like the homeless in Seattle, their needs were complicated. The best she could do for now was listen, take notes, answer questions, and offer advice.

Hum-Hum had not picked up his phone for weeks, and when he finally answered, Reade reported the happy news that their attorney had closed the deal: they owned the upstate farm.

"I ride Butter for an hour. Buckeye-follows. I see the

red tail hawk, flicker, catbird, oriole nesting by the barn, cardinal nesting by the driveway, flocks of goldfinch, house swallow, the screech owl, and the blue heron fishing in the pond."

"Is the barn cat still around?"

"Yes," he said. "She appears when I set down the bowl of milk."

"Do you have enough to eat?"

"Wild carrots, onions, chickweed, nettle, spicebush, dandelion, garlic, watercress. I swim with turtles and frogs and walk undisturbed in the woods and fields five miles a day. And I play pickleball with the neighbors."

"What's that?"

"Like ping-pong or tennis. But this week I took a ball in my eye—I have a black eye. The neighbors dropped off slices of cake, ears of corn, and homemade bread. I'm fine, Reade. Thank you for bringing me into your home."

The old men in the village clumped in groups in the shade all day long, fingered their worry beads, or played cards. The Greek Orthodox priest said mass over a scratchy loudspeaker on Sundays and Wednesdays, reaching everyone whether they liked it or not. AM sketched the children as they slept and Reade weeded the herb garden. AM taped her drawings on the kitchen wall. Billie's drawings, too. Reade watched the sunlight penetrate the rocky depths of the seafloor as he swam between the points of the crescent-shaped beach, and their salty suits and towels dried stiff on the balcony railing.

Kermit called about the upcoming 19th Century European Art Auction. The catalog was online. Specifically, Kermit was excited about a beautiful painting by Émile-René Ménard, *The Three Graces*, owned by the Pittsburgh Athletic Association. He read in the notes that Ménard was a student of Bouguereau and exhibited at the Salon des Artistes in Paris.

"This beautiful Ménard was inspired by his 1923 travels to see the Greek antiquities," Kermit said. "It is expected to sell between thirty and fifty thousand. But this picture is worth much more."

"We saw a Greek sculpture of *The Three Graces* in one of the Athens museums," Reade said. "The painting is beautiful, but my hands are tied until I sell the Flinck. I haven't heard from Tomas or Merilla."

"We still have two months to make a decision," Kermit said. "I will partner with you on it, fifty-fifty if you like. By the way, Lulu and I will be at my London flat for the month of August. You should fly over with the children for a week to visit us. And in case you need anything at the gallery, Mark is in the office Monday through Friday."

Tomas called from Athens to invite Reade and his family to lunch in the town of Samos the following day. They had visited Victoria's family in Rome prior to a weekend stay in Athens with their five-year-old son, Jason, and young daughter, Jaya. It was a casual restaurant on the harbor, something new for Reade and AM, with a small beach for the kids to play in the sand. It was a leisurely two-hour lunch in a shaded garden. As they ate salad and spinach pie, Tomas described the holy light of the oculus in the Roman Pantheon—the burial site of Raphael—and their visit to the Capuchin Church, as per Reade's suggestion.

"When the priest wasn't looking," Tomas said, "I was able to steal a look through the slot behind the altar where Granet painted the chapel. The yellow light of the window, the New Testament with its red text open on the pedestal, looked exactly like the painting—except that the pews were empty. No monks."

Vicki spoke up: "I insisted that we wait in line to see the crypt beneath the church. Jason asked a lot of excellent questions about the flowers made of skulls and ribs."

"No!" cried Jaya. Billie had stolen Jaya's shovel. Reade set down his glass of mint tea, but Tomas squatted in the sand and sorted out the problem. Both Jason and Jaya had Vicki's deep-set eyes, like the portraits on the walls of the Samos house, eyes complemented by a sculpted nose reaching full, articulated lips.

"Louise Bourgeois was an early inspiration," said Vicki. "Especially her large-scale sculptures. And her cloth work at the end of her life interests me. Her family was in the linen business, and she turned the family linens into anatomical cloth sculptures inspired by psychoanalysis. Take a look at her cloth book, *Lullaby*. It really twisted my heart."

AM licked her honeyed fingers as Greta began to fuss. "What about Hilma af Klint? I saw her Guggenheim show several times, exhibited in her dream building, which didn't even exist in her lifetime. She inspired me to make a drawing a day ever since seeing her exhibit. Her *Tree of Life* grows in my head."

Lunch was over too soon: time for their flight back to Athens. AM and Vicki promised to stay in touch. When Reade finished wiping Billie's sticky cheek with a wet napkin, Tomas handed him the check.

"The Flinck belongs in the Amsterdam Museum," he said. "Come visit us!" He waved as they climbed into a cab.

Reade studied the auction catalog before calling Kermit at his London flat. He understood what Kermit meant about Ménard. *The Three Graces* were not painted statues, as was tradition, but nude women in the setting of an ancient ruin. This was what Kermit talked about at the Yom Kippur dinner: a view of nature through windows in religious paintings that paved the way for modernity: landscapes, and nudes.

"That's very good, Reade," Kermit said when he told him that Tomas had purchased the Flinck.

Reade smiled into the phone. "I'm happy it worked out. Are you still interested in partnering on *The Three Graces*? If so, what's our ceiling?"

"Bids for the Ménard might go as high as $80,000,

more than twice its estimated sale price, and I believe its market value is even greater."

"OK," Reade said. "If the Willapa farm sells in the next two months, I'll go as high as $40,000."

"Excellent," he said. "How are the children?"

"Enjoying themselves!"

"And little Greta?"

"She kicks and coos. Billie runs circles around her and makes her laugh. I'll have to send you a picture, Kermit: in the Greek sun, Greta's dark hair has beautiful red highlights."

"Thank you, my friend."

THIRTY-SIX

AM RECEIVED notice that twenty boxes of donated supplies for the refugees had arrived at the airport, only half of which fit into the rental car. Reade made the necessary trips back and forth from the airport to the Refugee Reception Center. Weekly supplies were expected into the foreseeable future, and Reade asked the director at the new Visitation Center to recommend a driver, someone with a cell phone he could call when he got notice of a shipment.

As he headed back down the mountain, a small spit of land fought over by the Turks and Greeks for four hundred years came into view. Tomas had mentioned that at low tide this channel was swimmable. Reade continued down the dirt switchbacks to the small beach, half-expecting to see rafts of asylum seekers struggling to cross the mile of open green sea between Greece and Turkey. Instead, there were tourists. Wading into the water, he noticed the couple next to him holding hands and speaking French.

"Have you swam this before?" Reade asked.

The man nodded. "Every summer. The view of Mount Kostos is very beautiful from the island."

"It's shallow most of the way," said the woman in a red bikini.

The three waded together until the bottom dropped off. As Reade dove in, he was shocked by its swift current. He heard Jim's voice: *lock your eyes on a visual marker and swim for it.* Focusing on a group of bathers resting in the sand ahead, they seemed only a short distance away, almost as if he could reach out and touch them. But no. The swim was strenuous. Out of breath, he landed two hundred feet beyond his marker. On his back on the hot sand, he took in the view of the lush green chain of Samos mountains, including what looked like a snow-capped Mount Kostos, a stark contrast to the flat barren land of Turkey to the east.

Once he caught his breath, Reade stood. He was surprised that the French couple was not resting among the handful of others in the sand. They hadn't arrived. *Perhaps they turned back*, he thought. But squinting into the distance, he saw their waving arms: dragged by the current, they were headed out through the strait into open sea. Without hesitating, he dove into the water he had just crossed and swam back to Samos.

"Rescue boat," he yelled in English, running across the beach dotted with napping adults and children playing under umbrellas in the sand. "Two swimmers are drowning!"

A gangly teenager nodded and signaled for Reade to follow. Together they pushed open a boathouse door and dragged a skiff out into the water's edge. The boy released the motor lock to lower the outboard engine and pulled the cord. The motor sputtered. He adjusted the choke and pulled until the engine caught and they sped out into the channel. Crouched on the bow, Reade pointed to the open water as the boy pushed full throttle into the rough sea. Small waves crashed over Reade and into the boat as he searched the water. The French-speaking couple was nowhere in the fast-moving current. As the waves turned to swells and the boy steered the boat up and over each one, swerving and swaying, the propeller lifted out of the water until gliding down the other side. Reade shook his head and the boy cut back to the rocky cliff of the Samos shore. There, stitched to the rock face halfway up the steep terrain, he spotted something red: the French woman's bikini. The couple clung for their lives. Nosing the boat straight away, they crashed through rough surf at full speed until the hull scraped against the cliff. Grabbing a small tree root, Reade balanced the boat. The boy killed the engine, lifted the anchor, untied the rope, and heaved it over his shoulder. The Frenchman, fifteen feet from the woman, seemed to be encouraging her to hold fast as the boy scaled the cliff to the top. He tied the rope to a large tree, tugged hard on it, and then let the rope drop. The Frenchman, after a few swings, grabbed the rope, his bare feet kicking off the sandy face of the cliff when he swung too close. Sometimes, pushing too hard, he dangled wildly over the water. Finally, swinging near the boat, the Frenchman let go, skinning his legs and shoulder on the boulders under the sea. He grabbed the side of the boat and hurled himself aboard.

The boy was now on his belly at the top of the cliff, dangling the rope, swinging it close to the woman over and over as she held fast to the small clumps of rock and tree roots: she dared not let go to grab the rope. Only when the boy lowered himself to her did she latch her arms and legs around him. He slid down the rope with her on his back, burning his hands. The Frenchman grabbed the woman's legs as she fell on top of him, landing at the bottom of the boat. The seas slapped over them as they clung to each other, whimpering until they caught their breath.

The dinghy sank dangerously low as the boy stepped into the rear. The engine caught, and he steered close to shore. Reade noticed the anchor line left hanging off the cliff. Reaching the safety of the beach with its umbrellas and the parking lot, the French couple retrieved money from their parked car, thanked Reade and pressed money into the boy's bleeding hands.

Before heading home, Reade drove the rental car up Mount Kostos as far as he could maneuver the rough roads. The sky was clear like the Aegean. It felt like the edge of the world, with a view of Sappho's island, Lesbos, just to the north. To the east was Ephesus, an ancient archaeological site in Turkey, now closed to tourists because of the chaos and violence. He paused to study the channel he swam and the open sea beyond. Beneath Mount Kostos, literally beneath his feet, was an elliptical-shaped reservoir built in the sixth century BCE, with two eight-foot-wide tunnels a mile long that still carried drinking water to the city. Driving back down the mountain, Reade found an official-looking gate unlocked. He drove in. Walking inside to the cave-like opening of a triangular tunnel, he noted the numerical calculations and symbols carved into the stone slabs that leaned against each other at the ceiling. The Pythagorean theorem, worked out on Samos all those centuries ago, was still in use today.

Upon arriving home, AM reported that Greta, now nearly six months old, had a well-baby check-up with a pediatrician who spoke English at a clinic in the City of Samos. She was twenty-and-a-half pounds, which was excellent. Her ears, heart, skin, lungs, and eyes all checked out fine. After her vaccinations, she was cranky for twenty-four hours. Other than that, she cried like all babies—when she was hungry, tired, or in need of a diaper change. Her eyes followed her brother everywhere, even if she could not crawl after him. She grabbed her feet and tried to roll over.

AM expressed and froze her milk for Reade to feed her when she made her rounds with her translator,

Giglia, visiting the women and children living in tents and old shipping containers. Legal issues, health concerns, and schooling were their priorities. The women asked that sanitary napkins, bras, underwear, and other personal items be brought directly to them as they could not speak to the men at the Refugee Center about them. One woman spoke up about wanting a padlock for her tent zipper at night. Others agreed. Violence was escalating. The women slept with whatever cooking knives they owned, sharpening them on rocks in case they needed to defend themselves and their children.

AM asked Giglia: "Is there a social worker or psychologist willing to come into the camp?"

Giglia was silent. She adjusted her headscarf over her forehead and looked up at her new colleague. "All the doctors I know on the island are men. But there is a woman in the village of Kokari who delivers babies and counsels the local women. Her name is Miray Abaci."

"Maybe we can introduce her to the women as a group first," AM said. "They can ask their questions and all find some consolation. Those who have been raped or are in need of individual counseling can set up appointments."

"She is old."

"The Foundation can pay her," AM said. "I will pick her up and take her home."

Giglia nodded. "I will ask if she can come on Monday."

Saturdays Rena babysat Billie and Greta for a few hours, allowing Reade and AM to walk from village to village, swim together naked in the twilight, or pick the fruit that grows in the brambles at the side of the road. They climbed up to Pythagoras' cave from 507 BC, built in an extinct volcano, that served as both his home and the school where he taught philosophy. They visited the shrine of Aesop in the town of Samos and bought honey at the side of the road; they peaked into the temple of Hera, her birthplace, which was under renovation, and lunched at a mountaintop village surrounded by grapevines; they explored the Vronta Monastery, home to three monks, its large stone chapel designed with harmonious proportions, with frescos from the seventeenth century. The monks had posted a story about a statue of the Virgin Mary, stolen and years later, that it washed back onto the beach and was now considered more precious for her cracks and lines of repair. Reade and AM missed Hum-Hum. They spoke regularly with him about Butter and Buckeye; the fox and deer drunk on mulberries; Katrine and Dan's two fillies sleeping in the field surrounded by mares. They placed honey and fruit for the Greek monks beneath the statue of Mary in Hum-Hum's honor.

"Hum-Hum is for Humphrey, as in Bogart," said AM. "Binh is my father's middle name. It means peace."

Reade smiled. "Hum-Hum taught me the three Buddhist words: respect, acceptance, and appreciation."

AM lifted her eyebrows. Reade was beginning to

realize AM's close life-long reverence for her father, even if she knew him only from a distance.

Jeff texted that he and Bonnie were heading south. The old kitchen floor was replaced. The entire contents of the house, barn, garden shed, and cottage were packed in storage, burned, or given away. When Nancy, the realtor, called with a lowball offer, Reade accepted it, and JT scheduled a closing.

"Kermit," said Reade. "How are you and Lulu? How's London?"

"Fine, Reade. How is the family?"

"Great. My Willapa farm has a buyer. Are you still interested in partnering on *The Three Graces*?"

"Yes, of course. It is the most beautiful picture in the catalog."

He smiled into the phone. "With a high bid of $80,000."

"Very good," Kermit said.

As the fiery sun dipped between the two dark peaks, AM worked in the studio. Her sonnets for *Imaculatta* had been printed and the proofs approved. The exhibit was scheduled to travel the U.S. beginning in October, and Vivian Boo of Gallery A agreed to speak at the openings in AM's place. The press for the upcoming season of six debut performances at the Honey Dearborn Art Center was positive. AM was confident about her selection of artists. Her solitary hours now included the study of Greek and Arabic, usually until two in the morning when Greta awakened for her night feeding. Her sleep schedule was still on New York time, even as they had prolonged their stay on Samos.

Reade selected a book from the shelf on the ancient astronomer of Samos, Aristarchus, but his eyes closed after only a few pages. The moon rose bright as the sun, its big round orb visible even through his eyelids. He got out of bed and pulled Frank's small black journals from the bookshelf. Reade still believed him a monster for, above all, rejecting his mother's love, but curiosity drove him to brave the inner sanctum of his one-time neighbor. He figured the black books ended up in his hands for a reason.

The stone patio still held the warmth of the sun and now, was bathed in moonlight strong enough to read by. Unwrapping Frank's books at the table, he pulled loose their knotted string: a tinge of smoke rose like a genie from the Honey Dearborn conflagration and dissipated in the salty air.

Frank Dearborn, January 1, 1989.

Remembering Frank's obituary, Reade calculated that he was sixteen in 1989, the age he ran away from his Connecticut boarding school to live in Florida with a group of artists. He expected Frank's books to hold tales of his recklessness, but turning the pages, Reade couldn't make out anything. He tapped the light on his phone, only to discover page after page of abstractions, small neat symbols, and squiggles—lines bending as all waves bend. By narrowing his vision to a light beam's width, Frank's pages seemed to touch something universal. Cracks, irregularities, and bumps interrupted his lines, creating ghosts and echoes. *It's a self-portrait,* Reade concluded, like AM's drawings of him without skin, his nerves, sinews, muscles, bones, and arteries visible. Frank must have discovered his vulnerability and decided on a fleet of vintage cars for protection.

As the moon set, Reade retied the string around Frank's books, wrapped them in their plastic, and set them back on the shelf. He stepped into the shower and soaped his body in the lukewarm water, his thoughts turning to his father's paralysis. Even as he could not lift a finger, his big macho lessons on bullying, fighting, drinking, smoking, and womanizing had a lasting impact. He remembered his father's grip as the rogue wave toppled them, and they were ripped apart. Somehow, it took all these years for Reade to understand this as a show of his father's love: his dislocated shoulder was an act of tenderness, his attempt to rescue Reade, not hurt him. Drying off, he opened his phone and dismissed his Pa's last irritating instruction: he deleted his Bully List. And reaching in the dark for AM, he fell asleep. Hum-Hum. Humble. At peace.

The boisterous teens rounded the corner of the house, turning darkness into wakefulness through their sheer exuberance. Billie ran into their bedroom and hid beneath the covers to sleep again. AM stirred at Greta's cry, her milky sweet smell filling their room as she nursed in the still black night. Hours later he woke to the sun's rays slanting through the wooden shuttered window, mixed with stripes of a brilliant blue Grecian sky.

Kaliméra! The neighborhood chorus chimed as the women began their chores.

Two-year-old Billie spread like a cartwheel across half the bed, his brown hair curled with sweat. Greta slept in the nautilus shell of AM's knees and arms. Wrapped around her was Reade, his hand on the curve of her hip. He remained still in the morning light until he could no longer.

"*Hallelujah, Anna Magdalena,*" Reade whispered. "*Kaliméra!*"

The End

ABOUT THE AUTHOR

Maureen McNeil is a writer, artist and activist based in Brooklyn and the Hudson Valley. In 2021, her story, *A Strange Breathless Stunt*, was a finalist for the Tiferet Fiction Prize; and *Cooper and Corinna*, won second place for the Barry Lopez Nonfiction Prize. McNeil's first collection, *Red Hook Stories*, was published in 2008; *Dear Red: The Lost Diary of Marilyn Monroe, A Work of Fiction*, in 2017. McNeil lectures on writing, and designs and teaches workshops in partnership with arts and cultural organizations, such as PEN America, The Anne Frank Center USA, Prison Public Memory Project, Yad Vashem, the Morgan Library, the Woodstock Day School and Hudson Area Library.

        instagram.com/maureenmcneil5
        linkedin.com/in/maureen-mcneil-a3611010